# Black Beauty's Family

**by Josephine, Diana, and
Christine Pullein-Thompson**

illustrated by Elisabeth Grant

In this companion volume to
*Black Beauty's Clan*, the Pullein-
Thompson sisters write again about
Black Beauty's relations.

Nightshade, a thoroughbred
born in the reign of George III,
tells of his life as a racehorse, and
of robberies and violence on the
roads when he found himself carrying a highwayman.

Black Romany's story is set in
the 1840's and tells of life in a
stately home, of a visit from Queen
Victoria, and a hunt with the Consort, Prince Albert.

Blossom's story is of a lost
foal, of carting coal, and then, at
last, of unexpected success.

land Pony Club. Diana and Christine are married, and have two and
four children respectively, who also
like horses. Among them the sisters have written nearly one hundred books. They live in England.

# BLACK BEAUTY'S FAMILY

*Also by*
*Josephine, Diana and Christine Pullein-Thompson*

BLACK BEAUTY'S CLAN

# BLACK BEAUTY'S FAMILY

❀

by Josephine, Diana
and Christine
Pullein-Thompson

❀

*ILLUSTRATED BY
ELISABETH GRANT*

McGRAW-HILL BOOK COMPANY
NEW YORK   ST. LOUIS   SAN FRANCISCO

Library of Congress Cataloging in Publication Data
Main entry under title:

Black Beauty's family.

CONTENTS: Pullein-Thompson, J. Nightshade.—Pullein.
Thompson, D. Black Romany.—Pullein-Thompson, C. Blossom
    1. Horses—Legends and stories. 2. Children's
stories, English. [1. Horses—Fiction] I. Grant,
Elisabeth. II. Pullein-Thompson, Josephine.
Nightshade. 1980. III. Pullein-Thompson, Diana.
Black Romany. 1980. IV. Pullein-Thompson, Christine.
Blossom. 1980.
PZ10.3.B563  1980  [Fic]          80-23731
ISBN 0-07-050914-X

123456789 DODO 876543210

First published in Great Britain 1978 by Hodder and Stoughton Ltd.

First published and distributed in the United States of America 1980 by
McGraw-Hill Book Company.

# Contents

FOREWORD

BY POT BLACK

*Black Beauty's great-great-great-great-great nephew*

page 7


NIGHTSHADE

*by Josephine Pullein-Thompson*

page 9


BLACK ROMANY

*by Diana Pullein-Thompson*

page 109


BLOSSOM

*by Christine Pullein-Thompson*

page 199

# Foreword

BY POT BLACK

*Black Beauty's great-great-great-great-great nephew*

The three stories discovered by my late sire, Black Abbot, and published under the title *Black Beauty's Clan* brought a great spate of letters from horses believing themselves related to Black Beauty and a deluge of hoof-written manuscripts.

Checking the authenticity of these relationships and life stories has been a heavy task, but I am now in a position to set a further three bona fide autobiographies, written by members of my extraordinarily talented family, before the public.

Nightshade, a thoroughbred born in the reign of George III, writes of his life as a racehorse, of the robbery and violence of the roads when he found himself carrying a highwayman. He describes the world of factory children and chimney sweeps, which he saw when a manufactory owner's horse and finally the part he played in the Home Defence during the Napoleonic war.

Black Romany's story is set in the 1840s and tells of life in a stately home, a visit from Queen Victoria, a hunt with the Consort, Prince Albert. She goes on to relate her incredible adventures when trekking across England: confrontation with a ghost, near-death by drowning.

Blossom, a great-great niece of Black Beauty, starts a life full of problems caused by the unfortunate marriage of her dam, Black Tulip. Forced into drudgery as a work-

7

ing horse at the end of the nineteenth century, Blossom's story is of a lost foal, of carting coal, working in the fields and then, at last, of unexpected success.

I have appended that portion of our family tree which shows the relationship which our three storytellers bear to Black Beauty.

# NIGHTSHADE

✳

*by Josephine Pullein-Thompson*

# Contents

ONE   Thorngate Manor   13

TWO   The Lovelace family   19

THREE   A racer's life   27

FOUR   Triumph and disaster   35

FIVE   A gentleman of the road   48

SIX   'To be hanged like a dog'   61

SEVEN   A more respectable life   75

EIGHT   'The French have landed!'   88

# ❧Black Beauty's Family❧

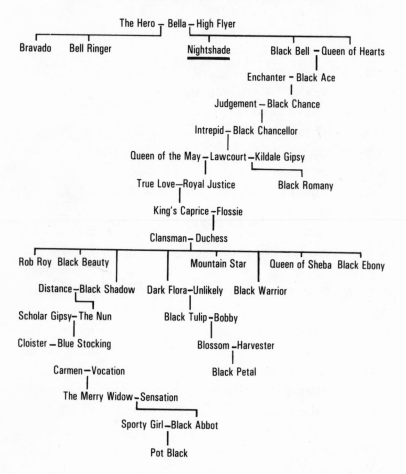

The Hero — Bella — High Flyer

Bravado   Bell Ringer

Nightshade

Black Bell — Queen of Hearts

Enchanter — Black Ace

Judgement — Black Chance

Intrepid — Black Chancellor

Queen of the May — Lawcourt — Kildale Gipsy

True Love — Royal Justice

Black Romany

King's Caprice — Flossie

Clansman — Duchess

Rob Roy  Black Beauty

Mountain Star

Queen of Sheba  Black Ebony

Distance — Black Shadow

Dark Flora — Unlikely  Black Warrior

Scholar Gipsy — The Nun

Black Tulip — Bobby

Cloister — Blue Stocking

Blossom — Harvester

Carmen — Vocation

Black Petal

The Merry Widow — Sensation

Sporty Girl — Black Abbot

Pot Black

## CHAPTER ONE

# Thorngate Manor

When I was young I thought myself a very lucky horse. I seemed to have been born into a perfect world. Squire Lovelace, my owner, was a great man in our locality and his estate, Thorngate Manor, was situated deep in the countryside far from any town or city. We, a peaceful party of mares and foals, lived among grassy hills and stately trees in a wonderful state of contentment.

All through my foalhood I was proud and happy. My mother often told me that we were aristocrats among horses for we were descended from two of the great arab stallions that had been brought to England from over the sea. Both my parents were thoroughbreds with pedigrees and their names were in the new Stud Book. My name was to go in the Stud Book too: Nightshade, black colt, by Highflyer out of Bella. All this made me walk proudly and carry my head high and I am afraid that I boasted and bragged of my breeding to the less high-born foals.

My mother, Bella, was still quite young; I was only her third foal. She was bright bay with a broad white blaze on her face and white socks. I thought her very beautiful.

My sire, Highflyer, was a very well known racer and I early showed that I had inherited his exceptional turn of speed. I was overjoyed when I found that I could outpace the other foals with the greatest of ease.

The leader of our group was an old grey mare called Cobweb. She had been the Squire's favourite hunter until lamed in an accident and, though not well-bred or fast, she was very wise and I noticed that my mother always listened to her with great attention.

Cobweb could remember the Squire as a young man when things had been very different. Our park had been the common field where the villagers grazed their cattle and ponies and their pigs, with rings in their noses that they might not root about too much and spoil the turf. The Squire had bought out the commoners' rights, fenced and improved the land and made the long, winding drive, that visitors might have plenty of opportunity to admire the house before they reached it.

We would graze early in the morning and then, as the day grew hot, retire to our shelter of thatch and poles to escape from the flies, which were a great plague to us foals with our soft and tender skins, and to the mares, who, except for my mother, were all cocktails. One day I asked my mother why she alone had such a fine, full tail and she told me that all horses were provided with them by nature, but it was the fashion for all but racers to have short tails, so men cut them off. And, not content with cutting off the hair, they cut through the bone of the tail so it could never grow long again.

'It saves our grooms the trouble of brushing tails and they think it is safer for driving as the reins cannot be caught under a cocktail,' said Rosetta, a brown mare who was chiefly used in the Squire's carriage.

'I have heard that its main purpose is to make our backs grow stronger,' added Cobweb, 'but it is difficult to see why a racer does not need an equally strong back.'

Whatever the reason, I was very glad that being a racer meant I could keep my tail.

Rosetta was a stout, talkative mare with an opinion on everything. My mother said that carriage horses travelled

14

a good deal and saw much of life and Rosetta had stayed at inns as well as private houses and even in London, for several months once, when the Squire had taken a house for the season.

Snap was even more heavily built and drew the coach or chariot with three other chestnuts when she was not in foal. She pointed out to us one day that Mischief, her filly, was a much finer, better bred looking animal than she was. 'Up-breeding is all the rage nowadays,' she told us. 'I heard Squire talking to Buckle a little time ago and he was saying that with more and more turnpike-roads coming into use all the carriage mares must be put to finer-bred stallions, for it was speed, not strength, that would be needed in the future as the better roads encouraged the building of lighter, more elegant carriages.'

'True enough,' agreed Rosetta. 'I well remember the effort it used to be to drag that heavy, old, broad-wheeled carriage. And the roads! We'd be stuck fast half a dozen times between here and town in the rainy season, but now, once you're on the hard surface of the turnpike, the carriage spins along with no effort at all.'

15

'Yes, it is very well once you are *on* the turnpike,' said Snap, 'but if you take these modern coaches into the more remote areas, along the old fashioned byroads, their wheels sink deep in the mud where the old broad wheels would have gone over the top, and you dare not take to the fields on either side as you used to do when the road became impassable.'

'But all these new hedges and fences prevent that anyway,' Rosetta pointed out. 'They force the road to continue along its usual track even though a drover taking two or three hundred cattle up to the meat market in London has just turned it into a hock-deep quagmire.'

'These new fences are a confounded pest in the hunting field too,' Skylark told us. 'Leaping from morning to night, that's all the young men think of nowadays and the Squire's grown nearly as bad. When I started a couple of stiles and a few ditches would be all you'd meet in a day's sport, but now every other field is fenced. And the speed they go! A hunter has to be almost as fast as a racer these days.' She looked at Ringleader, her foal. 'His sire *was* a racer so he should be fast enough for them.'

The abundant grass enabled our mothers to give us plenty of milk so we foals grew apace and were very strong and forward. In the cool of the evenings and early mornings we would race and wrestle and, as we grew older and dared to venture from our mothers' sides, we would make our way down to the fence that ran close to the drive, and watch the comings and goings.

Elegant carriages and chariots, curricles and chaises would bring the neighbours calling and relations and friends from further afield for longer visits. Our own horses took the Squire's wife and daughters to the town or to repay the calls and visits, in equally elegant vehicles.

The Squire and his sons did most of their travelling on horseback and they would start out across the fields rather than bother with the long, winding drive.

As I have said I was possessed of an exceptional turn of speed and I would frequently challenge the other foals to races and beat them easily. Even Ringleader, whose sire was a racer, could keep nowhere near me. Sometimes I would let them all start and then, coming from behind, I would exert myself to the very top of my speed and flashing by them in turn, be the victor once again.

My mother would not praise me for these efforts, but the other mares looked on and talked admiringly of my spirit and 'bottom'.

'He'll be a celebrated racer and no mistake,' they told my mother.

She would only blow and sniff as she grazed. 'So he ought to be,' she admitted at last, 'since his sire and dam and his grand-sires and grand-dams have all been racers before him, but it's not much of a life.'

'Why not?' I asked. To me racing with the wind in your mane and tail seemed the height of happiness, far better than drawing carriages, dragging carts or even being a hunter.

She stood staring into the distance, a few blades of grass dangling from her lip as she answered me, 'It is wonderful enough when the cheers of the crowd are ringing in your ears and you are in the lead; when you gallop first past the post to the delight of your jockey and master; but it is not always like that.'

'Why not?' I asked disbelievingly as I tried to imagine the sound of a cheering crowd.

'Because you can lose. You can gallop for all you are worth, until your lungs are bursting and your brain is dizzy with the effort, and still the other horse is ahead. The whip cuts your flank as you struggle to catch up, but the cheers are for the other horse and you stand, spent, with heaving sides and watch him led in in triumph.'

'*I* won't ever lose,' I told her. '*I'll* be the fastest horse in the land.'

My mother had sighed. 'You have a great deal to learn, Nightshade,' she said.

The other mares liked my answer, they said I had plenty of 'bottom'.

When I asked my mother what 'bottom' might be, she answered that it was really another name for courage and perseverance. 'It is the spirit and doggedness,' she went on, 'that keeps some horses galloping though they are struggling for breath and scarce able to see; it makes them keep going through a long day's hunting or pull and pull to get their cart out of a slough. That is what men call "bottom" and they are full of admiration for it, in horses and in each other.'

I was very glad when I heard this that I had 'bottom' and I determined to practise having it so that I possessed more and more.

## CHAPTER TWO

# The Lovelace family

My first summer passed without event. But in the autumn I began to see more of life for Ringleader and I, with our mothers, were taken into the stable each night.

Two stable boys, generally Bob and Dick, would come across the park calling us and shaking a sieve of oats. They would put halters on the two mares and lead them to the stables with Ringleader and me trotting along behind.

We would go through a gate into the back drive, past the midden and the forge, past the barns that held the hay and straw, the granaries and the coachhouse into the stable yard. This was a modern brick-built square with stables below and grooms' quarters in the lofts above. Two turrets faced each other, one holding a dovecote and the other a clock that struck the hours. Above the clock, a gilded weathercock showed where the wind lay.

The stables were thought very fine, fitted up with every modern convenience, my mother said, and Mr Lovelace brought any new acquaintance to see them and to admire every detail.

As the weather grew colder my mother and Skylark would trot across to meet the boys and when winter came on they would find us waiting at the gate whinneying at them to hurry and take us in.

One night instead of sharing a stable with my mother I was put in with Ringleader, just the two of us shut away in a great loose-box. A feed of crushed oats was put in the manger and soft, sweet hay in the low hay rack, but we felt very indignant at this trick and neighed at the tops of our voices, wanting our mothers and our accustomed milk. We heard their voices neighing back from distant stables, but they did not come. At last, worn out by our protests, we ate the food provided and lay down disconsolately together in the thick straw.

From that night our mothers vanished from our lives. We spent a few mournful days together in the loose-box and then Bob and Dick led us out to a little paddock behind the stables. They told us that we were grown horses now and must stop crying after our mothers, for they would be having new foals in the spring and must gather strength for that and not feed great colts like us with their milk.

We saw a good deal of life from our paddock and perhaps this was intended, for a young horse, reared in some very secluded pasture or moor, is likely to be in a continual state of fright when taken into the larger world and will spend much of his time starting and shying. We had something to watch every minute of the day. Besides all the carts and wagons belonging to the estate there would be visitors like the miller, his men and horses white with flour, the coal fetched in carts from a barge on the canal. Wagons from the cities bringing new furniture and carpets and once, when Mr Lovelace's old aunt died, mourning coaches and carriages drawn by black horses with black plumes on their heads; we thought this a very fine sight.

The children's ponies: Squirrel a red chestnut, Fidget a dun, elegant bay Julius, and tiny brown Sparrow, were often turned out in the paddock next to ours. Squirrel and Fidget belonged to the two younger boys, Georgie and

Harry, Julius carried Miss Polly and Sparrow, who was not as tall as Ringleader and me, had taught all the Lovelace children to ride and now belonged to the youngest, Miss Cassy. Mr Tom, the heir, who was almost of age, and Mr William both had several hunters and a road horse apiece. While Miss Lovelace, the eldest daughter, had a very pretty mare called Grace.

When the Christmas holidays came we saw a lot of Georgie and Harry for they liked the company of our stable boys and a great deal of boasting, wrestling and sham fighting would go on in the hay barn beside our paddock. If Mr Buckle caught our boys at it he would soon send them back to work and then, with no playfellows, Harry and Georgie would get their guns and blaze away at everything that moved. No bird was safe from being blown to pieces and they would fire at the stable cats and stray dogs if no other targets offered themselves.

Ringleader and I spent a good deal of time talking to the ponies over the fence, for they, Sparrow especially, knew a great deal about life and about the Lovelace family.

We learned that there had been eleven children born, but four had died of one thing or another, as was quite common, and Mrs Lovelace was thought lucky to have as many as seven children living and all in good health.

Fidget said that he couldn't answer for Masters Georgie and Harry remaining in good health much longer. He and Squirrel were being rammed at every new fence they met and he thought it likely that both boys would have broken necks before the season was over.

We saw Mrs Lovelace only occasionally. Sparrow said that she kept to the house in bad weather. She looked to us quite an elderly lady, much older than the short, square, red-faced Squire, but Sparrow explained that she was in poor health, mostly due to having borne eleven children.

The whole family gathered at Thorngate Manor for Christmas and Mr Tom came from his University, bringing with him a Bull Terrier and a fighting cock. The dog was renowned for killing rats and we learned that this was a popular sport among university men. They would put a dog in a pit, specially made so the rats could not get away. Then they would empty in a whole sackful of rats and time how long he took to kill them, laying wagers on which dog would kill the most in the shortest time.

Mr Tom's dog had become the champion and Sparrow, who went up to the house each day to take Miss Cassy out, reported that the Squire was as proud of Mr Tom for possessing the champion rat-killer as many fathers would have been if he had passed his exams or gained some great honour for learning.

The fighting cock was less fortunate. It seemed he was only a second rate bird and not worthy of the big fights that the Squire attended, but before long Mr Tom managed to arrange a match with an untried cock.

The weather being fine, they made a ring with boxes and trusses of hay between our paddock and the barn and the Lovelace sons, their friends and our stable boys assembled to see the fight. We all leaned over the fence to watch. We saw the cocks, two very fine looking birds, taken out of their baskets and some very long metal spurs attached to their legs. Squirrel and Fidget, who had experience of being spurred at large fences, were very much shocked at the length and sharpness of these weapons and said the birds would tear each other to pieces.

When the cocks were thrown into the ring we could

not see very clearly, for the excited spectators jumping up and down obscured our view. But we saw the cocks leap into the air and meet with savage fury. We heard their flapping wings as they prepared for fresh attacks. We caught glimpses of them pecking fiercely at each other's heads, we saw the blood on their combs and wattles. We could tell how the battle went by the cheers or silence from our family and our stable boys, who supported Mr Tom's cock to a man.

The great flapping of wings grew weaker as the combat went on, but the excitement of the watchers became more feverish.

At first all seemed to be going the way of Mr Tom's bird and he and Mr Will were betting heavily on their victory, but then there came a change of fortune and the voices on our side began to swear and call on the cock to show some pluck.

Then suddenly there was silence and then, in the midst of the silence, came a triumphant crow and we knew that the fight was over. The winning cock was taken up by his owner and carried away to his basket. Our bird lay on the ground until Master Harry picked him up and asked if he might not be revived with brandy.

'No, dead as a doornail,' said Mr Tom. 'Give him here,

I'd better save the spurs.' And, having unfastened them, he took the poor bird by the legs and flung him up on the dungheap.

'I'll get myself a better one, with more bottom to him,' he told Master Harry and then called to his friends to come up to the house and try the strong beer.

My second summer came. Ringleader and I were yearlings now and growing fast. He was a beautiful gold chestnut, I a sober, shining black with one white sock. We were no longer biddable foals and we would play up Bob and Dick, rearing and bucking, trying to break away from them as they led us in and out of the stable.

The Squire and Mr Buckle had a conference and decided that we had better be made obedient to man's will and accustomed to wearing saddles and bridles before we grew any stronger or more unruly.

After that Stephen, the second man, took us in charge and we were made to go round on the lunge rein, to wear saddles and bridles and taken to the forge to have our feet trimmed. We were also put in separate stables and every day we were tied up and made to submit to a thorough grooming.

I did not care for all this discipline, but most of all I hated the bridle, the feel of straps over my head and a bit in my mouth, was a great source of irritation. And, when we were led out in our bridles, the boys had far greater control over us and we were forced to walk soberly, without horseplay.

Looking back now I see that the Squire was right. If a horse has to submit to the commands of man it is better to teach him to do so early rather than to wait until he is a strong and rebellious horse, accustomed to liberty and with a will of his own.

Mr Tom was the focus of all events that summer, for it was his coming of age. He was not universally popular with Squire Lovelace's people for he showed little consideration to those beneath him. His orders were not given with politeness and they were often followed with, 'and look sharp about it,' which annoyed the older men, while his habit of forcing his attentions on laundry maids and dairy maids caused frequent uproars. But most of all it was his constant need to be best at everything that was disliked. A man had only to say that his horse could trot so many miles an hour for Mr Tom to cry out that he had one to beat that easily and suggest a match. He would bet on how many miles he could run, how many bottles of wine he could drink, before falling in a stupor under the table, and one day, on how many swallows on the wing he would shoot in half an hour. I think his friend, another university man who was staying in the house, felt certain of winning this one for Mr Tom finally agreed to shoot twenty in as many minutes.

But fetching his guns and Mr Will to act as loader, he stationed himself by the barn and shot the poor birds as they flew in to feed their young in the beautiful little nests under the eaves.

The friend lost his money, the birds lost their lives and the fledglings must have starved to death, but Mr Tom went off very pleased with himself at this clever idea.

The coming of age was a great occasion with the quality entertained at an elegant ball in the house one day, and the tenants and work people and all the poor from the villages for miles around invited to a great feast in the park the next. A whole ox was roasted on a huge fire and great quantities of ale were drunk.

We horses heard the proceedings very plainly, but we saw little save the glow in the sky, for we had all been taken out of our stables and put in farm buildings and barns for the night. Our stables were bedded with fresh straw and given over to those who were too drunk to make their way home, of which there were a great number.

Next morning we heard nothing but groans and complaints and the yard was full of people waiting to put their aching heads under the pump. Our stable folk were among the sufferers and it was several days before life returned to normal.

Soon after this our early education was considered complete and Ringleader and I were turned out in a great meadow that took in two sides of a valley as well as a copse. Here we were reunited with the colts we had known as foals and joined a number of hunter geldings turned out to rest.

## CHAPTER THREE

# A racer's life

The spring that I was two years old I was separated from my friend Ringleader, which was a great blow to me, but it was on Squire Lovelace's orders.

He came round the stable one morning, with Mr Buckle as usual in anxious attendance, and, looking at Ringleader said that he would grow into a valuable hunter by and by and had better be turned away for another year. But that Nightshade, being destined for the race course, had better be sent over to Clinton Lacey to commence his training with Simpson; it having become common practice of late to race two- and three-year-olds.

I could see that Mr Buckle did not like this overmuch, but he did not dare argue with the Squire; he mentioned one or two horses who'd raced very young, but whose successes had been short-lived.

'There may be truth in what you say,' admitted the Squire, 'but it suits my plans to have a good horse on the turf as soon as possible. I need some return on the enormous sums these animals are costing me and I count on Nightshade here to provide it.'

Clinton Lacey was a matter of ten or twelve miles from Thorngate Manor, but the countryside was very different. The village was in a hollow below a high, bare down, growing nothing but the short, sweet grass so beloved of sheep. Their baa, the bark of dogs and the whistles of shepherds were the sounds that filled the air.

The house was a comfortable sort of farm house which

had been given over to Mr Tom as a hunting box. It was considered good enough for him in his bachelor state, but the Squire was said to have great plans for turning it into a gentleman's residence should he decide to marry.

The racers, of whom there were upwards of half a dozen, were kept at some distance from the house in a new-built stable block and I soon found that we were kept very much apart, our large comfortable loose-boxes being entirely cut off from each other, to avoid the spread of coughs and other distempers.

Simpson, the Squire's training groom, was a thin man with a limp, blackened teeth and a crooked nose from being thrown in various accidents. He had a very quick temper, not that he vented it on the horses. It was kept for the poor stable boys and he would lash out at them with a whip for the most minor of faults.

I was given a little lad called Andrew. He was some years older than he looked, being about twelve, he thought. But lack of proper food had made him small and stunted, though with a rather wizened and careworn face. He was fair with blue eyes and, being very timid, lived in mortal terror of Mr Simpson. I was the only horse in Andrew's care, but he was expected to groom me to perfection and his lack of strength and stature made it hard work for him.

I found my new life, shut up in a loose-box on my own, very hard to bear. The four walls quickly became a prison to me and I fretted for my lost freedom and companions. The door of my stable was always kept shut and the window was set too high for me to see out, so there I lived in solitary silence and, after being my own master in the meadows at Thorngate Manor, I found it very terrible.

I made a friend of Andrew and would listen hopefully for his coming as the long hours dragged by. He understood horses and would talk to me as he groomed. 'Mr Simpson's in a rare old mood,' he would tell me or, 'Two of the boys 'ad a turn up and Christopher's nose won't stop bleeding though they've 'ad 'im under the pump these ten minutes.'

After a few days of being driven round on the lunge and led out in a saddle and bridle, Mr Simpson decided that I was ready to be backed and Andrew was legged up into my saddle. He weighed nothing, but it seemed very extraordinary to have him perched up there and I felt I must move with extreme care lest he should come tumbling down. But having seen so much riding and driving going on, I thought it quite the usual thing and was not terrified as wild horses are, so I raised not the slightest objection and very soon the feeling of strangeness passed off.

After that my education went on apace. I was taught to turn and stop and set off again at signals from Andrew's reins and legs and, when I understood them, we went on to trotting. Soon Mr Simpson, who was always there overlooking the proceedings and shouting furiously at Andrew, damning him for this and that if he made the least wrong move, decided that I was ready to go out with the general string of horses.

This made a great improvement in my life for I now had company for some two hours a day. At first I was so excited by the sight of the other horses that I almost tipped Andrew off with my prancing about, but recollected myself just in time. When he was back in the saddle and Mr Simpson had ceased his shouting and swearing, I was allotted fifth place in the string and we set off up a miry lane to the Down. Mr Simpson led the way on an old grey nag, followed by a full grown stallion and two three-year-old colts and behind me came a couple of very pretty fillies and a boy on a pony.

I found carrying Andrew up the long hill to the Down very hard work and I was glad when I reached the soft turf of the training area, that no galloping was required of me. I and the younger of the two fillies were walked about while the other horses galloped and Mr Simpson cursed and roared.

Andrew told me that one of the colts was half brother to me. He was a beautiful bay like our dam and I felt very proud when I saw his fine carriage and his turn of speed.

I settled down to my new life fairly well after this and, after I had been ridden up and down to the Down for a few weeks, Mr Simpson said I had to start my training proper and, to this end, I was physicked. The forcing of a ball of evil-smelling medicine down my throat with a long stick was bad enough, but the next day I developed terrible pains in my stomach. Andrew was sorry for me, but he said that it was for my own good and the physic would drive out all the bad blood and humours from my system. After a day or two's ill health I recovered, but I cannot say, in all honesty, that the medicine did me the smallest good.

Now I began to be fed on a rich diet of rye bread and split beans as well as oats and cut grass and carrots and I joined the older horses in their gallops. I enjoyed carrying Andrew and sharing the feeling of speed. I enjoyed the wind in my mane and the soft turf beneath my hoofs and the feeling of strength and power that grew in me as I became fit.

One day the Squire came to see us gallop. Mr Simpson

paraded us with pride, pointing out our glossy coats and hard muscles, and then we were lined up.

We set off steadily and at first Andrew held me in behind the other horses. My brother, Bravado, was the leader and we thudded across the Down in a close-knit bunch.

There were whitewashed stones to mark the furlongs and, at the third, Andrew began to ride me on. The other horses quickened too and we began to race, all delighting in the feel of speed. Then Andrew urged me on again. I lengthened my stride and suddenly I was amazing myself with the speed at which I could travel; I seemed to be flying. I flew past my stable companions one by one. I galloped neck and neck, stride for stride with my brother. Then, at Andrew's urging, I drew away and suddenly I was alone, out in front; the winner.

We pulled up at the appointed place and turned back. The Squire was full of excitement, his red face glowing with triumph. He dismounted and hurried to slap me on the neck and praise Andrew. Then he began to talk about the horses I might be matched with.

'He'll beat any horse in these parts,' he told Mr Simpson, 'and the best of it is we'll take them by surprise. You must bid the boys keep quiet upon pain of dismissal. I'll plunge heavily and win a fortune on his first appearance. You must put him into full training at once, Simpson. He's too fat; you sweat him well and he'll beat any horse in the kingdom.

'Bella's colt! I knew Highflyer would be right for her. We'll put him in next year's Derby; how should you like that, Simpson? To train a Derby winner, eh?'

'You don't think we should keep him for the Derby, Squire?' asked Mr Simpson. 'A dash race like that is far less strain on a young horse than the old system of heats. It would be a shocking pity to knock him up by asking too much of him.'

'Oh damn you for an old cosset,' said the Squire. 'Look, I'll tell you plain, I can't afford to go on laying out money with no return. With Mr Tom's debts on top of my own, I'm in no position to wait. Nightshade must win me a packet, and quickly.'

From that day I was exercised all wrapped up in horse clothes and a hood. I did not enjoy my sweating sessions overmuch and at first I looked very askance at the exotic food I was being offered. The best oats were dressed with beaten eggs, a dozen at a time, Andrew told me, and ale, and I was given drinks of barley water flavoured with syrup of lemons and syrup of violets. While every day at noon my legs were rubbed with oil.

It seemed that Andrew was not to ride me in my race.

The Squire had decided that he dare not risk his money with a greenhorn in the saddle and had engaged an experienced boy, called Sam Tilney, who had many races to his credit, and he would come and ride me in a trial gallop.

Andrew was very disappointed at this, but when the day for the trial came he was mounted on a pony and came to watch, while I carried Sam. Sam was taller than Andrew, but being dreadfully thin, weighed much the same. He had a dark, gipsy-looking face and no front teeth, which made him talk with a lisp. He was very much a man of the world and was soon setting our boys right about all matters to do with the turf.

It seemed that I was entered for a plate for two- and three-year-olds at Newbury. The prize was only fifty pounds but Mr Lovelace was known to have made several large wagers with other gentlemen, notably the owner of the favourite, a grey called Pegasus.

Sam was a more forceful rider than Andrew. He was always pushing me on or holding me back or thrusting me through a small space between Lady Jane and Bravado and he seemed to be up to all sorts of tricks like making a great noise with his whip to put them off their stride. Not that we needed tricks, for I just galloped away and left them standing.

The Squire and Mr Simpson seemed well-pleased with this trial and it was settled that Andrew should lead me over to Sir Peter Cardew's stable, where I would stay overnight, and then walk me to the course next morning. Andrew was given very strict instructions by the Squire. He was to sleep in my box and let no one come near me lest they tried to ruin my hopes with a nail in the foot or a last minute bucket of water.

'And don't go bragging about his chances,' finished the Squire. 'Keep your mouth shut and if anyone questions you play the clodhopper. If all goes well you shall have a handsome present.'

CHAPTER FOUR

# Triumph and disaster

I enjoyed the walk to Knighton Park. We set off early in the morning when all was fresh and dewy and made our way through lanes and byroads with one stretch along a turnpike, for which Andrew had to pay one penny at the tollgate. He said it was for me as pedestrians paid no dues.

At Knighton I was kept very much to myself and being a young, untried horse did not cause much of a stir. Mr Simpson sent my food over in a little cart so that I should have no change of diet. On the morning of the race Andrew gave me toast soaked in wine, which was supposed to give great energy. 'Most boys drink the wine themselves,' he told me, 'but I 'aven't, not one drop.'

It was late in the morning when we set out for the course and when we reached it I was amazed to see all the people and bustle. There were a great many booths and little tents erected everywhere; gipsies told fortunes, strong ale was sold and many other things.

A large number of gentlemen and farmers were there on horseback, careering all over the course, the ladies were mainly seated in carriages that were placed in a row along the rails to give a good view.

Andrew asked for the rubbing house and when we came to it we found Mr Simpson and Sam waiting for us. Then Andrew got to rubbing my legs with oil and Mr Simpson offered me more toast soaked in wine, while Sam took my saddle and went to be weighed in on the scales by the rubbing house.

I looked with interest at all the activity. The great crowd of gentlemen, in their round black hats and frock coats, clustered round the betting post, the quieter ladies with their long dresses billowing out around them and their wide-brimmed hats.

The Squire came to watch me saddled and Sam, very elegantly dressed in a red and white striped silk jacket, breeches, boots and a velvet jockey cap, was legged up. Mr Lovelace's face was a deep red, his talk louder and his oaths more frequent than usual. Though he had told Andrew not to brag of my chances he never ceased from doing so and all his friends were called over to inspect me.

Many of the gentlemen were in an even greater state of drink and excitement and thieves were picking pockets in the most open way, the crowd seeming to view it as the most normal thing and doing nothing to stop it.

Sam cantered me down to the start alongside Pegasus who was still favourite to win. The starter, a portly man in breeches, frock coat and a high-crowned narrow-brimmed hat, came forward carrying a flag. He spoke severely to the jockeys about lining up correctly and not trying to break away before the others.

Ignoring the great crowd of horsemen pressing round us, I watched the flag with Sam and when it fell I leaped forward and there was no need for the sharp jab with the spurs he gave me.

Two miles is a long way and Sam did not want to make the running so he tucked me in behind the favourite and we stayed there easily enough.

At the mile post Pegasus began to quicken and Black Tommy and I quickened with him, but the other two, Merryman and Defiance, had shot their bolts and fell back out of sight.

I stayed with the leaders very easily and when Sam began to make a lot of noise with his whip on his boot, I drew alongside Pegasus, leaving Black Tommy behind. As we came to the carriage stand the two of us raced neck and neck and the roar from the crowd was immense. When Sam urged me on I swept by Pegasus and raced on alone, proud of my easy stride and the speed that put lengths between us.

As Sam pulled me up I felt a hero. Many people cheered as we walked back to the rubbing house, though some were too busy cursing the loss of their money.

I was soon surrounded by my own people who seemed delighted by my success and as Sam went off to be weighed again, Andrew got busy, scraping the sweat from me with his old piece of sword blade and then rubbing me with a cloth.

I was munching wine and toast when the Squire came over, so cock-a-hoop that one would have thought he'd run the race himself. Then the wagering began again and Andrew told me proudly that I was now favourite. After about fifteen minutes I was saddled and I realised that I was expected to go through the whole performance again.

Down to the start we went and though I did not feel quite the same enthusiasm for the race, I did not think that any of the other horses could beat me.

This time I jumped off smartly to avoid a jab from Sam's spurs. Black Tommy took the lead and Pegasus followed right on my heels, which I did not like at all, while Defiance and Merryman pressed close on either side of me and in this way we proceeded steadily for the first mile. Then the other jockeys all seemed intent on putting me off, they all banged their boots and crowded in on me. But Sam held me very steady for another half mile and then he began to ride me. I was still game and responded willingly enough, lengthening my stride, I burst out of the knot of horses and raced away. Not one of them could keep with me. The crowd roared with pleasure and I passed the post two lengths ahead of Defiance, who came second.

The effort had been considerable and my head was not so high, nor my step so proud as I walked back to the rubbing house for the second time. But my people were even more jubilant as all the weighing and scraping and rubbing down was gone through again.

I thought that having won twice should be proof enough of my superiority, but I soon learned that I had to run *yet* again.

'Win once more Nightshade and you'll be the clear leader and won't 'ave to run again a fourth time,' Andrew told me as he walked me up and down to prevent me stiffening after all my exertions. But I didn't feel like running again. Four miles is a long way for a mere two-year-old, which cannot have the stamina of an adult horse, and I felt tired out and saw the possibility of defeat.

Mr Simpson saw it too. I heard him advising the Squire to hedge his bets as he was afraid that I might not pull it off for a third time, but the Squire would have none of it. Purple-faced and reckless, he shook Simpson off angrily, 'The other animals are just as done up. Take a look at Defiance, if I ever saw a horse cooked it is him.'

Wearily I cantered down to the start, without enough energy left to study the condition of my rivals. I resolved to do my best, but if that did not win me the race I was not going to care. I had proved myself the fastest horse and this running again and again seemed senseless cruelty to me.

We all started slowly. We galloped, but not near so fast as previously. The way seemed very long and my breath grew short before the first mile was done. As we went into the second mile it seemed to be Sam who was holding me together. I could feel myself rolling and lurching, my breath came and went in painful gasps and the green track ahead seemed to stretch on for ever and ever. Another panting, grunting horse came alongside me, and we seemed to be almost leaning on one another for support as we staggered on and on. Winning or losing meant nothing to me now; I just kept going. Sam was sawing on my snaffle, spurring my sides. Then he began to lash me with the whip, burning, red-hot cuts on my

heaving sides. I made one last effort to escape from the pain. Then it was over. We pulled up.

Head down, panting for breath, I stumbled back to the rubbing house too exhausted to care for cheers. I was still trying to get my breath as Andrew began to scrape and rub.

'You won, you beat the favourite. Well done, Old Nightshade,' he was telling me.

Interested bystanders and sporting men came to inspect me. 'What a turn of speed!' they said. 'What bottom for a youngster!' Only one man looked sadly at my hanging head and mangled sides and spoke angrily against the butchery of heats; wishing that they might be abolished in favour of dash races, for the sake of the horses.

As I recovered from my exhaustion I became more and more conscious of my spurred and lashed sides. I walked back to Knighton in a very dejected state and not at all pleased with my triumph.

Mr Simpson beat up eggs and ale into a drink and poured it down my throat through a cow's horn, Andrew brought me a warm mash and bathed my torn sides, my straw bed was made thicker than ever. But none of this attention could make up for what I had been through and it was several days before I regained my spirits.

Back at Clinton Lacey we fell into the old routine and it was some time before the date of my next race was decided. Andrew told me that Mr Simpson constantly pleaded for its postponement as he felt another severe trial so soon would destroy me, but the Squire, who cared for nothing but the restoration of his fortune, insisted that I ran at Hungerford Races.

This time I started favourite, for my fame had spread. But, knowing what lay ahead I husbanded my strength, winning each heat by the narrowest of margins.

The day ended with the Squire triumphant and drunk, his face purple, his wig askew, while I was spent and exhausted and in much pain from Sam's reckless use of spurs and whip.

So my life went on. The Squire, regarding me as invincible, backed me heavily every time I ran and it was soon being said that I had earned him some forty or fifty thousand pounds.

Fortunately Simpson managed to convince him that the modern dash race would preserve my strength longer and Andrew and I walked many miles through the countryside that summer to reach the courses where they were held. Those walks were very pleasant to me for I enjoyed the new surroundings and the escape from my hot, solitary stable.

When winter came I rested quietly, but great events were taking place in the outside world. The French people, who had been in the throes of a revolution for some time, cut off their King's head and declared war on England, but, though it was said that both prices and taxes had risen alarmingly, things seemed to go on much as usual at Clinton Lacey.

In the spring I reached three years of age. Mr Simpson wanted to give me one or two dash races before the Derby, but the Squire, who was running short of money again, had other plans.

It seemed that I had become altogether too well-known and people did not want to match their horses or lay bets against me. There had been talk of a brilliant three-year-old from one of the midland shires and a four-year-old from Oxford, but their owners were not prepared to take the Squire's vast wagers at even weights. They demanded that I should be heavily handicapped and, much against Mr Simpson's advice, the Squire agreed.

I never care to remember that day. My heart sank from the moment I was saddled and Sam legged up, for I felt the weight of the extra lead that I was to carry in my weightcloth. I knew at once that I had been given a very severe penalty and the wet state of the ground made the extra weight even more of a burden.

I won the first heat, but only with great labour. I carried off the second heat too, but only by a nose and I was totally exhausted by this hard fought battle with the Oxford horse – Baytree – who was a year older and carried no dead weight at all.

When the half hour of scraping and rubbing was over, I could scarce drag myself down to the start of the third heat and then, try as I would, and despite all Sam's spurring and lashing, I just could not draw ahead of

Baytree. We battled together the whole way up the course, we fought for every inch and, at the end the weight told and he just managed to get his nose in front.

I had won two heats and been second once, Baytree had won once and been second twice. Gold Dust was out of it, but if Baytree won the final heat and I was second it would be a draw. If he won and I was only third he would win the match.

The Squire came over half drunk and in a very ugly mood. He cursed Mr Simpson for not having me fit and then he turned on Sam and said if he did not win next time he would never employ him again.

'I'll do my utmost, sir, but the weight is telling on the horse,' Sam answered respectfully.

'Damn the weight,' roared the Squire. 'I've wagered a fortune on this race. You get that horse first past the post. I don't care if it kills him, you're to win, boy. D'ye hear me?'

'Yes, sir,' said Sam, 'I'll do my utmost.'

He did. When we came to the last mile I began to fail. I was grunting for breath and rolling in my stride, but I suppose the other two were in much the same state, for they did not pass me, though Baytree seemed constantly alongside.

With five furlongs to go I could no longer see. My breath came in hard, unbearably painful gasps, my legs were scarcely under my control, but the cruel spurs and whip forced me on and on. I think I was slowed to a stumbling trot when I passed the post and when the whip and spurs stopped I staggered and fell.

For a time I hardly knew what went on around me, but gradually the mist over my eyes cleared and I found

Andrew stroking my neck and Mr Simpson calling for wine or ale.

I cared nothing for the crowd pressing round me, all telling each other that I was done for and advising Mr Simpson that it would be a waste of good wine to pour it down my throat. I just lay there in a state of exhaustion, unable to move.

Then I heard the Squire's voice, 'Is he done for, Simpson? Well, small matter, he's more than paid for his keep. If you do get him on his feet, sell him for whatever you can get. I doubt if he'll make a full recovery.'

I could feel Andrew's tears falling on my cheek and as I moved my head a little to escape them he called to Mr Simpson, ''E moved. There's life in 'im yet.'

'Can you lift his head? Some of this might revive him.' I was quite indifferent as to whether I lived or died, but Andrew and some of the bystanders heaved me into a position from which they could raise my head and pour wine down my throat. Then they let me lie again and I could hear talk of sending for the knacker's cart.

But, gradually the wine did revive me. I stirred and found I could raise my head and look about me. And then, after about ten minutes, I felt able to get to my feet.

Andrew, seemingly overjoyed, put on my horse cloth and led me slowly to Knighton.

'What will the Squire do when 'e finds you 'aven't sold Nightshade?' he asked Simpson fearfully as they fed me that evening.

'He won't remember, men don't when they are three-parts drunk as he was. He'll never say a word if the horse recovers. I'll only hear about it if he lingers on an old crock, but he won't remember.'

Andrew nursed me back to health, but there was now

no hope of my running in the Derby and indeed it seemed as though all my old fire and spirit had gone. I would walk up to the Down with the rest of the string, but when they wanted me to gallop with the other horses I became very nervous. Sweat would pour off me as I ran backwards and refused to start. Andrew did his best to calm me, but it was no use; I could no longer bear the thought of running in a race.

'He's turned sour,' said Mr Simpson, 'I knew it would happen. All we can do is take him steady and hope he comes right in the end. I'll talk to the Squire.'

I suppose the Squire thought he knew better, for I found myself in training again and suffered the indignity of being chased by boys with great branches of furze or gorse when I ran backwards and refused to start.

I gave up this fight mainly to oblige Andrew, but though I consented to canter gently with the other horses I had made a firm resolve that I would never try to win a race again.

Mr Simpson could see I had changed, but when the Squire came to watch he said that the fault lay with Andrew, who wasn't man enough to put me straight, but with Sam in the saddle I'd stop all that nonsense and show my old form.

When the day came to set off for the next race meeting both Andrew and I were in very low spirits. We knew what sort of man the Squire was now: he would kill me in order to win, but as his anger at losing would be uncontrollable, the outcome was bound to be unhappy.

When we reached the course, when I saw the booths and tents, the white rails and the people, I began to sweat and shake with anxiety. Andrew tried to calm me with stroking and soothing words, but it was no use. The dreadful memories of my last race kept flooding back and filling me with a terrible agitation.

Mr Simpson took one look at me and went off to tell the Squire that he must hedge his bets before my state was generally noticed.

Sam's face also became glum at the sight of me.

'Try to use him gently,' said Mr Simpson, legging Sam up, but I knew that I was not going to trust myself to him again. I was not going to race and I did not care what they did to me, it could not be any worse than the treatment I had gained by trying to win.

I went down to the start lathered with sweat and in a great state of turmoil. I began to lash out as we lined up, confusing the other horses with my display of anger. The starter shouted at Sam to control me, but I had no intention of being controlled and when the flag fell I was facing in the wrong direction, kicking and plunging as I had never done in my life before. When Sam dug in his spurs and began to lash me with his whip I became almost unrideable. I flung myself backwards like a mad thing, I reared, I plunged, I kicked and bucked. I no longer cared for the safety of my rider and, when he persisted in his attempts to make me join the race, I redoubled my violence until at last I threw him off. Then, still half crazed by painful memories, I fled into the crowd. Eventually I found Andrew and let myself be caught. I was disqualified, disgraced.

The Squire came purple-faced, almost bursting with rage.

'Pole-axe him, knock him on the head,' he roared at Simpson. 'He's cost me thousands, the damned, sour faint-hearted screw. He can have his eyes put out and turn a mill-wheel, that's all he's fit for. Get him out of my

46

sight, he'll not even do for stud now he's disgraced himself.'

Andrew hurried me away and, acting on the assumption that the Squire was three-parts drunk, Mr Simpson didn't have me pole-axed, but told Andrew that he might ride me home.

## CHAPTER FIVE

# A gentleman of the road

I never knew what took place between the Squire and Mr Simpson. But it soon became plain that my career as a racer was over. The Squire's revenge was limited to having me gelded. I suppose he thought that I had not bottom enough to father future racehorses. Then I was turned out in the familiar valley meadow at Thorngate Manor with a collection of untried colts and lame hunters for companions.

I was more neglected than I had ever been in my life. There was grass in summer, hay in winter. A stream for water, a copse for shelter, but as for oats and beans, eggs and ale, toast soaked in wine, I never saw them. I was unkempt and ungroomed, but wonderfully happy.

As the weeks stretched into months and the months into a year I began to feel that I had been forgotten. But one day as summer ended, when autumn mists hung over the valley and little children came with baskets and pails to pick the mushrooms that had suddenly sprung up everywhere, I saw Dick, quite a man now, coming across the meadow and he was calling my name.

In the stable Mr Buckle sighed over the white hairs that had grown where the spurs wounded my sides and told his boys to get to work on me. In no time I had a short tail, a trimmed mane an almost clean coat and a set of shoes.

Life was different now. After the horrible process of physicking had been gone through I started exercise, walking and trotting round the lanes with a string of hunters. I had become an ordinary horse, living in a stall and treated just like the others. I missed my loose-box at night, for I could no longer lie down and stretch out, but the pleasure of having the other horses all round me made up for this.

I was not looking forward to my career as a hunter for the Squire and Mr Tom were known as hard riders who cared little for their mounts. Only Mr Will, it was said, spared a thought for the horse that carried him. But then something occurred to change my life.

The Squire came home from Scotland in a high good humour having shot more birds than any of the other gentlemen in his party, but this mood vanished when Mr Tom returned from foreign parts and confessed to having run up gaming debts of a considerable sum. The uproar over this had scarcely died away when a young man calling himself James or Jem Lovelace appeared at the house.

There was great excitement in the stable over this visitation for the young man was known to be a bastard son of the Squire's – it was said he had six or seven – who had come to claim relationship and assistance.

He was a pleasant well-dressed young man and his likeness to Mr Will struck Mrs Lovelace and the young ladies so forcibly, that they pleaded for him to be allowed to stay the night at the house and not turned straight out into the storm as the Squire intended. The result was permission to sleep in the stable. He came in with us hunters, his face black as thunder at the reception he had received from the Squire, and, wrapping his cloak around him had flung himself down on a pile of straw in an empty stall.

But when all was quiet and our boys asleep in the loft above, Jem Lovelace rose up and began to prowl about the stable. He obtained a lantern and went from stall to stall closely inspecting us horses.

At length he seemed to decide on me and, to my amazement, I was saddled and bridled and cloths were bound round my feet. Then, with the utmost caution, I was led out and across the yard, the cloths muffling the ring of iron on cobblestones. Outside, by the barn, he mounted and, in the grey cold of first light, we cantered silently and swiftly up the back drive. Behind I heard the voices of my friends calling to me, but I left willingly enough. I felt that any master would be preferable to Squire Lovelace.

At the end of the drive Jem stopped to pull the cloths from my feet and then we rode on, but at a less rapid pace.

Dawn came; a wet, misty morning, and from the light coming behind me I knew that we were heading westward. My new owner seemed very pleased with himself and with me. Several times he patted my neck and then he said, 'Nightshade, by Highflyer out of Bella, quite an aristocrat and a very fine piece of horse flesh, if I may say so. What do *you* think of carrying a by-blow, a Lovelace bastard? Or don't such things concern even aristocratic horses?

'You are my Patrimony, Nightshade,' he went on after a pause. 'My Father flung me a guinea and said I might eat in the servants' hall, so I have stolen the fastest horse in his stable, a good saddle and bridle, a pair of pistols and set myself up in a business more to my taste than the apprenticeship he provided. I am too much of a Lovelace to be content with putting up a draper's shutters and sweeping his shop.

50

'I don't suppose you've heard of the Foundling Hospital, Nightshade, but that is where I was brought up. Neither parent having the least use for me, my Father paid ten guineas that I might not starve. Ten guineas! How does that compare with what he has spent on the education and pleasures of my proud brother Tom? But never mind that, I begin to feel more equal now that I am mounted on a fine horse. And we must go to work for I have nothing but the Squire's guinea, having spent every penny I possessed on fine clothes to impress my family.'

By noon we'd left our tame and cultivated country with its frequent villages, its rectories, farms, manors and halls and entered a wilder, bleaker county. Windswept hills and downs stretched away on either side of us and the turnpike-road lay ahead. My master rode along singing cheerfully, showing no haste to begin the work he had spoken of, until he caught sight of a tollgate. Then he said, 'We had best save our penny,' and, riding me through a weak half-grown hedge, took to the fields.

Some way on, well out of sight of the pikeman, we regained the turnpike and found ourselves approaching a small market town.

'A two hour bait for you, Shady and a good dinner for me,' said Jem as we clattered into the innyard. He called for the ostler, in a very confident and gentlemanlike way, and stayed to see me watered and fed before vanishing into the inn.

I was glad of the food, but did not get much rest owing to the great noise and constant comings and goings. The clatter of hoofs, the harsh rattle of the iron tyres of the carts on the cobblestones, never stopped for a moment and the voices of men calling for ostlers and ostlers calling for stable boys were near as bad, while the cries of the traders selling their wares in the market place added to the general turmoil.

When I complained of the uproar to a stout chestnut horse in the next stall, he looked at me in surprise, 'O 'tis nothing,' he said. 'You want to come on fair day, then 'tis bursting over and you can't get in nor out of yard for carts.'

Later, when my master called for me, a new saddlebag was strapped to my saddle and when we had made our way down the main street, which was as crowded as any race course, and out into the open country beyond, he began to talk. 'I laid out the rest of my money in town, Shady. I am equipped with powder, ball and the means for casting more. My father's pocket pistols shall earn us a good living.'

I was glad to hear that the pistols were to earn our living and went on happily enough, enjoying the new scenery that constantly unfolded before my eyes and listening to my master's songs, which he sang very cheerfully, considering they were all about being crossed in love or dying young.

We saw few people for this was grazing country and great numbers of workers were not needed, just cowmen and drovers for the cattle. No great armies of people to plough and sow and harvest. The hamlets we passed through were very poor places. One-storied hovels, built of mud and straw, housed the people. The doors stood open to the road, for there were no chimneys to let the smoke out, and the window was frequently covered with paper or rags for want of glass. The difference between these one-roomed cottages and elegant houses like Thorngate Manor struck me very forcibly and I could see that the Squire's horses had been better fed, housed and clothed than the ragged families who came to their doors to watch us ride by.

My new master seemed to know where he was going. Once he asked for directions from an elderly crone gathering cresses from a stream and once from some ragged children picking up sticks, to whom he threw a penny. We rode down green lanes and across fields and then, on the crest of a hill he halted and exclaimed, 'The Bath road, Nightshade. That is where we commence our business.'

The road was still some distance away, across a stretch of grass, and Jem suddenly urged me into a gallop. I was quite happy to show my paces and I think he was amazed by my speed and the way we covered the ground. When we pulled up he patted me delightedly. 'You'll do excellently, Shady,' he said. 'I'd defy anyone to catch me when riding a horse of your speed. I foresee a very long and profitable partnership between us. We will both live like gentlemen for very little toil.'

I was surprised to find Jem a practised horseman and wondered at the time how a foundling apprenticed to a draper could have accomplished this, but later I learned that the draper, being in business in a very big way, had kept a stable of horses, mainly for deliveries, in which Jem had started work as a stable boy.

When we reached the Bath road my master became nervous and uncertain. He said we must find a suitable spot, but this proved far from easy. One place was too close to a house, from another he could see a church spire, a third offered no hiding place. He had almost settled on a hollow at the foot of a long hill, when he recollected that most coachmen 'spring' their horses, that is whip them into a gallop, at the foot of a hill so that the carriage is taken half way up by the momentum, and this would not suit our purpose. We climbed to the top of the hill and Jem found a spot there that would do.

'Those coming up the hill will be blown and those coming the other way will be going slow and wondering whether to put on the drag,' he said, 'and there is that clump of trees for us to lurk in.'

We went into the trees and there he took out his pocket pistols and inspected them in turn. Then he waited, listening and watching the road with impatience.

We heard a rumbling, the sound of hoofs and bells and soon a covered wagon heavily laden with goods and drawn by six great horses came in sight. Rattling and clanking on its great broad wheels it passed slowly by. Behind it came two farm horses, clopping leisurely. A smocked carter sat sideways on one and there was a smell of new shoes about them. My master fidgeted and sighed. Then, as dusk was thickening, we heard the rattle of light wheels and the spanking trot of well-bred horses. In a moment my master tied a piece of black crepe round his face, his eyes seeing through two slits, drew a pistol and urged me forward into the road.

A handsome carriage drawn by four roan horses was slowing as it came to the downhill; a private carriage with two postilions in blue jackets and jockey caps riding the nearside horses.

'Stand!' shouted my master in a loud and commanding voice and riding into their path, he pointed his pistol at the leading postilion's head. He was a decrepit grey-haired old man and the other just a boy so they offered no resistance and came quickly to a halt. My master rode to the carriage door and pulled it open. The lady and gentleman inside were both middle-aged and agitated.

'Sir, Madam,' said Jem in very polite tones, 'I am sorry to inconvenience you but, being the natural son of a gentleman with no fortune of my own, I must extract contributions from those in happier circumstances. Your money, sir.'

'Money, yes, of course. Let me see . . .' The gentleman searched his pockets and held out a handful of coins. My master took the two golden guineas from among them and said, 'Your purse, if you please,' thrusting his pistol into the carriage to emphasise his words. The lady screamed and the gentleman began to scuffle hurriedly inside his coat and brought forth a small leather bag. Jem looked inside and seemed well satisfied. 'Thank you, sir,' he said. 'May I wish you a pleasant journey.' And, wheeling round, we took to the fields.

Safely away we stopped to count the coins. 'Eleven guineas, Shady! Eleven guineas. That is the beginning of our fortune, though I should have taken their watches too, but clean forgot in the excitement. Still, guineas are a good deal safer. Well, that is our work done for today. We'll go on towards Bath and find an inn.'

We put up at a small inn some distance from the highway. I found myself stalled between a bagman's pony and a doctor's horse that had lost a wheel off his gig and was waiting at the inn while the wheelwright carried out repairs.

The landlord's son, aged about ten years, was our groom. He brought me a large feed and an armful of choice hay, gazing at me all the while with great admiration. I don't think he had ever had a thoroughbred in his care before.

The bagman's pony, a hairy bay with a ewe neck and a hollow back, was a very talkative fellow and when I confessed that I had no notion of what a bagman did for a living, he soon explained. It seemed that many villages were beginning to have a shop for the first time. This saved the poorer sort of people from a long trudge into town every time they ran out of tea or some other grocery they could not produce for themselves. The bagman rode round these village shops taking their orders and collecting the debts on previous deliveries of goods which were sent by wagon or pack pony.

The bagman's pony said that it was a good life except that his master was a terrible rider, 'By my troth 'e'd be off an 'undred times a day if I didn't see after 'e. As for stumbling or starting I just daren't risk the like of it, 'e'd pitch straight over m' 'ead for sure.'

When my companions enquired as to the occupation of my master, I found myself saying that, as I had only been his for one day, I hardly knew as yet, but he seemed a very pleasant young fellow and might have private means.

As I lay down on my thick bed of bracken, I thought that my master's profession was going to involve me in many lies and deceptions and I wished, most heartily, that he had chosen some respectable occupation.

For the next few days we rode about the countryside, dining and sleeping at different inns, while my master seemed very taken up with observing the lie of the land and studying maps.

Then one day he told me that our money was running out and towards evening we set off purposefully and came at length to a highway which he said was the Exeter road.

By reading the milestones, we found a particular spot which was midway between two post houses, the inns where the stage coaches and the post-chaises changed their horses. It was a very lonely place, without a habitation in sight, and there was a thicket close to the road in which we took up our station. There Jem checked his pistols and put on his crepe mask.

We waited. The faint wintery sun sank behind a hill, the evening closed about us cold and damp; my master shivered.

Then we heard hoofs. A great number of hoofs and the rattle of several carriages. I waited ready to swoop out into the road, but the order never came.

'Outriders,' said Jem, as two grooms in green livery on matching chestnuts went by, and he cursed under his breath. Then came a very handsome chariot, also drawn by chestnuts and with postilions in green livery, then more liveried grooms. They were followed by several less outstanding carriages, carrying children and nurses, servants and boxes, while more grooms brought up the rear. We could see that it was a rich family moving from one estate to another or coming home from a visit.

'There were far too many of them for us to take on,' said Jem as the cavalcade passed out of sight.

It was not long before we heard a single set of hoofs coming along at a very brisk pace, as though anxious to reach home before dark.

As we burst out of our hiding place I saw that it was a very stout, hairy-legged grey, ridden by an oldish man, with a lady in a long cloak and a bonnet riding behind him pillion.

'Stand!' called my master. 'Stand, sir, or I fire,' and he waved his pistol aloft in a very threatening manner.

The man reined-in the horse, but the old woman shrieked at him to take no notice, but gallop on and she

was belabouring the horse's rump with the bag she carried.

'Strike the villain with your whip,' she cried. 'Ride him down, he'll not fire.'

But the man, I took him to be her groom, was grey faced with fright and dared not ride on. He shook his head, when Jem demanded money again, 'I've but a few pence,' he said through chattering teeth.

'Madam, your money,' said Jem pointing his pistol at the lady.

'You won't frighten me, that's never loaded,' she answered scornfully.

'If you try my patience much further, Madam, you

shall have proof that it is,' said my master in a cold voice. 'I will begin by putting a ball in your old horse,' and he clapped the muzzle of the pistol to the horse's head, which I felt very unfair. Let the humans rob each other as much as they like, I thought, but they should leave us horses out of their quarrels. So I backed away and resolved to rear up if he fired and make the ball go wide.

However the lady had been convinced by Jem's manner and was fumbling inside her cloak. She brought out a little bag on a string and handed it over with many scoldings and threats that she should see Jem hanged before long.

'Thank you, Madam,' he said bowing. As we galloped off I could hear her berating the poor old groom for his cowardice.

'Six guineas,' said Jem stopping to count them. 'And now I think we will move on, for that ferocious old woman will be back if she can find a few stout lads to help her.'

We rode westward. It was almost dark, but soon we heard a carriage and saw lights approaching. Jem stopped to put on his mask and draw his pistol, then we took up position in the middle of the road.

'Stand!' shouted my master very loud. 'Stand and deliver or I fire.'

The postilion, there was only one for it was but a pair of horses, tried to whip them into a gallop. My master fired a shot over his head and quickly drew his other pistol. The chaise window opened and a deep voice called, 'Pull up, postilion, we want no loss of life.'

'Your money, sirs,' said Jem looking into the carriage.

'I am afraid we have but little on us,' said the deep voice. 'We have met with so many accidents and delays on the road that we are almost penniless.' He rattled a few coins in his hand.

Jem ordered them both out and told them to stand by the carriage lamp. They were well, but soberly, dressed. City men by the look of them for they had white hands and faces and none of the ruddiness of country folk.

They turned out their pockets eagerly, demonstrating their emptiness in the most affable manner. Jem brandished his pistol and ordered them to take off their coats. They stripped off great coats and frock coats and waistcoats, the last most reluctantly for the night air was cold. Still finding no hidden money bags, Jem ordered them to take off their boots.

The sudden fall in their spirits told me that he had hit upon the hiding place, and, as the boots came off, a shower of guineas fell upon the ground.

'Hand them up,' ordered Jem and when he had been given some twenty-five he seemed satisfied and, apologising for the great inconvenience he had given them, we set off westward again.

He kept laughing to himself as we walked slowly along the dark road, hoping for the moon to rise. 'An excellent evening's work, Shady,' he told me. 'I'll never forget their faces when I hit upon the boots.'

## CHAPTER SIX

# 'To be hanged like a dog'

For some weeks we went on in much the same manner. We kept on the move, never robbing two nights in the same spot and changing frequently between the Bath and Exeter roads so that the poor travellers might never know where to expect us.

As winter came on there were fewer travellers. Though the regular coaches, The Salisbury Diligence, The Green Dragon, The Expedition, went up and down our roads with great horn blowing as they went through the villages or approached the post houses, my master did not like to take them on single-handed. He said they all carried an armed guard as well as the coachman so it only wanted one stout-hearted passenger with a pistol for him to be outnumbered. Instead we took to preying on the farmers going home from market and, since they had frequently drunk away some of the proceeds of selling their cattle and corn, they were easy victims.

At the post inns we could sometimes gather information about the travellers staying overnight and several times we rose in the early morning and waylaid our fellow guests a few miles along the road. Again my master was cautious; *one* naval man, newly paid off and travelling home alone, he would attack, but *two*, travelling together, might keep their money.

'I want to live to be an old man, Shady, and to die in my bed,' he told me, 'so discretion shall be the better part.'

As the winter grew increasingly bitter, he decided that

we needed more permanent quarters and we made our way to the Cranborne Chase, a great forest on the borders of Hampshire and Dorset and there we found an isolated farm that took us in.

It seemed that this was a very desperate and lawless neighbourhood, which welcomed such a man as my master. I soon heard tell of the terrible bloody battles that took place when the poachers went after the deer, for Prince and Queenie, the two stout ponies that stood next to me, were used to carry home the carcases when the poachers had made their kills.

They had witnessed many ugly scenes and battles, for the gamekeepers and poachers would kill and maim each other without a thought, and they told me their stories on the long winter nights, when the wind moaned round our stable, the rain pelted down or the snow fell, thick and silent.

We were fairly comfortable inside. My master had procured me a horse cloth. It was a little faded and moth-eaten, but warm enough and as the farm boy slept in the stable with us, he had taken great trouble to stuff all the cracks and crevices with rags and make the place snug.

But outside many people lost their lives, for the cold was intense and we even heard of folk being frozen to death on their way home from market.

I was always happy enough if I had good food and company and there it was strange company. For sometimes at dawn the smugglers' ponies, carrying tea and lace and spirits that had come into the country without paying duty, would arrive and hide away in our stables until darkness enabled them to move on again with their packs and panniers of contraband goods. They had many stories of fights with the Excise men and though the smugglers themselves were often desperate men, the buyers of the contraband were most respectable people and the ponies said they left many a cask and package on squires' and parsons' doorsteps at dead of night.

It seemed that my master was keeping company with a very pretty milkmaid and had decided that during the cold weather one or two robberies a week should be sufficient to keep us. We continued to terrorise the folk going home from market, but as we took a different market each week, no sooner had one set of people decided to arm and organise themselves, than we had gone elsewhere.

At the first sign of spring my master became restless and irritable. As the days grew longer we would ride to Salisbury and watch the cockfighting or bull-baiting. The second was a very cruel sport, I thought, for the poor bull was fastened up by a chain and then the dogs were set upon him. As he could not run, he had to stand and fight and, with the dogs sinking their teeth into him in the most ferocious manner, he would toss or gore them with his horns.

I longed to tell them all to stop, for this was a fight purely got up for the pleasure of men, who watched in a great state of excitement and laid wagers on the result, which was frequently the death and maiming of several dogs as well as the death of the bull. I never saw bear-baiting, though a lot of it went on, but I was told it was much the same and very horrible to watch.

One day my master bought a fine new suit of clothes, which put him in a very good humour. Then he paid the carter to trim my mane and tail and give me a very thorough grooming, and, soon afterwards, we set out on our travels again.

I was sad to part with Prince and Queenie and the pretty milkmaid sobbed most pitifully to see us go.

As we rode through the countryside I was very much shocked to see the state of the animals that had wintered out on the commons belonging to the villages. Many of them were walking bags of bones and had evidently not seen oats or hay all through the bitter weather. Ponies, donkeys, cows and goats, it was pitiful to watch them searching for each new blade of grass as it came through, there being not a scrap left to eat on their bare pastures.

One day, when my master was drinking a mug of ale at the door of an inn, I talked to a starved pony that had been put to pull a cart, despite his condition, and looked so feeble that it seemed to be the shafts that held him up. He explained that he belonged to a cottager who had but a very small amount of land on which he grew vegetables for his family, but had no room for hay or oats. His master had grazing rights on the common, but so had all the other village folk, and their great quantity of animals over-grazed it even in the summer, with the result that in a hard winter like the last, many animals died of starvation.

In one village we passed through there seemed to be more organisation and the whole common was given over to geese. A great flock of several hundreds honked and grazed and two or three very little boys and girls were minding them.

Yet another common was newly fenced and my master enquiring about it was told that the villagers had sold their rights to a rich farmer under the enclosure laws. But now, having spent the money, they deeply regretted what they had done for they had nowhere to graze their cows and when they sold them, no milk for their children. Added to this they had lost the right to cut furze for their fires and now many cottages were without fires for days on end and those that had them would be boiling their neighbours' kettles as well as their own.

As spring came on with balmy air and flowers and blossom everywhere, my master talked to me about his plans. He had heard that there was talk of setting up a special patrol to capture him and earn the forty pounds paid to thief takers, so he had decided to leave our old neighbourhood and move across to the Southampton road.

We kept on the move all that summer and robbed a great many travellers. Though I had grown accustomed to sleeping in a different stall every night, I often felt the want of a regular stable and some of the ostlers were careless, some rough in their grooming and others dishonest. If my master did not stay to see me fed, it was quite likely that I would get nothing but hay, my feed of oats being spirited away in a sack to be sold or fed to the ostlers' own goat or poultry.

When winter came we returned to the Cranborne Chase. There I enjoyed the company of Prince and Queenie and the local farmers, coming home from market with their hard-earned guineas, were again at the mercy of my master.

It was sometime during this winter that Jem Lovelace took up with another highwayman called Edmund Evershaw. Evershaw had been robbing coaches on the Norwich road and then moved to Hounslow Heath and now being wanted for the murder of a guard, he had come to lie low in the Chase.

His previous horse having gone lame on the journey, he had turned her loose on a common and stolen a good chestnut hunter, called Harkaway, who was now stabled next to me.

I did not like Evershaw. He had a hard, cruel face, deeply pitted with smallpox, and he cared nothing for Harkaway except as a means of conveyance. I also feared his influence on my master, who was younger and had seen less of the world.

Of course it was understood that with two of them, they could take on greater numbers and more reckless endeavours and Harkaway and I soon began to feel a great dislike for the night's work.

Evershaw had a double barrelled pistol of which he was very proud and he would fire it in the wildest manner. On one occasion the ball went through the window of the carriage, narrowly missing the people inside and causing an elderly lady to faint, and all this after they had pulled up and were handing over their valuables.

Another night we robbed two clerical gentlemen coming up from the cathedral at Exeter and Evershaw swore most horribly at them when they failed to hand over as many guineas as he expected. Having had almost all their clothes off, he seemed inclined to kill them out of spite, when he found that they were speaking the truth and had no more money hidden. If my master had not been there to drag him away, I am convinced there would have been bloodshed.

And once he was very cruel to a lady who could not remove the ring from her finger. He threatened to take the finger too, if she did not hurry up and actually got out his knife.

Then, as summer came on, the rogue somehow heard of a mail coach that would be carrying vast numbers of bill notes from a bank. He knew that there would be a guard travelling with it and perhaps two, both armed, so he persuaded my master that another highwayman should be asked to join them.

When we set out for the scene of the robbery, it was to take place somewhere near Andover, a loutish youth, called Billy Hind, came with us. He was a great bragger and before we had gone many miles we were all heartily tired of hearing how much his pistols had cost him and how fast his lumbering gelding could trot.

After some disagreement, they settled on a suitable spot and my master checked his pistols and put on his mask. Evershaw never wore a mask. I suppose he thought his ill-favoured countenance almost as good a weapon as his pistol.

Poor Harkaway was very nervous and kept sighing and wishing that he could return to his life as a hunter, while Billy boasted in a loud voice how many pints of ale he could drink at a sitting.

We waited and the drizzle which was falling thickened into rain. The men swore and turned up their coat collars; we horses bowed our heads and tried to put our tails to the wind.

At last we heard the coach, the four horses trotting briskly. It wasn't dark, just wet and dismal, and, as we burst into the road with our masters shouting 'Stand! Stand and deliver!' we could be seen quite plainly.

Evershaw, who always carried at least three loaded pistols, fired off one of them, the ball passing dangerously close to the coachman. The guard fired in return and Billy Hind cried out and dropped his reins. My master closed with the guard, demanding his blunderbuss and making him and the coachman get down from

67

the box. Meanwhile Evershaw was getting the passengers down.

When they had all the people lined up my master stood over them, a pistol in either hand, the reins knotted on my neck, while Evershaw searched hurriedly through the mail bags and swore at Billy Hind to stop blubbering about a ball through the arm.

Finding the bag he wanted, Evershaw swung himself up on Harkaway and placed it across his knees. My master was engaged in collecting a few guineas from the passengers, when the sound of approaching hoofs was heard and three young men came riding through the dusk. The passengers called out for help; the guard broke away and was shot down by Evershaw. The young men drew pistols and charged. The commotion was terrible. Pistols banged, ladies screamed, men shouted. The black smoke from the gunpowder hung in the air. There was no time to reload, so they closed in, using their whip handles and pistol butts as cudgels. Hats were knocked off, men swore and shouted, we horses reared and plunged in fright.

Above the uproar my master called to Evershaw to break away and gallop for it. We were heavily outnumbered and he had seen the coachman pick up the guard's blunderbuss; in a moment it would be reloaded.

'I'm going, Evershaw,' my master called again. 'Break it off, you fool.' Then to my relief he did go. We took to the fields. Never had I galloped so willingly. Shouts and thudding hoofs followed us, too close for peace of mind. I hoped that they had had no time to reload.

The country was strange to us but my master rode as though he had a place or point in mind and we took the obstacles that appeared in our path as best we could. I was

not sure of myself as a jumper, but I managed to scramble over several ditches and hedges and when we came to a stretch of grass, I covered it at full speed, confident that no ordinary horse could keep near me.

But it was darkness coming down that saved us, though we were soon lost ourselves, in a strange place with no moon.

My master dismounted and led me, walking boldly until he came to the darker blackness of a wood or hedge, then he felt his way as best he could, stumbling over rough ground, tripping over roots and losing all sense of direction.

Our progress was very slow and there was no light or other sign of habitation to make for. At length he gave up.

'We'll rest and hope for a moon, Shady,' he said, slackening my girth and taking the reins over my head. 'You must graze as you can for I fear a shelterless and supperless night lies ahead; at least the rain is warm.'

I cropped the grass which was short and sweet, he ate some crumbs of bread and cheese from his pocket and we waited.

There was no moon that night and though once or twice we moved on a little, it was more to warm ourselves or to find me fresh grazing, than in the hope of making any progress.

Dawn found us cold and wet through, but at first light my master began to lead me forward and, as the sun rose, he mounted and we went on, heading south-west towards a heath. On the heath he stopped to look at his map, while I listened to the birds, all singing noisily at the sight of a new day.

When Jem was certain of his way we set off again, still going south-west, and we kept going steadily for several hours. We halted once or twice to drink at streams, but not for food, and I began to wonder if we would ever be able to enter a comfortable inn again.

We came at length to the Weymouth road and, crossing over, made our way into the hills of North Dorsetshire and, beyond them, we came to a vale. Here we were quite unknown and when we stopped at a small inn I was more hungry and more weary than I had ever been in my life.

We rested there in the vale for several days and then, our money beginning to run short, we began to rob again.

King George was at Weymouth taking the sea air, so many fashionable people belonging to the Court and politics were travelling up and down the road, and my master seemed well satisfied with his takings. Away from Evershaw he had resumed his former polite air and we had no shouting or threats. But I think he was in some anxiety about his friends for he went out of his way to get hold of newspapers and looked through them in a very apprehensive manner.

One day we rode right into the town of Weymouth. It was very early in the morning, but there were people everywhere and all the shops open. When my master enquired the reason they told him that the Queen, who was a strange old body and wore a cloak and bonnet just like any other old woman, rose up at five every morning and went sea-bathing with her daughters. And the whole population feeling that they must rise with her, the shops were all open by half-past six.

I was very much taken with the sea, never having seen it before, but my master seemed more excited by the people parading about in fine clothes and the bands which appeared as the morning progressed, and played for the king. Farmer George, as he was called by the populace, had been very ill and many people were pitying the poor old man and wishing that he might be left in peace. But the music went on all morning; we heard *God Save the King* played six or seven times and the trumpets being sounded as he went down to bathe.

From that day my master had no peace of mind either. For, while still in Weymouth, he got hold of a newspaper that announced the capture of Edmund Evershaw. He had been arrested in the act of changing bill notes taken in the robbery and was in prison awaiting trial. But, worse than this, it was now known that my master had also been involved and a reward of two hundred pounds had been offered for his capture.

He read this several times, turning very pale, and then he began to curse the day that he had met Evershaw. Until, suddenly recollecting where he was, and realising the danger, he mounted hastily and hurried from the town.

'Two hundred pounds, Shady,' he said, slowing me to

a walk as we reached a quiet byroad. 'Two hundred pounds! It is a great deal of money – a fortune to some. Shall I ever be able to trust anyone again?'

The next few weeks were very uncomfortable. We travelled great distances and lived rough, sleeping out at nights and stopping at small inns for but one meal a day. Otherwise I lived on grass and became quite lean.

We robbed solitary travellers on the byroads, choosing those who would not put up a fight. My master swore at the paltryness of the sums he took and was very sad and restless and irritable.

Then came more bad news. Evershaw and Billy Hind had been tried and sentenced to death. It seemed they were in prison near London and my master suddenly resolved that he must go there; he must see Evershaw before his end.

By this time we were both very rough-looking and my master's fine clothes were very much the worse for wear, but staying only at the lowest sort of inn, 'dogholes' Jem called them, this did not attract attention to us. It was only to those who knew a good horse, that I looked too superior for my station, and for them my master had an answer ready: I was a broken-down racer he had bought for a song.

I do not know if Jem managed to see Evershaw in prison. But he was desperately low spirited for days on end and, not knowing what to do with himself, hung about a disreputable tavern gaming and drinking Geneva spirits.

When the day for the execution came we rode to the common near London where the gallows had been set up. There were four of them, for Evershaw, Billy Hind and two other wrongdoers.

I did not see the horrible business myself. Jem left me to be baited at an inn and went on foot, for together we were more likely to be recognised. But I had seen the great crowds of people gathering and, when the wagon carrying the prisoners appeared, I heard the shouts and boos that greeted it. I heard the terrible excitement of the people enjoying the spectacle of men being hanged.

When my master came to fetch me he was pale and much shaken. 'Oh God, Nightshade, this will not do,' he said, as we hurried away from the place. 'I could not bear an end like that. To be hanged like a dog for all the world to see. And now his body is to be gibbeted! Hanged in irons from one of the gibbets on the heath. Horrible!

'To think of his body swinging there until it rots away and bits of him stolen by the old witches for their spells. Oh God, I could not bear such a fate. And Billy's is little better. His body has been given to the surgeons for their dissections.'

My master rode on towards London in this very agitated mood and then gradually he seemed to come to a decision.

'I must leave the country,' he told me. 'I must go to the colonies, the Indies, America, anywhere, and start again under another name. I must sell you, Shady; it grieves me, but it has to be done. You will pay my passage to a new life.'

I was apprehensive at the prospect of a new master, but I did not see how things could go on as they were for, without a settled existence, we would starve or freeze to death when winter came.

I do not know how my sale was managed, I suspect it was through a friendly inn-keeper, but a buyer was found, and as Jem Lovelace gave me a quick pat and hurried away, a brown-liveried groom, who said that he was Mr Samuel Packington's man, came and took me in charge.

## CHAPTER SEVEN

# A more respectable life

I soon learned that Mr Packington lived in one of the suburbs of London where the newly rich merchants and owners of manufactories were building large modern houses. I also learned that Joseph, his groom, had been sent to London on two errands.

The first errand was to buy a riding horse, my predecessor having died of colic, the second to escort a party of parish children from one of the London workhouses to Mr Packington's manufactory in Kent.

Joseph was a neatly made, small featured man, wearing his own black hair. He was a fair rider and a good judge of horses and, being of superior intelligence, was entrusted with many business matters by his master.

Greatly dissatisfied with my appearance, Joseph soon began to trim me up. He also put an ostler to work grooming me and a stable boy to cleaning my saddlery, with the result, that when we set out next morning, I felt and looked a different horse.

We went straight to the workhouse. A huge grey, gloomy building in a dismal street, it housed the poor, the old and children who had no parents to see to them. Orphans, foundlings, unwanted bastards and children whose parents were too poor to keep them, were all shut away and paid for by the parish.

As Joseph told his business to the man at the door, our two wagons, drawn by six horses apiece, came trundling up the street.

'You've got the leftovers,' said the man on the door. 'All the best ones get taken as servants or apprenticed to trades. Very rough lot you've got, and mind you keep 'em, we don't want to see 'em back in London. The Poor Rate's 'igh enough as it is.'

The children came marching out in a very orderly fashion, boys being directed to one wagon and girls to the other. They quickly piled in, as though glad to get away. They were very young, about eight or nine years of age, with pale faces as though they never saw the sun and, though clean and not ragged, their clothes were of very poor quality and seemed either much too large or too small.

As soon as they were settled we set off, Joseph and I leading the way through the busy streets. Carts and carriages were crowding us all the time and some of them becoming very impatient at the lumbering pace of our wagons.

The children were all in a great state of excitement and fighting for places where they might look out, round and under the wagons' canvas awnings. They seemed as happy as if it were a pleasure trip. They sang songs and hymns and shouted remarks at the passers-by.

Their favourite shout was, 'Guinea pig!' for since powder had been taxed one guinea, to help pay for the war, many men had given up wigs and it was the fashion to wear your own hair and unpowdered. Men of the old school who stuck to their wigs were nicknamed guinea pigs.

The two carters, who wore brownish smocks and carried whips, mostly walked beside their horses and from time to time Joseph dismounted and walked with me, which rested my back and stretched his legs.

Towards dinner-time, we went on to warn a small country inn of our arrival and then while Joseph ate in the inn and I was baited in the stable, the children were given bread and cheese and tea in the barn.

They seemed very disappointed with this fare and it gradually came out that the overseers at the workhouse had given them great expectations of their new life. They'd been promised roast beef and plum pudding every day and told that they would earn enough money to buy gold watches and fine clothes.

Joseph was very much shocked at the wicked lie. He told one of the carters that the unfortunate children were going from the prison of the workhouse to the slavery of a factory, and that Mr Packington would not pay them a penny until they were twenty-one. Until then they must work long hours for their clothes and keep. And poor keep it was.

A coach would have accomplished the journey to Critley in a few hours, for the better roads and the quick and constant changes of horses enabled them to cover eight or nine miles an hour in flat country. Our wagons' steady plod, with the same horses taking us all the way, could not do better than three miles an hour and so it had been arranged that we should spend a night on the road, Joseph and I putting up at an inn, the children sleeping in the wagons.

Bred in the city, the children did not seem to like the look of the country overmuch, but when at length we reached Critley and drove through gates, with *Packington & Tucker* writ very large on the archway above, and they saw the factory, a great, tall, ugly building, with the noisy thump of machinery never stopping for a moment, they were very cast down indeed. The sight of the two bleak,

grey barracks they were to live in was an even greater disappointment and many of them burst out crying.

Joseph was very unhappy at their distress, but there seemed to be nothing he could do for them, so when he had handed them over to the overseers and seen them counted, he said we must be off at once for we had a long way to go.

Mr Packington's house, number 22 Park Drive, was a good deal closer to London than it was to Critley and I was very tired by the time we turned in at the gate and saw the tall modern house standing in a garden, with a coach house and stable to one side. In front it looked across a common, but there were no cattle or geese grazing there. Instead avenues of trees had been planted and walks laid out, but the air was fresh and not thick with smoke and dirt as the city air is.

I soon found myself in a stall, with companions on either side, and a boy called Rob unsaddling me.

I was quite glad to have a regular stable again and soon settled down in my new home. Mr Packington did not keep a very large establishment, Joseph being coachman as well as head groom and Green helping in the garden as well as the stable. Rob was a dull, sandy-haired boy with light eyelashes, who had to be given every order twice, but even so the place was run in a very orderly manner.

The carriage horses were a well-matched pair of bays, called Madcap and Tomboy, but they did not live up to their names, being very staid animals. There was also a small pony, a sturdy, cheerful, dark brown called Jolly Roger, and a larger grey, Snowstorm, who was rather a weary, grumbling sort of pony, much afflicted by worms.

In the general way Mr Packington took the carriage when he went to the city, for there, Joseph said, he had to look the big man, but when he visited the manufactory, which was three or four times a week, he rode me.

Joseph rode me a good deal too, generally on errands for his master, and Mr Sidney, the elder son, was to ride me when he came home from school.

There were four other children: Violet, Rosamund, Myrtle and a little boy of five who was the curled and spoiled darling of his Mamma. According to Jolly Roger, Master Clarence was a good deal too free with his whip and when Rob, who was his riding master, took the whip away he made a great outcry and said he should tell his Mamma that Rob had not treated him with proper respect.

At first I much enjoyed the rides to Critley, but, as I grew used to the road, they became rather monotonous. Mr Packington, who was a well-built man in his forties, with black, bushy eyebrows, a large nose and a severe mouth, never thought of changing his route or giving me a gallop. He was not much of a rider, being unable to get into the rhythm of the thing, and always pulled on the reins as though force was needed. But, worst of all, he never spoke to me and we would go all the way to Critley and back in perfect silence.

When I had lived at 22 Park Drive for some months a great outcry against the conditions of factory children was raised and taken up in Parliament and the newspapers.

It came out that the children at Packington's worked for twelve hours a day, six days a week and the men whom they assisted, being on piece work, would do almost anything to keep them awake and busy. They often beat them and soused them with cold water if they were slow, or dropped off to sleep.

It seemed that such great labours at a very young age (some of the local people sent their children to work in the factory at six or seven years) often caused malformation of the bones and many had crooked knees and grew up quite lame and crippled. The heat and dust also brought on consumptions and many of the children died young.

Mr Packington did not seem much perturbed by this outcry. He pointed to his two grey barracks and said that they were well-conducted by respectable overseers and the boys and girls kept strictly apart. That the children were given a plentiful supply of bread and porridge, with either bacon or cheese every day and meat on Sundays. Every child attended Sunday school or church and the long hours of labour at least kept them from idle habits and mischief. And many people, agreeing with him, and feeling that the parish children should earn their own bread from the age of nine onwards, the protest died away and nothing was done.

I think I had been with Mr Packington about two years, when disaster struck his own family.

As the spoiled Master Clarence grew older he had

become more and more disobedient and one day, when being taken out for a walk by his nurse, he ran off and, in a moment had entirely vanished. The poor woman hunted high and low for him and then, hurrying home in a great state of distress had called on the whole household to assist in the search.

When they failed to find the boy, Joseph mounted Madcap and rode to Critley at breakneck speed to bring Mr Packington the bad news. I was saddled at once and we hurried back to Park Drive to find Mrs Packington in hysterics and the boy still missing.

Mr Packington went off with Snowstorm in the gig to tell the magistrates and have the Bow Street Runners informed, for it was now feared that the boy had been stolen.

It was quite a common thing to steal little children for their fine clothes, which could be sold, and sometimes gipsies took them away to distant parts of the country and they were never seen again, but Mrs Packington feared that Master Clarence had been sold to a chimney sweep. It seemed that the newspapers had reported a shortage of climbing boys, for the tall modern houses had narrow chimneys with small flues (nine by fourteen inches was said to be the usual size, but some had been built only eight or nine inches square), which needed a very small child indeed.

With all the master sweeps wishing to advertise 'Little boys for small flues' on their trade cards, they were paying parents as much as two guineas a child and taking them as young as five or six. But, since the better sort of parent did not want to inflict such hardships on their own children, a trade in stolen children was thought to have grown up.

Green, who was frequently in and out of the house with flowers and vegetables, reported all that took place there to Joseph, so we were kept well informed of Mrs Packington's fears and vapours, of Mr Packington's rages and of the dismissal of the poor nurse without references.

When the first shock and upheaval was over a more systematic search was organised and a handsome reward was advertised for the return of the boy safe and sound.

I found myself constantly searching some squalid quarter with either Joseph or Mr Packington, for there were many poor areas between Park Drive and the centre of London and some very desperate districts near the river.

To relieve Mrs Packington's fears we called on every chimney sweep that we could hear of and, though I had stayed at low inns with Jem Lovelace, nothing I had seen hitherto had prepared me for the misery and stench of the dreadful streets I now visited.

The buildings were all crushed together without gardens or fields and every house was crowded with people; incredible numbers packed into every dirty, damp room, and frequently without proper beds or any sort of furniture.

Outside there were middens or dungheaps close to the houses and they were piled high with every sort of refuse; dead cats and dogs, as well as soil from the privies, all decaying together and stinking most horribly, while the open drain that ran down the street smelled far worse than the dirtiest stable.

The sweeps worked very early in the morning. This was so that the fires might be put out at night, and the chimneys have time to cool down, and yet the whole operation be over and the fires lit again in time for break-fast. We began our search in the late morning expecting to find them returned home.

But, though the master sweep was often there, waiting for his dinner, the poor boys had frequently been sent out to walk the streets crying 'sweepo, sweepo,' in an attempt to get work for the future and we did not see them. This made us change our tactics and we began to go out at all hours in order to get a look at the boys themselves.

Black all over, ragged, barefoot and carrying the great, heavy sacks of soot on their backs, they were a sad sight. They were all thin and starved, for a well fed boy would not be able to elbow his way along the smaller flues, and with their red eyes and coughs, bent backs and swelled knees, they looked a good deal worse than the factory children.

One day Mr Packington stopped and talked to three little sweeps walking without their master and he asked them how they came to this work. One had been apprenticed by the parish when eight years old, another by his father when his mother died and the third said he was the master sweep's stepson. He looked just as ragged and dirty and starved as the other two and he told us that his stepfather ill-used him, his mother did not want him to be a sweep, but was powerless to stop it.

Another time we saw a little curly-headed sweep crying pitifully and I felt Mr Packington's hopes rise that he would find his son under all that dirt and soot. It wasn't Clarence, but when Mr Packington asked him why he cried, he answered that he had only just started as a climbing boy and, being afraid of the dark, could not bear the long climb up, the scraping and brushing away, all the

time in the black stifling chimneys. And yet, if he did not climb, his master threatened him with beatings, pinched his feet or, lighting damp straw in the fireplace below, half choked him with smoke. He showed us the raw wounds on his elbows and knees caused by climbing.

But the bigger boy who was with him said he'd get used to it by and by and after a few months his elbows and knees would heal and the skin harden. Then he showed his own scars. Some were caused by falling down a chimney. The others when he had lost his way in a connecting flue and got by mistake into the chimney of the next door house. There he had knocked down soot into a lighted fire, causing it to flare up and burn him most severely.

Though a hard man, Mr Packington seemed much affected by the misery of the climbing boys' lives, but, beyond handing out pennies, he did nothing for them, though, Joseph said, he was spending larger and larger sums advertising rewards for the safe return of Master Clarence. He also spent many hours out looking for the boy and, when his own presence at business was essential, he sent Joseph out on me to search in his stead.

Joseph would rise early and we would be on the road at dawn. So I became accustomed to seeing the sweeps at their work and hearing the cry of 'All up!' and seeing an arm and scraper waved at the top of a chimney, to show that the boy had done his duty and gone all the way to the top.

One day we had the address of yet another sweep and, going to his dirty, tumbledown house, we found a little boy lying in a cellar on a bed of soot sacks. He said he was ill with sooty wart, a horrible disease confined to climbing boys, but did not want to go to hospital. He said his master had taken on a new little boy in his place, quite lately and told us the street where they were working.

We gave him a penny and left. Joseph said he was certain to die, for without an operation soot wart was fatal, and hurried me through the streets in search of the new little boy.

We found the house easily enough for the back door was open and the place in an uproar, with servants running about not knowing what to do, for the climbing boy was stuck fast in a flue and could not be shifted. The kitchen window was open and we could hear the sweep shouting at the boy. He was threatening to fetch a barrel of gunpowder and blow him out if he did not come down immediately. When this failed the sweep told his other boy to strip off his clothes and fetch the first one down. So, wearing but a hood over his head, he vanished into the chimney too.

Joseph hitched me to the railings and went down the basement steps into the kitchen. The sweep was telling the second boy to tie a rope round the first one's ankles

85

and, when this was done, he began to pull on the rope in an attempt to drag the child free. But the boy could not be moved an inch and his screams were terrible to hear. Joseph was trying to prevent further use of force, the kitchen maid was in hysterics, when the master of the house, awakened at last, came down in his night clothes. He took command and while a servant was sent running for a doctor, Joseph and I were dispatched to fetch a mason, who lived further afield.

We hurried through the early morning streets, fearing all the while that it was our Master Clarence stuck fast in the flue. We knocked up the sleepy mason, throwing stones at his window, and Joseph impressed on him the urgency of the matter, but he was dreadfully slow and we had to wait while he wakened his boy and loaded his handcart with tools.

We found everyone at the house waiting in great anxiety, for not a sound had been heard from the boy for some time, and the mason was hurried to work, knocking a hole in a wall with his pick, somewhere up on the first floor.

At length the poor boy was brought out and the doctor arrived in time to pronounce him dead of suffocation.

He wasn't Master Clarence, but Joseph and I rode home in very low spirits all the same.

Our search went on all summer without success and, as winter followed, the hardships suffered by the climbing boys were much increased.

We found that frequently they had no coats, no shoes or stockings and went to work at two or three in the morning without so much as a slice of bread. It was terrible to see the shivering little boys walking barefoot on frosty ground, or through snow.

One day when we came upon a bigger boy carrying a little one on his back, Joseph stopped to ask the reason. The big boy said that the little'un had been crying so dreadfully about his feet and displayed them to us, all red and raw. Joseph asked if the people at the large houses did not give them the cast off shoes and stockings from their own children? The boys said that this often happened, but, as their master immediately took them away and sold them, they preferred to be given food.

As time went on we all began to give up hope of ever seeing Master Clarence again. In his absence all his faults and spoiled ways were forgotten and even Jolly Roger mourned his loss.

The troubles of the country were also in the forefront of everyone's mind, for the war was sending all prices bounding up and up and now the French were thought to be contemplating an invasion of England. Joseph said that Mr Packington was much taken up with raising money for the defence of the country and had subscribed very handsomely to the Lord Mayor's fund for this purpose.

Mrs Packington had less to distract her and, as her hopes of finding her son faded away, there began to be fears for her health. First they tried ass's milk, then the doctors said that there were symptoms of a consumptive decline and she must be taken on a sea voyage.

After much discussion, Mr Packington decided on taking his whole family to Lisbon and, since the future was uncertain, and his wife could no longer bear the house with its memories of Clarence, he dismissed the servants and put both the house and the horses up for sale.

## CHAPTER EIGHT

## 'The French have landed!'

In a very short time the establishment at 22 Park Drive was split up and we all went our separate ways.

Mr Tucker, who was to run the business in Mr Packington's absence, decided to take on Joseph; Rob was sent home to his parents. Madcap, Tomboy and the carriage were put in a sale, Jolly Roger went to some children living near and Snowstorm found a comfortable situation with two elderly ladies.

I was quite well known locally and several offers were made, but a close friend of Mr Packington's was determined to have me for his brother-in-law and brought him to try me.

I liked Mr Maitland directly. He was a thin, spare man of medium height and a great deal lighter than Mr Packington. He wore his own silver hair quite short and was exceedingly courteous to those around him.

He congratulated Joseph on my general condition, Rob on the cleanliness of my coat and me on my manners and paces, but, to the disgust of his brother-in-law, he seemed very doubtful about making the purchase.

'What should I do with such an elegant animal?' he asked. 'I do not propose to join the fashion parade in Hyde Park, or lead a regiment, or dazzle some beautiful lady. All I need is a steady conveyance and you find me a magnificent thoroughbred. Neither I nor my horsemanship are worthy of such an animal.'

'Nonsense, Maitland,' the brother-in-law was very

firm, 'I know that you are unworldly, but other men judge each other by appearance and you will procure far better attention at an inn, riding a horse of his stamp, than on your usual decrepit nags. In addition you will find a well-bred, well-made horse far less tiring to ride; a man who travels the distances you do, should not condemn himself to the joltings of a common animal.'

In the end, this second argument prevailed, for my new master admitted that, as he grew older, he did have to look more to his comfort. So I was sold and it was settled that Joseph should ride me to my new home, which was some distance to the south of Critley and not far from the sea.

In London, where there was constant talk of invasion, nothing much seemed to be done about it, but as we came closer to the coast there was a great deal more activity. We saw semaphore signalling devices on the hill tops, looking very much like gibbets, but said to take the news of a landing to London in an unbelievably short space of time. On every church lych gate and nailed to a tree on every village green was a poster headed INVASION with instructions on how the people were to burn the crops and drive the cattle with them and many other things.

Here and there we came across materials for building barricades piled at the roadside, ready to be pulled across and obstruct the approaching army. There were also many little fortifications, made where a bridge was to be defended or a crossroad held.

When Joseph stopped for ale the talk was all of armies massed along the French coast, only twenty miles away, and of the thousands of flat bottomed boats that were to bring them across the channel. It was said that there was hardly a tree left in that part of France; they had all been cut down for boats.

Everyone seemed a good deal afraid of the French leader, Napoleon Bonaparte. Boney they called him for short. All day long you could hear mothers using him to threaten their children. In London they were threatened that the sweep would get them, here it was Boney.

When we reached my new home, The Croft, there was quite a party of people to welcome me. Mr Maitland smiling and joking about how much in awe he was of my elegance and how he must mend his ways and buy a new coat. Mrs Maitland saying that she wanted a kind horse that would bring him home safely and she could see from my eye that I was just the thing. Three maidservants all crying out in admiration at my appearance and, to my great surprise, a black man. I had seen quite a few in London, runaway slaves who begged for a living and were known as St Giles blackbirds, after the district where they congregated, but never one who came up and, patting my neck, made jokes about the master riding in the St Leger now he had a racer.

I was led into a stable, where a pony neighed greetings to me, and put into a loose-box which to my great joy had a half door so that I could look over and see the rest of the stable and the row of stalls where the pony was tied.

Joseph handed me over to my new groom, Mr Howard. He was a short man with white hair, a long serious face and even older than Mr Maitland. There was also a boy called Pat with a screwed up, monkey-like face and dark hair. He seemed very pleased at my arrival, but whenever he tried to do anything for me Mr Howard drove him away, saying that he was to see to the pony and that a scamp like him was not fit to look after a thoroughbred.

When I had been watered and fed I was left to rest and Joseph, saying goodbye to me, was taken into the house for a meal.

My fellow horses at The Croft were two stout mares called Jenny and Poppy. Jenny was a very irritable brown, who would bite at the least thing. She said she had suffered very cruel treatment from a farm boy when she was young and could not forget it. She often bit Pat when he was grooming and harnessing her, but he took his bruises in good part.

Poppy was bay and a hand taller, so they did not match very well when they drew the carriage, but for the greater part of the time they were employed on a little farm that was attached to the house. Poppy was sweet-tempered, but when she moved she threw out her forelegs in a very ugly way, called dishing, which would not do for a carriage horse in smart circles.

The pony was a piebald, called Magpie, who did the errands and was driven by Mrs Maitland in a pretty little cart.

I soon learned that Mr Howard was a great singer, but only of hymns and psalms. He thought songs very wicked. He was a chapel-goer and lectured Pat a great deal about the error of his ways and the certainty that he would go to hell and be consigned to the flames. The boy took it all in good humour and did not seem at all in awe of Mr Howard, answering back very pertly at times and making faces behind his back, in a way that Mr Simpson would not have stood for a moment.

After a day's rest, Mr Maitland took me for a ride round the neighbourhood. The whole of our village

Hurstmore, seemed very excited by the event of a new horse and the people all left what they were doing and came to give an opinion on me. It seemed to be generally agreed that I was a great improvement on any horse Mr Maitland had owned before.

My new master was constantly apologising to me for what he called his 'ambling ways' and hoping that I was not hankering for my life as a racer. He also apologised for his horsemanship and sometimes I wished that I could speak and set his mind at rest on both counts.

To me, absent-mindedness was his only fault. He seemed to ride in a dream, his mind entirely taken up with other things, and would frequently lose himself through lack of attention. I did not like retracing my steps so, when I grew to know his habits I would take charge. But when we went on longer journeys into strange neighbourhoods I had no idea where to take him and I began to shy a little, jumping sideways at the rustle of a bird in the hedge or the bark of a dog on a chain, when I wished to regain his wandering attention.

Jenny, Poppy and Magpie were not much interested in the nature of Mr Maitland's work. Having been born and bred-up close by, they had seen very little of life and all three had a very rustic outlook, but I gradually learned from the conversation of the people around me that my new master was very taken up with reform. It seemed he had modest private means and so was able to give all his time to societies for the improvement of the prisons and the abolition of the slave trade.

He was also a very religious man, but in a different way from Mr Howard; I never heard him threaten anyone with hellfire or eternal damnation.

One week when Mr Howard was called away to Tunbridge Wells in a great hurry because his brother was very ill and like to die, Mathew the black man was constantly in and out of the stable.

He was a very cheerful person full of jokes and stories. When he groomed me he talked all the time, so from this and what I heard him tell Pat, I gradually pieced his history together.

It seemed that he had been born in Africa and, being captured by another tribe when very young, had been made a slave as was the custom there. He had served a black mistress in Africa until he was eleven or twelve years old, but then she had sold him to a white man. In the black family he had been treated more as a servant than a slave, but now he was dragged away to a slave ship and forced into the stifling hold with hundreds of slaves, packed tight and chained, so that they could scarcely move.

Without exercise, or fresh air or proper food many, more than a third, had died on the voyage, but he being young had been allowed on deck a good deal and so, though frightened, sad and sick, had survived.

They arrived in the West Indies, where they were intended for the sugar plantations, but a British naval officer had liked the look of him and bought him for forty guineas.

He had then gone to sea with the navy, serving the officer, learning to set the sails and to fire the guns and even to navigate the ship, of which last he was very proud.

He had grown very fond of his master and served him well. As a slave he received no pay and even his prize money (all the crew had a share when they captured a ship in battle) belonged to his master. But he had not minded about this for he expected that when he was twenty-one he would be set free. There being no slavery allowed in Britain he thought he would be treated as an apprentice and they were always free to work for whom they pleased from that age.

When the time came, they were in an English port, but when the ship's company was paid off he was not allowed ashore. His master, now a Captain, held him prisoner, the law on slavery not applying to ships, and sold him to another Captain who was returning immediately to the Indies. When they reached a West Indian port he was sold again, this time to a merchant.

It had been very terrible to find himself a slave again, with all his expectations dashed, and, as he had looked upon his master as a friend he felt that it was a great betrayal of trust.

However, his new master had given him a responsible position and had not objected to him doing a little trading on his own account, so, after another fifteen years slavery, and saving every penny, he was at last able to buy his freedom.

The white men there hating and distrusting freed slaves, he had come to England, and Mr Maitland being well-known for his efforts to have slavery abolished, had sought him out.

He was employed in quite a lowly position, but he made himself very useful to Mr Maitland, who was inclined to neglect his own affairs in favour of reform, and they worked for the abolition of slavery together.

Mathew told us many stories of the cruelty with which the slaves were treated on the plantations. How they were flogged for the most minor misdeeds, had all their teeth pulled out as a punishment for eating the sugar cane, and how, if any black man ventured to strike a white man, he was tortured and hanged, even though the white man was in the wrong.

'They treat them far worse than horses, Nightshade,' he told me. 'Though I can see that you have been ill-used by these white hairs on your sides.'

Mr Maitland made good use of me in his own quiet way. We often went miles to see some lady or gentleman of influence who might help his cause, or to discuss his latest pamphlet with a fellow worker.

We also visited many prisons up and down the country and I would be put in the stable while he was shown round. He took many notes and was always full of ideas for improvement of the conditions, which were often very bad as you could tell by the stench, it being worse than any farmyard or pigsty.

Some were damp dungeons with little air and the poor prisoner lying there, fettered, on dirty straw, he would tell me, and at some the jailors were dishonest and did not give the prisoners even their meagre allowance of bread. He was always much affected by seeing bad conditions and would talk about them all the way home, musing as to what could be done.

The worst of it, as he was always saying, was that these prisoners were usually foolish or unfortunate men who got into debt and, instead of being allowed to work and pay what they owed, they were confined in these dismal circumstances until ill health or jail fever carried them off.

It seemed that felons: thieves, murderers, highwaymen and the like, were only kept in prison until their trials, then they were either hanged or transported, while minor offenders and runaway apprentices, were sent to bridewells where they had to work very hard, but only for a short period.

Sometimes we went to London to see members of Parliament about new Bills and Acts, but more often Mr Maitland took the coach, a thing rather frowned upon locally, for men of his standing, carriage folk, were expected to travel post and hire expensive chaises. But being unworldly and not caring the least for show, he could not see the need.

Pat was always happy when our master was away for he was the only other person to ride me. Mr Howard, though too old and stiff to take me out himself, could not bear to see Pat on my back. He was certain that the boy would let me break my knees on the road or over-gallop me on the grass and we never went without terrible warnings or returned without an inspection of me from head to tail.

Except for the war and bread going up to seventeen pence a loaf and a mad dog going through the village and biting dogs and pigs, all of which had to be killed, our life went on smoothly.

Then came a great surprise. Peace with France was

declared. At first it was not believed, there having been no suggestion of it until that moment, but when the coaches from London came through our little town bearing banners saying *Peace with France!* and the coachmen and guards wearing sprigs of laurel in their hats, then we began to think it could be true.

There was great excitement everywhere with the Militia firing cannons in the market places and church bells ringing everywhere and those who could afford it putting lighted candles in their windows at night.

In London, it was said, the Post Office had lighted six thousand lamps, but in Hurstmore we contented ourselves with a bonfire and ale. It was very different from the Lovelace celebration, there being only two people too drunk to get home and they being much frowned on by the chapel-goers. Mr Howard threatened poor Pat with hellfire for days, because he had seen him at the bonfire, a pot of ale in his hand, singing *Rule Britannia* at the top of his voice.

Soon after this all the notices about invasion came down and all the part-time soldiers were disbanded and stopped drilling on the village greens.

Mr Maitland, feeling that people would now have more time to consider the horrors of slavery, arranged a great many meetings. Mathew came with us on Poppy, leaving Jenny to do the farm work, and spoke on the misery of being a slave from his own experience.

Mainly the speeches were given in Town Halls, but once or twice they spoke in market places, telling of the dreadful slave ships, of the toil and floggings, of the fetters and chains, of the shocking fact that in America it was a crime to teach a slave to read or write.

Once a man shouted that factory children were slaves

too, and nearer home, but most people agreed that slavery was very wrong and that something ought to be done. The difficulty was to *get* anything done and sometimes Mr Maitland became very despondent, but this would pass quite quickly and soon he would be making new plans and full of hope again.

So life went on very happily until, after a year had passed, England and France fell out again and the war re-started.

Many people felt that the peace had been a trick and that France was now all the more ready to invade us. Rumours came every hour of armies and boats gathering in France for the crossing.

In our part of the world all the arrangements for defence had to begin again. The Militia was recalled, the Fencibles or Home Defence re-enrolled, the invasion notices put up again.

This time Mr Maitland, being one of the chief men locally, was asked to take command and I was kept very busy taking him hither and thither, for he seemed to have to spend every minute of his day at some drill or meeting.

Mathew joined the Home Defence. Pat was very angry that he was too young. They would take no one under fifteen years or over sixty. Mr Howard seemed quite glad to be too old and did not at all object to driving Jenny and Poppy in our largest wagon and going in the parson's party. It had been settled that in every village the women and children should be put in wagons and carts, and, led by the parson or curate, should drive inland to safety, keeping to the lesser roads and lanes, so that they did not slow up our army advancing to battle with the invader.

The skilled men, blacksmiths, wheelwrights, masons and such trades, were put into a pioneer band. They were to knock down bridges and build barricades to slow up the enemy advance, and yet another group were to drive the cattle inland and fire the ricks so that Boney's army found little or nothing to eat.

Then we got down to making our beacon on Hurstmore Hill. There was to be a chain of beacons covering the whole country. When the watchers on the cliffs saw the enemy ships approaching they would light theirs, and, seeing theirs, we would light ours and all the people would know to leave off work or rise from their beds and take up arms.

In the daytime wet hay was to be used to send up a smoke signal, at night it was to be a good blaze.

Jenny and Poppy and some of the neighbouring farmers' horses dragged up the wagon-loads of mouldy hay, faggots, old barrels and pieces of old timber that would make a sudden blaze. The children all thought it rather a holiday and begged rides on the wagons so that they might come up and help build the beacon. But Mr Maitland was very serious about it all and said that he prayed God we might not have cause to light it, for he feared we were very ill-prepared to meet an invader.

Every week we held drills and once there was a parade, which included all the wagons and carts that were to take the women and children. Jenny and Poppy were fetched from their hay-making and Mrs Maitland drove Magpie and they all paraded round the village green before lining up. Mr Howard caused great annoyance by singing *Soldiers of Christ, Arise* very loud, and keeping it up after the military gentlemen who had come to inspect our efforts had arrived. However the Home Defence men with their six muskets, proudly carried by the best shots, in the lead and followed by those armed with staves, while those with pitchforks brought up the rear, marched very well and behind them came the pioneer band with axes and picks over their shoulders.

On Saturday we had a sham fight with the Home Defence men of several other villages and quite a few old scores were settled when the men began to battle with their staves. Mr Maitland was riding up and down the line calling, 'Steady, there' and, 'Let us not be too realistic, we want no broken heads,' in the hope of calming things.

At night we manned our hill and put a guard on the road by the bridge and I would take Mr Maitland on his inspection of these outposts. When there was a good moon I enjoyed it, but on dark nights scrambling about on the hill was not so pleasant.

The fear of invasion was very real and some of the older folk could scarce sleep at night for anxiety. People feared for their lives and their children and their money which it was said they were drawing out of the banks and burying in their gardens. Every day there were new rumours, a plot to capture the King, landings in Ireland, landings in Wales, to keep the people in a perpetual state of fright. It was a good summer with a fine crop of corn, but it was said that we were only harvesting it for Boney.

Then, one warm October evening, ships were sighted out at sea, and it was the fish ponies, galloping their fresh fish to London in relays, that passed on the news that the French had come.

It was after dark when the news reached Hurstmore and it caused a dreadful panic. People were running from cottage to cottage crying out that the French had come. Men, boots in one hand, weapon in the other hurried into our yard shouting for Mr Maitland.

Mr Howard, already abed, for he thought late hours ungodly, appeared very flustered in his nightshirt and cap and called for Pat to come down at once and saddle the horse.

Pat came, dressed but half asleep, and saddled me with Mr Howard shouting all the while for him to make haste and harness the pony.

I could hear Mr Maitland's voice outside, telling people to calm themselves and asking how the news had come and whether it was from a reliable source.

Pat led me out with my bridle all twisted, the throat-latch round the cheek-piece, and forgot to tighten my girth. So when Mr Maitland tried to mount the saddle slipped round and added to the general confusion.

However, gradually things began to be sorted out and the men were assembling in the churchyard while the wagons gathered on the green.

Then it was found that many of the women were bringing great bundles of household possessions, and in some cases birds in cages, as well as six or seven children and a baby in arms. When they were told the wagons could not take all of it there was a general outcry and complaint. This added to the babies' crying and the mothers calling for the bigger children, who constantly wandered away into the dark and were soon lost, made the most terrible uproar.

Mr Maitland kept calling for order and silence and tried to keep the two parties apart so that the men might concentrate on defence rather than lost children.

At last, having collected most of our force, we marched away to the bridge. It was pitch dark, there being no moon, but a good many of our party carried lanterns. Mr Maitland asked everyone to be quiet and listen for the sound of church bells and to watch the south for the sudden flaring of beacons. Then he reminded everyone that we were to hold our position on the far side of the bridge as long as we could, but when forced to retreat we had to knock the bridge down, in an endeavour to slow up the French advance.

We had not been long at the bridge when it was discovered that Pat, armed with a pitchfork, was with us. He said that Widow Todd from Well Cottage had been forgotten by her wagon and finding her screeching that she'd been left to be murdered by Boney, he'd given her his place in Magpie's cart and come to join us. He made himself useful holding me while Mr Maitland settled which of the great elms was to be felled across the road

when the moment came, posted two men further down the road as look-outs and some more in the fields on either side, and then inspected our first casualty, a ploughboy who'd put his pitchfork through his foot in the general excitement.

By this time we had settled down, all were outwardly calm, and there was great laughter when Thatcher Brown was heard to challenge one of Farmer Chapman's cows.

But then there was a sudden glare in the black sky and everyone called out that the beacons were lit, that Boney really was coming and panic broke out again.

Mr Maitland called for order, very sharply for him, and pointed out that it was *our* beacon on Hurstmore Hill that was lit. 'Can any of you see any other beacon burning?' he called out urgently, as he climbed on me to look from the greater height.

We scanned the hills to the south carefully, but there was no other fire to be seen. Mr Maitland said, in great distress, that our men must have done it without waiting for orders and now the whole country would be thrown into a state of panic through our error. 'Every beacon to the north of us will be lit on our signal,' he said, 'and what Frenchmen have we seen?'

We all began to feel a great sense of shame that our village should have done such a thing and several men offered to run up the hill and put the fire out, while others suggested that a messenger be sent to Bilbury Hill to explain the mistake. But it seemed that both actions must be too late to be of any use, until the blacksmith thought of me.

'Yon Nightshade were a racer,' he said, ''e might do the distance in time. 'E's our best 'ope anyways.'

'Our only hope,' agreed Mr Maitland, 'but who's to ride him? I cannot leave my post. Is there anyone here who can gallop a thoroughbred?'

Lanterns were held up as the men looked at each other's faces, but for most of them a jog trot was the fastest pace they used.

'I'll go, sir,' said Pat's voice.

Mr Maitland did not seem very happy to send such a young boy, but there was no one else and so, as Pat climbed up and shortened my stirrups, he wrote a note and signed it plainly. 'Give that to the men on Bilbury Hill,' he said, 'provided the beacons to the south have not been lit meanwhile. Are you certain of the way?'

Pat said he was and we set off, both very pleased at the importance of our mission. It was dark away from the lanterns, but not as dark as it had been earlier for the moon was rising. We cantered through the deserted village and took the track to our hill. From there we would follow the drovers' track that led over the hills for miles.

We galloped up the track to the hill, for we both knew it well, and came quickly to the blazing beacon.

'Douse that fire,' shouted Pat in a commanding voice. 'Mr Maitland's orders.' He waved the note, 'It never ought to 'ave been lit.'

'But Mr Howard said . . .' figures, black against the orange flames, came forward to argue.

'Who can read?' asked Pat, waving the note again. 'The fire is to be put out immediate.'

As soon as they were convinced of the order we galloped on. The hills looked wonderfully dramatic, very strange and mysterious under the climbing moon. I could see where I was going, but not where I put my feet; I hoped that we would not find ourselves in a rabbit warren and turn head over heels.

Then Pat found a wide track, mercifully it was dry and not too poached by the hoofs of the droves of cattle.

We galloped as I had not galloped for years, pulling up pretty sharply once when the moon vanished behind a cloud, but setting off again the moment it reappeared.

Pat let me choose my own speed. At first I think he was a little frightened by our pace, never having ridden at racing speed, but he grew to enjoy it and only slowed me up once, saying that I must take a breather, I was an old horse now, and the master wouldn't want me galloped to death even for the good name of the village.

All the time we watched the hill ahead, waiting for the flames to burst forth and pass on the false alarm, knowing that when that happened our gallop would have been in vain. We knew it *must* be a false alarm now for, every so often, Pat looked to the south and nowhere could he find the smallest glow in the sky.

Our reckless speed brought us to disaster at last. We had left the main track and were going down into a hollow before beginning to climb Bilbury Hill itself, when I felt a forehoof sink into a rabbit hole and sprawling forward collapsed upon my nose, pitching Pat over my head. He landed heavily, but fortunately the turf was soft and, though both much shaken, we quickly scrambled to our feet.

Pat felt my forelegs and then led me forward, looking with great anxiety to see if I was lame. The leg seemed undamaged and he looked round for a hollow to stand me in so that he might climb back into the saddle.

We went on more slowly, convinced now that we must be too late. As time passed it seemed more and more extraordinary that the Bilbury beacon was still unlit. Had the guard been asleep, or had they had reason to disbelieve our signal?

As rather blown and tired I climbed the last stretch of hillside, we could see torches and hear the angry voices of men cursing each other. A thin spiral of smoke rose from the beacon and the ashes of burnt straw smouldered below a great pile of unburnt wood.

We cantered up and delivered our written order.

'Well that do be a mercy for sure,' said the rustic in charge and burst into a loud cackle of laughter. 'Here lads, the Hurstmore beacon shouldn't 'ave gone up at all. "It were lit in error". There b'aint a Frenchie in the place. Perhaps it were a good job arter all that old skinflint Thomson sent up green wood.'

'Green and wet too,' said an indignant voice.

We learned that they had been struggling to light their beacon for the past twenty minutes, but had burned every bit of their straw without getting the green wood to catch and the poor men had become quite desperate in their efforts, feeling that through them the whole country would go unwarned and hundreds be murdered in their beds by the advancing French army.

We parted in a state of great mutual relief. Pat and I made the homeward journey at a very gentle pace and found Mr Maitland and his troop much pleased with our success, though quite unable to guess how it had been achieved.

Pat and I were sent home with some of the other men, no longer needed, for it seemed certain now that the alarm had been a false one. The Mail coach had brought a report to town that the ships sighted were East Indiamen.

Next day the villagers, the bundles, the children and the birds in cages all came home again and gradually things settled down. With much grumbling Jenny and Poppy hauled another load of wood up the hill and we rebuilt our beacon.

It soon got about that it was Mr Howard who had caused the trouble. It seemed that the old man, feeling certain of invasion, had thought the beacon forgotten in the excitement and taken it upon himself to give the order to light up. It was said that Mr Maitland had taken him to task very severely, speaking uncommon sharp and calling him an interfering old man.

Pat and I were more fortunate. We came in for a good deal of praise for having ridden so fast and saved the good name of the village. Not a great deal was said about the green wood.

About the same time as our false alarm Admiral Nelson had been fighting a great sea battle and a week or so later, news reached us of a glorious victory at Trafalgar, where the French navy were totally beaten. But the rejoicing over this was very much dampened by news, that came at the same time, of the death of Lord Nelson. This was a very heavy loss and was felt by many as though it were the loss of a member of the family.

The war was by no means over, in fact many hard battles remained to be fought, but, from that day there was no longer any dread of England being invaded, for our navy had control of the seas.

All the Home Defence were disbanded again and Mr Maitland went back to his prisoners and slaves and his endeavours to improve the lives of one and abolish the other. I continued to carry him on his journeys until we were both so old and grey that we were forced to retire, he to his armchair and papers, I to my paddock, where I spend the days happily enough, thinking about the past and those far off days when crowds roared my name or I carried a highwayman.

# BLACK ROMANY

*by Diana Pullein-Thompson*

I wish to thank *The Times* and the *Leicestershire Chronicle* for their reports on the visit of Queen Victoria and Prince Albert to Belvoir, and also Miss Barbara Smith of Hodder and Stoughton who kindly transcribed much of them for me.                                              D. P-T.

# Contents

ONE    A visit from the Queen    113

TWO    I hear news of a journey    124

THREE    Lost in the dark    130

FOUR    I swim for my life    139

FIVE    Trouble at an inn    153

SIX    I become a wild horse    162

SEVEN    Charlie says farewell    173

EIGHT    Life on a Cornish farm    181

NINE    A happy ending    191

# ❦Black Beauty's Family❦

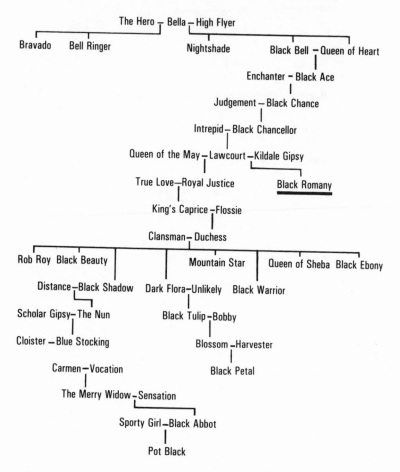

## CHAPTER ONE

# A visit from the Queen

Looking back now I see that my life began to change in December 1843 at the time when Queen Victoria and her German husband, the handsome young Prince Albert, visited my home at Belvoir Castle in the county of Leicestershire.

Up till then the days had run smoothly into one another, and I can truthfully say that the first six and a half years of my life passed with few worries and only small mishaps.

I was born in a large stable kept for foaling mares. My mother, a Cleveland Bay thoroughbred cross, was pitch black apart from a sparkling white diamond on the centre of her forehead. My father was pure thoroughbred, black, too, with a remarkable turn of speed and a proud nature. I inherited strength of physique, depth of girth, wide cannon bones and a placid temperament from my mother and a slender curving neck, long sloping shoulders and swift action from my father. I was black, too, with a white diamond on my forehead exactly like my mother's, but I would rather have been bay or, best of all, grey with dapples and a steel-dark mane and tail. However, the Duke of Rutland particularly liked black horses especially to pull his carriage and to carry outriders on grand occasions.

I grew up in meadows near the park in view of the castle which was partly castellated, but had been largely rebuilt and redesigned after a fire some years earlier. And there was always much to see, people coming and going, horses being schooled and jumped, shooting expeditions, hounds being exercised or the hunt actually crossing our fields with the sound of horn and the cry of hounds echoing across the countryside.

After I had left my mother, my chief friend was my half-brother, Pioneer, a handsome bay with black points. We shared the same father, but his mother was without thoroughbred blood so he was heavier than I was, but fast and nimble for his size and with high spirits that matched my own. We were broken-in at the same time by old Mark Bampton, a gentle teacher who took us slowly, step by step, so that we were never frightened or dismayed. Of course we were accustomed to seeing our friends and relations pulling all kinds of vehicles or being ridden, so none of our training came as a surprise to us.

Paddy, my groom, a cheerful and affectionate Irishman, took me hunting for the first time when I was five and a half and afterwards I was usually ridden by one or other of the Duke's sons, being too strongly built to take his daughter; my favourite being the intelligent Lord John Manners, who stammered. Meanwhile Pioneer was used mainly as a carriage horse, although sometimes he would carry a rider to hounds for half a day. In the summer of 1843 he was sold and disappeared from my life, and in the autumn when I was six and a few months I was allowed to stay out with hounds all day if a second mount was not available.

Then at the very beginning of December there was a tremendous air of excitement at Belvoir among the servants and tenants of the estate. Carriages and chariots were brought out and cleaned, extra stables, some of them recently built, were prepared for visiting horses.

Carts, vans and drays delivered extra provisions to the Castle, the Duke's private band practised at all hours, and the gardeners were busy clipping shrubs into perfect shapes and tending the flowers. Paddy seemed to take longer each day in grooming us and much time was spent cleaning bits, buckles and stirrups with silver sand until they shone like silver.

The grooms talked over the impending royal visit and we learned from them that the Prince was coming to hunt with a fast pack, so that the British people could see that he was a brave and accomplished horseman. Our stud groom said that some of the gentry and also a few noblemen suspected that the Prince was a cowardly and ineffectual horseman partly on account of his nationality, for they believed that the English were the only people who could truly understand horses and hounds, with the Irish coming a poor second. A German might ride beautifully in a ménage, but would show little sense, skill or courage in the field.

On December 3rd six of the Prince's best horses arrived with two grooms and later one or two belonging to the Duke of Wellington – I cannot recall the exact number – and there was much discussion about the decorations which were being put up to celebrate the visit. We heard that the Prince intended to hunt his thoroughbred, Emancipation, but there was some uncertainty about whether the Queen would go to the meet. A triumphal arch was built of evergreens at the entrance to the park, and the tenants made plans to acclaim their Queen.

On December 4th the quietness of the morning was broken by the boom of guns, and an old war horse threw up his head and neighed a warning, but we heard later that the noise was only a royal salute being fired at

Nottingham Castle in honour of the Queen's arrival in the town. She had come by train from Chatsworth to be greeted by hundreds of people and companies of soldiers. Horses were harnessed and away she went with Prince Albert, escorted throughout by relays of troops of the Enniskillen Dragoons. The first carriage horses were exchanged at Bingham for fresh animals and soon after eleven our master, the Duke of Rutland, set out to meet the royal carriage and I learned later from his horse that there was much waving and cheering by Belvoir tenants, two hundred of whom had lined the road near Red Mile, and that a local gentleman, named Norton, of Elton Hall had come too with his own tenants and had also escorted the royal party right to Belvoir, which they reached with a great clatter just before half past one. Afterwards there was a flurry and bustle in our yard as the steaming carriage horses were rubbed down, watered and fed. And later they, too, described to us the triumphal arches, the decorated houses and all the bunting and flags.

'Had we not been blinkered we most certainly would have shied,' one gelding told us, 'for the bunting was very frightening when the wind caught it.'

In the late afternoon the Duke's second son came to the yard accompanied by a young man of fresh complexion, with a friendly smile and gentle manner, whom he introduced to Paddy as Charlie Daintree, saying that the Duke had decided that he should hunt me the following day. The young man stroked my neck and patted me, saying that I was a fine beast, and Paddy asked whether he was staying at the castle and he replied that he was and explained that he was related to the Duke through his mother's side. Then he talked merrily of racing, a subject close to Paddy's heart, and stroked a black cat sitting on a mounting block, and I saw that this man was an animal lover and as a result I felt quite happy about carrying him to hounds the next day.

In the evening the Castle, which stands on a mound, was bright with lamps and candles, the fountains gushed water and carriages and coaches rolled up the private road. Paddy said a grand dinner party was being given attended by many noblemen and their wives, including Sir Robert Peel, the Prime Minister.

The next morning soon after seven o'clock as our grooms were bringing us out to drink at the trough a handsome elderly gentleman walked into the yard, and a whisper went round. 'It's the Duke of Wellington!' The hero of Waterloo was still tall and walked like a soldier; his face was remarkable with fine eyes and a hooked nose, and his charm of manner was evident in the way he spoke to the grooms. I felt him looking me over as I walked across the yard and raised my head higher and lifted my tail, wanting his admiration.

'He bends well to the bridle, your grace,' said Paddy turning to smile politely at the Duke, who nodded solemnly, his hands behind his back.

Presently we heard that the Queen had decided to attend the meet and would drive over in a landau with the Queen Dowager, who had arrived at four the previous day, and the Duke of Rutland. So four of Belvoir's best black carriage horses were prepared and others to carry the outriders who dressed themselves in the Belvoir livery. Soon afterwards Paddy saddled me up, for Charlie Daintree had decided to ride me over himself. He was now splendidly clothed in scarlet coat, white stock, breeches, boots and a top hat and his face and eyes shone with youth and excitement.

'I was presented to her Majesty last night,' he said excitedly. 'I had not realised she was so enchanting and so *kind*. She has the loveliest blue eyes! I actually *liked* her, almost *loved* her!' And Paddy, unaccustomed to young men talking so frankly and freely to him, merely smiled and advised Charlie to be gentle with my mouth which, he announced, was as soft as a ripe peach. As my rider sprang into my saddle a chariot set off to the Castle to take Prince Albert, the Duke of Wellington and Lord George Manners to Croxton Park to mount their horses which had gone on ahead.

'I should hurry, sir,' said Paddy.

Soon I was trotting along the private road in the wake of the groom who was hacking Emancipation over for the Prince. Meanwhile the Queen drove to the meet along public roads lined again with her subjects, and everywhere there was much cheering and, as she went, more and more people joined her until the cavalcade was at least three hundred strong. When I arrived at Croxton Park which was only a short distance from the actual meet I saw lots of decorations and mottoes such as 'God Save Queen Victoria and Prince Albert', and bunting running from building to building. Prince Albert and the Duke of Wellington were just mounting their horses surrounded by thousands of people and riders, for now another three hundred horsemen and women from a neighbouring hunt had joined us. However the Prince made his way through the crowd to join his wife and rode beside the landau as it was driven through Croxton Park to Waltham where hounds awaited us. He cut a fine figure on horseback, tall and slim, yet wide-shouldered with large blue eyes in a face hedged by sideboards. A thin brown moustache crowned his red upper lip and his

hair was the same light brown as the Queen's. She looked in contrast very tiny and young, sitting straight and demure in the landau beside her old aunt, Queen Adelaide. Her hair was parted in the middle and her blue eyes seemed to be watching the Duke as he cantered beside the landau dressed like Charlie in a red coat and top hat. At Waltham the cheers that greeted the royal pair were so loud that the Duke of Wellington's mount, which had been lent to him by the Duke of Wilton, became so disturbed that the old soldier had to dismount and ride one of his own instead, which fortunately had been brought over by a groom. Then we saw hounds and my heart began to beat wildly with excitement, and Charlie's time was taken up keeping me still. Someone proposed three cheers for the two Queens and at this my black friends pulling the landau threw up their heads and danced with excitement while the outriders were kept busy keeping the crowd back from the Queen.

Fortunately only a few minutes passed before the huntsman gave a toot on his horn and hounds moved off towards Melton, with almost six hundred riders in their wake.

Hounds found three foxes in Broom Covert and after a time, when one had left the wood, we all started galloping madly across the fields to the sound of their music. Charlie urged me forward until I was almost level with Emancipation, who was going like the wind with a long effortless stride, but, with so many people around, the fox was soon headed and we all turned back towards Melton. Soon we moved on to another wood where we failed to find, and riders drank from flasks and ate their sandwiches. Then hounds drew Waltham Pasture and found again and we had a ten minutes run jumping hedges, ditches and timber. We lost that fox in gorse but found another and then there followed a long run, with Charlie digging me with his spurs so that he could ride beside the Prince, whose horse was one of the fastest in the field. Now we thundered over the turf, five hundred or so behind us, the hounds streaming before us and the notes of the huntsman's horn ringing across the landscape.

We jumped a tall hedge with a ditch below, galloping a few yards behind the Prince, and a horse beside me fell, and then a post and rails. And, afterwards, a long meadow stretched out before us with the hounds moving closely together as though a table cloth could have covered the whole pack. Cries of 'Tally Ho!' came from a distant lane, beyond which we could see ploughed fields climbing to meet the grey sky; for an instant the whole of England seemed to lie before us, dreaming and beautiful with the trees dark, still and leafless and the sky pale as a pigeon's back. Oh, it was so lovely and so exciting that I felt the sweat breaking out on me all over! I strove then to make my legs move faster until I was beside the Prince and Charlie's hand was on my neck patting his thanks.

More hedges rose before me and wide newly dug ditches (for landowners were beginning to drain their fields) and timber fences and even a closed gate which Charlie put me at to get out of the way of other riders who were jumping the nearby hedge. All the time the noise of hounds and horn acted wildly on my brain driving me to greater efforts so that I would gladly have galloped until I dropped. Coming abreast of Emancipation I saw his ears flatten with annoyance, and his nostrils extend as he blew at me fiercely as though trying to say, 'You can't over-take royalty, keep back!' Then I felt Charlie's hand on my rein, 'Steady there!' At the same time a man in a top hat on a beautiful grey frowned and I dropped back a few paces, and catching my breath saw that the Prince was well accompanied by other young men: the Duke of Rutland's two eldest sons and also the Lords Wilton, Forrester and Jersey, all riding superb horses, and behind me there galloped a lone lady side saddle on a blue roan.

We leaped over a wall into a park across which we galloped like race horses our hearts pounding, our necks stretched out, our legs moving like clockwork, and then we came to ploughed fields and saw ahead of us a fine team of shires, their manes plaited with ribbons of red, white and blue and we realised by the way hounds paused and swung back that this team had headed the fox. Now our quarry turned off in another direction but was stop-ped by a dog, and changing his mind again made his way back towards Waltham, and then the huntsman's long wail on the horn told us that he had reached an earth and gone to ground. I looked around again at that moment and saw that the Prince was still riding determinedly and skilfully, sitting straighter than the English horsemen and interfering less with his mount on take-off. We jumped one last fence and were the first to arrive at the earth after the huntsman, his whipper-in and the Prince. And now I paused at last with my sides heaving and my hot breath rising like steam. I gulped and drew in a long sweet draught of air and, dismounting, Charlie turned my head to the wind.

'You're a great horse, Romany, and I wish you were mine,' he said and then Lord George Manners came across to congratulate him on his horsemanship and he replied that he was all right when his blood was up. 'But I was just a passenger today, this willing beast did it all.'

Men drank from their flasks again and horses stretched their necks and nibbled what grass they could find. The Prince, whose cheeks were red now from his exertions, commended the huntsman on his skill, and everyone talked about the run which had actually lasted forty minutes. Presently the Marquis of Granby suggested that we called it a day and we set off for Belvoir along with the Prince while hounds took a slightly different route. Charlie was most attentive and opened all the gates for the other riders, until two ladies joined our party and then, after being introduced, he chatted and joked with the prettiest all the way home with hardly a pause.

Gradually the intoxication caused by galloping in the wake of hound and horn died in me and by the time I reached Belvoir I was as quiet and calm as an old donkey back from a regular journey, but pleased none the less to see Paddy and plunge my muzzle into the warm gruel which he had prepared for me. The Duke of Wellington's hunter was anxious to know about the day as his master had turned him back after the first covert was drawn and the landau horses were interested because they had seen the start of the first run before returning the Queen to

Belvoir. So there was much blowing and talking between the bars that separated us that night while the band played at the castle; and, when dawn sent her first grey shaft through the window, it seemed only an hour or so since we had thundered so wildly across the Leicestershire fields as though we would die rather than be left behind in the chase which men call hunting.

## CHAPTER TWO

# I hear news of a journey

The next morning Paddy took me for a short walk in the park to loosen-up after hunting, and we saw the Queen, wearing blue velvet trimmed with white fur, walking arm in arm with the Prince who was in shooting dress. They looked to me like ordinary lovers and, although both were attractive, I could not understand why everyone made so much fuss about their visit.

Back in the yard, the grooms were discussing the Prince's horsemanship all over again, declaring that though he might be a German he did not lack courage. In fact he rode and walked with the stiff bearing of a soldier and, someone said, the proud valour of a Prussian.

There was another meet in the district that day and so the grooms were busy again hacking horses over and making gruels and mashes for their return. The Queen went with the Duke of Rutland to see hounds draw the first covert, while the Prince went shooting with the Duke of Wellington and the Duke of Bedford. I cannot sympathise with man's love of killing and was as usual greatly upset by the sound of guns firing, and the thought of the poor, beautiful birds falling to the ground with bloodstained plumage.

The next day the royal party left in the landau at eight o'clock, the Prince's horses having gone on ahead. They went to Leicester this time and were again cheered by great crowds. One triumphal arch, crowned by two stuffed foxes, bore the inscription 'Albert, Prince of Wales,

England's Hope', referring to the Queen's baby son whom the English expected one day to be king.

By this time I was tired of all the excitement and the endless talk of the royal family, and was looking forward to more hunting, without, if possible, any foxes being killed.

My wish was granted for Charlie Daintree rode me to hounds the next day, but, without the incentive of keeping up with Prince Albert, he proved to be an indecisive rider. He put me, for example, at a black bullfinch and then changed his mind and all but turned me back, and I only saved myself by snatching the reins and bounding forward to take off a stride too late. Then I nearly fell as I hit the top. Afterwards Lord George Manners angrily told Charlie that he should let me go on at the fences or risk an accident. But Charlie only smiled and said he was deuced sorry and would try to do better next time.

'I'm not in the saddle more than two or three times a month, so you must forgive me my occasional mistakes. I will try to mend my ways and would be much distressed if I were to damage Romany in the slightest,' he said in his light charming voice, which was hard to dislike, even when the words were irritating.

By the next day most of the house party had gone and the stables were getting back into their usual routine, with only members of the family driving or riding the horses. I love the place to be run like this, in the same way day after day. It makes me feel safe and secure and when I listen for Paddy's footstep I know he will not fail me. I can look forward to regular meals, and the chimes of the stable clock fill me with happiness for they seem to regulate the day and keep everything in proper order. Before first light each winter morning I hear the pump going up and down, as the sleepy grooms and stable boys wash under its gushing water, and the mewing of the black cat asking for milk. Lanterns swing in the murky darkness and feet crunch on the gravel or clatter on the cobbles, and then I hear Paddy's cheerful whistling and know that another day has begun. I raise my head and neigh for the hay he will put in the rack for me to nibble as he mucks out my stable, and I think of the food that will follow, the broad flakes of bran and the fine full oats, and the dull chaff that stops me gobbling. But this year of 1844 wasn't to be like that right through the winter.

In January I heard news of a change, when Charlie's name cropped up in conversation. There was talk of a bet, a wager to save his honour, and it was said that the Duke had agreed to lend me to him for a long ride down to Cornwall. My master had said such a trek might be the making of the young fool, who meant well but had no spine or perseverance. The Duke was a betting man himself, who often lost money on horses, so could understand Charlie's troubles. 'But he shouldn't play the tables,' he said. 'He hasn't the brains for that.'

Paddy was clearly upset at the thought that I was to be taken out of his care and left in the hands of a young man with 'as much sense as a louse', as he put it. 'Why, that young gentleman couldn't find his way from Red Mile to Nottingham, let alone from Leicester to Tintagel!'

Other grooms said that Cornwall was a wild and dreadful place, where I should doubtless fall into the hands of gipsies. They said the Duke was making a mistake in letting me go, and that he was too kind hearted, and that Charlie Daintree came of an unreliable family and had bad blood in his veins. Paddy said the fool was too fond of the bottle and a stable boy said he reckoned the ladies would be the young gentleman's downfall. Then Charlie came to the yard again and rode me out on the roads and tracks and across the fields for three hours, and spoke in so friendly a way to the grooms that for a time they began to relent and say that he wasn't such a bad young gentleman after all. Paddy told him that I needed feeding every four hours during the day and must always be offered a drink first, never afterwards. He told him I must wear two rugs at night and never be galloped over stones, and he warned Charlie that the Duke would be very angry if I was returned with any blemishes or splints or spavins. 'You've got a valuable 'oss there, a good 'un, who must be cared for like a child.'

Charlie promised that he would do all that Paddy told him, and that he wouldn't make me go too far, or let me sleep in draughty, dirty stalls. He said that he would make the ostlers at the inns clean my saddle and bridle so that they were always supple and comfortable. And, feeling better, Paddy said he would see that I had a fine set of strong shoes that would last me the whole journey, so there would be no problem about finding a farrier; he also said that he would take me for long rides every day at a hound-jog, so that I would be as fit as an athlete in training. He said I was just the horse to make a long journey and that I could beat any horse to be found anywhere in the whole length and breadth of England, and that Charlie's rival, Archie Hickstead, would not be able to find a comparable animal.

I heard that the journey was to start in February and that Charlie hoped to retrieve his lost fortune by winning and that the wager had been made before witnesses when Charlie and Archie were under the influence of drink.

The grooms said that in their grandfather's days the two young fools would have fought a duel instead. They then made several rude remarks about *young bloods* and *tom-foolery* and Paddy wished that the Duke had let Charlie have any other horse but me.

Such changes of attitude were unsettling. And I didn't understand exactly what was wanted from me, only that somehow I had to behave well and work hard for the honour of Belvoir, and that a long and arduous journey was before me; a ride which would be safe and easy enough if I was cared for by Paddy or his like, but would undoubtedly be difficult because of the poor judgement and unreliable nature of Charlie.

It was all very disquieting and yet in a strange way exciting for although the routine was, as I have said, comforting and pleasant, the prospect of change sud-denly seemed to stir me. I began to paw the ground in the morning if my hay did not come quickly enough and to nudge Paddy when he was slow tipping my feed into the manger. I suppose I realised that there was a challenge in the air and that quickened my blood and gave me a new impatience and feeling of importance.

January came to an end with rain and high winds, and my mother, who was expecting another foal, was kept in night and day, and there was much talk of a new drainage system for the fields. The Duke came to see me and feeling my muscles, declared me to be fit.

'The sure winner, if young Charlie keeps his head,' he forecast. 'I have a mind to lay a bet myself that he will be first at Tintagel.'

'But what a time of year to choose, your Grace,' the stud groom said.

'Ah, it would be far too easy in summer. These young

men want to test themselves, that's natural at their age. I admire them for it, so let it be.'

And that was the last time I was to see my true owner for many a month.

## CHAPTER THREE

# *Lost in the dark*

Three smart young men wearing fancy waistcoats, checked trousers, cut-away coats and top hats, witnessed our departure, their noses reddened by the keen February air. Charlie wore breeches, boots, a stock, plain waistcoat, beaver hat and leather gloves.

'Archie's riding a weed, you'll win easily, my dear fellow,' said one of the young men twisting his beautiful fair moustache.

'I *mean* to be there first,' said Charlie. 'I must win or flee the country. My debts, ah how my debts haunt me! You've no idea, the nightmares. Pray for me my friends.'

'That we will do!' exclaimed the owner of the fair moustache. 'My thoughts will go with you.'

'I back my brother as you know,' answered a man of sanguine appearance with dark sideburns, while the third who was neutral patted my neck. 'I wish you a safe journey and God's speed,' he said solemnly. 'It's a bold man or a fool who undertakes so long a journey at this time of year.'

Now Charlie turned and, with a little bow, wished his companions goodbye.

'I'm neither a fool nor a courageous man, just half way in-between.'

'Good luck! Keep away from the tables and the ladies and no tippling!'

His fair friend's warning seemed to follow us down the twisty lane that wound its way between hovels and better cottages as though made by the straying feet of drunken men. Clipped and cold, I was glad to trot briskly with my breath rising like steam in the cold air. Soon dark clouds rolled up across the sky and balls of hail fell, beating a tattoo on the hard surface of the road and the roofs of the cottages. Charlie turned up the collar of his cloak and pulled his hat lower on his head. Then quite suddenly the sky cleared and a sunlit patch of blue lay before us like a grotto in a dark cave.

At midday we stopped at an inn where a young ostler fetched me water and rubbed me down in a stall, hissing and muttering about the long journey that lay before me. I buried my head in a moist feed in which split beans had been added to the oats to give me extra energy. Meanwhile Charlie also ate well and came out about half an hour later with a swagger to his walk.

'To horse!' he cried dramatically. 'No time to waste!' The ostler put on the 'furniture' as he called my saddlery, and in no time we were on our way again, trotting and cantering down lanes and tracks through flat countryside almost empty of leaves and birdsong. I loved my home and did not want to leave Belvoir. The further I went the less eager I was to continue until Charlie used his spurs and I had no alternative but to go on.

We came to another inn at dusk and another ostler led me away to a warm stall where I stood next to a big chestnut who had just been taken out of a stage coach. He had galloped down hard roads and now his legs ached and he hardly seemed to know which to rest first. Later he lay down with his head stretched out breathing heavily, but I remained standing all night. I do not like lying down when I am tied or in a strange place. I dozed and was wakened by rats scuttling in the straw under my feet.

Big brown fellows they were with intelligent beady little eyes, bright as boot buttons. Had rats been found at Belvoir the head groom might have been dismissed, but that inn was a miserable place with holes in the walls and not a cat to be seen. In the morning my feed tasted of mice and the hay was yellow and rank. I had eaten what I could when Charlie appeared smiling with his cheeks still fresh from yesterday's ride.

'How's he doing? He's a nice horse and a great one with hounds,' he told the ostler, who replied that I was 'a fine 'oss, gentle as a baby.'

Presently I was saddled-up and another day of the journey began. A light drizzle of rain fell softly from steel-grey skies and Charlie sang old ballads. And I was happy then, for I love singing.

'On to the sea and I'll wager you've never seen the sea before,' declared my rider.

But he could not know that I had heard horses talk of it, especially a little mare who pulled the Duke's phaeton and had once lived in Brighton, taking a trap up and down the Promenade.

'We are going to win,' Charlie now went on. 'Two

hundred golden sovereigns, my dear Romany, think of that! And then I'm going to change my ways. I'm going to become a respectable country gentleman. I shall no longer be seen at the gaming tables nor the races. I'm going to marry a nice girl with a fine dowry, and settle down and rear a family.'

He patted and stroked my neck as he talked and for a time I almost forgot about Belvoir and Paddy.

That day we took a long time to find an inn for lunch and it was past three o'clock before I was settled in a stable with my muzzle deep in a manger, and, as I ate, it started to sheet with rain.

In no time at all Charlie was with me again.

'Just five more miles, Romany,' he said, as he swung himself into the saddle. 'I've looked at the map.'

He soon turned me into fields where he galloped me before the wind and the wild driving rain, until my heart was pounding with excitement and my sides heaving. At last he brought me back to a trot. 'Had enough?' he asked, his breath heavy with the smell of wine. My hot, wet body steamed, but Charlie complained of the cold.

'You are lucky not to have been born with fingers and toes. Man is most stupidly constructed.' He put a hand inside his cloak and took a few gulps from his brandy flask. 'Ah, that's better.'

We went through a gate and came out on a rough road, and presently we heard the rumbling of wheels and the clattering of many hoofs and a few moments later a coach and four came into view. In a trice Charlie had me standing in the middle of the road. Waving his arms he brought the sweating horses to a halt. They leaned forward trying to stretch out their tired necks, but their bearing reins were too tight to allow it; a little foam lay like cherry blossom around their mouths and flecked their wide chests.

A pretty girl with kiss curls leaned out of the window while Charlie asked the coachman how far it was to the next town.

'Five miles, sir.'

'Five miles?' Poor Charlie was incredulous.

'You must ride like the wind to get there before dark,' said the girl teasingly before drawing back into the coach.

'We will. Never fear!' said Charlie taking off his hat to her as the coach raced away into the gathering dusk.

'He can't be right,' said Charlie, bringing out his map. 'And I can't gallop you along that road or you'll spring a splint and then there will be no two hundred sovereigns to get me out of a hole. In actual fact I shall be ruined.'

He dismounted and, screwing up his eyes, tried to read the map in the fading light.

'We've taken a wrong turn. Ah, here's a short cut, up over a bit of downland, that couldn't be better. Can you gallop on a bit, Romany? You must or we shall be caught in the dark without a light.'

He stuffed the map away under his cloak, took another swig of brandy, sprang into the saddle and dug in his spurs. Away we went then with mud spattering our faces, rain whipping our backs and the sky above turning black as tar. And I longed for Paddy, who would never have allowed himself to be caught in such a situation.

After a mile or so we turned down a track into a wood, a deep wood with dark firs and the scent of wet pine needles. It was very quiet and the track seemed to go on and on, while the darkness came down through the trees and blackened everything. The night grew very still, as the rain stopped. And the boughs dripped, pitter patter

134

on the sodden earth. Then the track petered out and we were simply moving through trees, hundreds of trees, all slender and dark and not yet large enough for the forester's axe. Charlie shivered and I knew from his smell that he was frightened and that made me nervous. He stopped me and drank again from his flask and cursed, and his voice seemed very faint and young in the darkness of the wood. There was no moon nor stars only the rolling clouds, and the horrible quietness which seemed to suggest that we were miles from open fields or roads and tracks. Not a chink of light proclaimed a thinning in the trees which were now hard for me to see so that I was constantly brushing Charlie's legs against their trunks. Then, all at once, I felt a path under my feet and those regiments of trunks parted a little to allow a passageway. The air freshened, a tiny night breeze wafted the scent of lavender through the darkness, and I saw before me the solid form of a building. I stopped. It was very strange and I cannot now explain the sensation which came over me because there are no words to match my feelings. The trees seemed to move slowly away to reveal to my startled eyes a little dingle in which a tiny deserted cottage stood. And then I sensed that a strange being was with us. My heart thumped and my eyes seemed to strain in their sockets. A snort, my snort, rent the silence with the savageness of a pistol shot; the splintering of twigs told me that some wild animal was fleeing before us. I stood with legs straddled then, my skin flapping with fear. I saw a luminous figure dressed in ragged clothes rise from the walls of the cottage, and as she levitated her sad grey eyes seemed to look straight at me. Her lovely red hair lay about her narrow shoulders, and over her arm she held a basket full of lavender tied up in bunches ready

for the market. But she wasn't alive; she was transparent
and through her ragged skirts and shawl I could see the
darkness beyond. And I knew that her lily-white face was
bloodless. The poor girl was neither dead nor alive. She
was for ever between the two states.

'Romany, my dear fellow, have you seen a ghost?'
Charlie's voice came to me like the voice of sanity and
commonsense. More calmly I watched the tragic figure
float away among the still trees, while my eyes began to
feel more normal and my flesh settled. He had seen
nothing but the solid form of the cottage, the dripping

136

trees and the blackness of the night, to which his eyes had become accustomed. I straightened my legs. I tossed my head as though to cast out the memory of that ghost.

'There now,' said Charlie, dismounting. 'Dear me, you are in a sorry state. Fear not. Let me lead you on.'

He pulled my ears affectionately, stroked my neck and rubbed his bristly cheek against mine. 'Be a brave fellow. See, there's a hut where we can take shelter.'

He coaxed me forward, kindled a light with his tinder and found the door. The scent of lavender had faded to be replaced by the more natural smells of wet fir wood and damp earth. It started to rain again.

'Come on, inside.'

The cottage had just one room with a broken window and a pile of sacks or rags in one corner.

'A miserable place,' said Charlie, 'but at least it will afford us some shelter.'

He took off my saddle and bridle, rubbed me down with a handful of rags and patted my neck.

'Sorry my old friend but I am afraid you must go hungry tonight. Thank God for my brandy or I might have expired with the cold.'

He latched the door, drained his flask, wrapped himself up in his cloak, lay down on the earth floor and was soon fast asleep. But I could not forget the ghost and that night was full of fears for me. I could hear noises that no human ear could detect, and I stood close to Charlie until the dawn, wanting the comfort of a breathing, living thing.

I nuzzled him, as the light came through the little window, glad to break the loneliness of my vigil, and he awoke smiling.

'Oh heavens, where am I?' his voice was heavy with sleep. 'Oh Romany, what a night! I was dreaming. I was in London with the most wonderful girl with dark flashing eyes and such hair! But you're only a horse, you wouldn't understand, and I'm an idiot to speak to you in this way. Heavens, I'm cold!' He stretched. 'And stiff too! What a miserable place this is. I bet Archie managed things better, a hotel bed for Archie I'll be bound. And you're cold too,' he added, looking at me. 'Oh dear me, what a pickle, and all my own fault for drinking too much wine at that inn and not reading the map accurately. Have you seen any more ghosts, my dear fellow? You were rigid as a plank.'

As he spoke he picked up my bridle and looked at it with a perplexed frown on his face. 'Which way up? Well, the bit must be at the bottom. Open up, Romany, now you must be patient and good.' He spent a long time saddling and bridling me and when we left the cottage my bit was too low in my mouth and my girth back to front.

## CHAPTER FOUR

## *I swim for my life*

Now in daylight the wood seemed a friendly place, full of singing birds and flashes of green where clearings allowed the grass to grow. The path from the wood-man's cottage led us towards a break in the trees through which the early sun shone.

'That means we are heading south-east,' said Charlie. 'We should keep a little more to our right but I'm hanged if I'll leave this blessed path.'

I was hungry. My tummy rumbled and I longed for a bite of spring grass to freshen my dry throat. All the same I cantered willingly, being careful not to trip on roots and each moment the wood seemed to lighten so that we knew we were moving towards open country. Then at last we were out of the trees and galloping down a track towards a farmhouse which nestled against a brown hill, like a wild animal sunning itself on a ledge.

Soon Charlie was knocking on the old front door. 'Anyone at home?'

A woman came with a grey shawl over her shoulders. 'Yes?'

In a few moments Charlie had explained how we had spent the night and the woman had promised him a fine breakfast of bacon and eggs. A man was summoned and soon I had drunk deep at a trough before being settled in a stable with a good feed and a rack of hay. An hour later we were on the road again.

'It *was* a ghost you saw, Romany,' said Charlie. 'Poor

Mary, the lavender girl, who was betrayed by her lover, Joe the forester. No one will live in the hut now on account of her presence. It's very singular that you should have seen her and I should not.'

Feeling better for my feed, I trotted willingly enough and we soon reached the town where Charlie had intended spending the night. Here he left me tied by a public drinking trough while he went to buy a compass. When he returned a small crowd had collected around me.

'Is this the 'oss what's a travelling all the way down to Cornwall?' one swarthy man asked.

'Indeed, indeed,' replied Charlie with his good natured smile. 'But I was not aware that we were famous. News travels fast in these parts and no mistake. Have you heard of my rival, a dark haired fellow riding a mare with two white socks?' But no one had news of Archie, not here nor in any of the hamlets through which we passed during the afternoon. We kept to one road and the day passed uneventfully, and before nightfall we came to a manor house owned by Charlie's cousins.

'I promise you safe lodging this night. No ghosts, no haunted houses to set your flesh flapping, and I believe there's a horse from Belvoir to keep you company,' said Charlie as he turned me up a well raked gravel drive flanked by yew hedges.

The front door of the house opened and a stout barrel-chested man in breeches and gaiters looked out.

'So you are here on your mad escapade, Charlie Daintree,' he said gruffly. 'Our other guest overtook you on the road and brought news of you. Your horse will be in need of fodder and a good rub-down. Stanley! You must be patient. Our servants are getting old like us and don't move as fast as they did.' At that moment an old bow-legged groom came shuffling round the corner of the house. He took my rein, grunting disapprovingly at the mud and earth on my coat, and led me away.

He put me in a loose-box with a floor of blue Stafford-shire brick from which, looking through bars, I soon addressed my neighbour, a fine bay shining like mahogany. My whinny of welcome was returned, the long elegant head turned; fine nostrils were pushed between the bars.

'Romany!'

'Pioneer!'

How pleased we were to see one another. And how we longed to be closer so that we could feel each other all over with our muzzles. It started to rain as we began to talk.

'What's brought you here?' asked my friend.

And I told him my story and all the news from Belvoir, and then he explained to me that the Duke had sold him to Charlie's cousin at the Manor House.

'I am a horse of all work now. I carry him to hounds and pull the trap, and I have even pulled the mower that cuts the grass on the lawn, with rubber boots on my feet so that I should not spoil the turf. Oh, it's a quiet peaceful life, with just Joey, who taught my master's children to ride, to keep me company now and then. Yet I'm bored, Romany, really I am.'

'But you were bored at Belvoir,' I reminded him.

'Yes, but this is worse. But I hear that Master is short of money and I may be sold. They say I'll fetch a lot, because I'm reliable and lively and up to weight. I'm heavy without being clumsy.'

'I know, I know. That is what Paddy always said,' I cut

in. 'He talks of you even now. He says you are a great beast, a grand hunter.'

'And now I want to be in a larger place again, an estate, with carriage horses as well as hunters and all the bustle of a busy yard. How I hate these bars! Will men never learn that horses like to have windows, too? I want to push my head out into the fresh air and smell the spring! Oh, how well I remember the oaks at Belvoir, and all the excitement before a great house party. Standing here all day looking on that passage I hear so many noises, yet I cannot tell what they mean. I cannot see what's going on. Everyone is kind. No one ill-treats me. But Romany you are the first visitor for ever such a long time! And although Stanley is a good man he doesn't talk to me as Paddy did.'

'Charlie is kind, too,' I said. 'He talks and sings to me and I am growing to love him, but he's foolish, Pioneer. I can't trust him and I'm not sure where he will take me next. And he drinks too much liquor and yet and yet, there's something about him which makes me very glad of his company.'

We talked through much of that wet and stormy night, sniffing each other's nostrils and when I was saddled at nine o'clock next morning we looked longingly at one another and were sad to part.

The day was damp and grey. Standing outside the Manor House waiting for Charlie I felt the keenness of the February wind biting at my clipped flanks.

Stanley soon started to grumble. He threw a rug over my quarters and led me up and down, and every now and then he stopped to beat his arms across his breast against his sides to warm his hands. Ten minutes must have passed in this way, then fifteen, then twenty. A maid came out of the house with a tankard of frothy beer for Stanley. 'Don't let the master see it, drink up quick,' she said.

'I'll be in need of brandy soon!' he said.

Then we heard a familiar tinkling laugh in the garden and seeing the girl who had looked out of the carriage so prettily I knew the cause of our delay. Walking across the lawn with Charlie, she wore a long brown coat and a fur trimmed bonnet, and her eyes sparkled as she laughed up into his face. Presently they both went into the house through a side door and the church clock struck the half hour, and Stanley muttered something rude about 'young bounders'. I thought of Archie and the bay mare that I had never seen. And I remembered that the people and horses at Belvoir expected me to win. I wondered whether my rivals were already on their way and I recalled the warning given by Charlie's young friend about keeping away from the ladies.

''E'll be driving you that 'ard to make up for lost time, that 'e will,' said Stanley. 'Master should give 'im the boot.' Then it began to drizzle with rain, and the old man found another rug to put over my saddle to keep it dry. Pioneer neighed and I neighed back to let him know I was still around. And then the little old grey pony in the field neighed too, and a Newfoundland dog started to bark.

At last, as the church clock struck ten, Charlie came out full of apologies.

'I was delayed,' he said, pressing a silver coin into Stanley's hand.

'And we all know what by, that we do,' snarled the groom, keeping the money. 'I'm an old man to be 'anging about while a young bounder plays with the ladies.'

The girl stood on the steps smiling.

'Bon voyage,' she said, tossing her head and making a rude face at the groom's back.

'Au revoir! On to Tintagel and the ghosts of King Arthur and all his knights,' cried Charlie dramatically, swinging into the saddle and pushing me straight into a trot. At the bottom of the drive he turned and waved to the girl who stood on the doorstep looking like a brown china ornament.

'And now for the road!' he cried to me as though he were an actor playing a part rather than a real man on a long and arduous journey.

We had thirty miles to cover after a late start, but my rider remained cheerful. Indeed he soon started to sing and invent crazy poems about beautiful girls. Every now and then he stopped to consult his compass of which he seemed very proud.

'We won't get lost with this bit of magic on board! Oh, Romany, have you ever seen such a girl!'

Soon we took a gated road which led us through pleasant hilly countryside. We came to a farm where Charlie paused to buy me a feed, and soon afterwards we stopped to eat, Charlie having brought sandwiches and a bottle of ale from his cousin's house. Scenting food a little

dog came begging scraps of bread from my master. A terrier, mostly white, he had a brown patch over one ear, bandy legs and a short stumpy tail. He stood only about twelve inches high, but his eyes were spirited and he looked as though he could walk for ever, for his little limbs seemed to move automatically. Charlie made a great fuss of the dog, talking to him as though he were another human being, and patting and stroking him.

When the last morsel of sandwich had disappeared down the terrier's throat, Charlie mounted me.

'Now, home, dog!' he said. 'Go on, home!'

But the little dog only gazed up at us with astonishment, as though amazed that we could be so cruel and unfeeling as to send him away after he had offered us his adoration for life.

'Oh don't be silly, you must have an owner somewhere,' said Charlie.

But the little dog came with us, his bandy legs working like clockwork and his eyes full of admiration for Charlie and happiness that he had found himself a master.

After a time my rider dismounted and lifted up the dog so that he could ride on the pommel of the saddle.

'We'll call you Skip until we find who you belong to,' he said, and the little dog licked his nose, as if to say thank you.

Presently we came in pouring rain to a village perched on a hill above a rushing river. Charlie hitched me to a post and went to a shop with Skip in his arms. I turned around until I had my back to the wind. A carrier's cart passed by and a timber wagon pulled by three enormous shire horses, with brasses shining on their harness, and a couple of dogs yapped at me through a fence. Then Charlie returned still carrying Skip.

'It seems you will be staying with us for a while,' he said, patting the terrier. 'Can't *you* tell us where your owner is?' He fetched his map out from under his cloak and consulted his compass.

'We're behind-hand. Can you manage a ford, Romany? It will be quite deep.'

Feeling cold and impatient to be off, I pawed the ground.

'I suppose that means yes,' said Charlie, tucking away map and compass and turning up the collar of his cloak. 'And there's no time to waste. I've news of Archie; he's five or six miles ahead of us on the upper road.'

He mounted quickly putting the dog in front of him perched on the saddle with his paws on my withers.

'You're a fine brave horse and ten miles further on there's a capital lodging house with good fare for man and beast. But we can cut that distance by a third if the ford is passable,' he said, urging me into a trot.

Soon we took a lane which wound between bare thorn hedges, where the puddles lay like little lakes overflowing here and there to rush ahead of us down towards the valley. The sky rumbled with thunder while the clouds rolled above the hills and valley, and the trees shuddered under the fury of the wind.

We came to a fork with a choice of two lanes running almost parallel, before curving away from one another towards the river we hoped to cross.

'Right or left?' asked Charlie. 'I can't dig out the map in this rain.'

He threw down my reins and drove me forward, and I took the left for it seemed to lead towards woods and I wanted shelter from the storm. Now thunder growled like the guns of war, and lightning cracked the sky and lit the waving treetops. Our lane ran beside the woods not through them and Charlie was loath to lose time taking shelter. We had been climbing upwards for a while, but now we started to descend and the lower we went the wetter was the ground underfoot until the water came above my fetlocks. Little Skip, who had jumped down from the saddle earlier on, was all but swimming so Master pulled him up on to my back again, from which he saw the swollen river foaming and rushing before us and the trees tossing either side.

'The deuced thing is flooded – this, my dear Romany, is the ford!' cried Charlie. 'Just my luck!' He pulled me to a halt, fetched out his flask and drank deeply from it, then he poured a little liquor into each of his boots to warm his wet feet.

'Dammit! We should have delayed until April, waited for fairer weather. What fools we were, what hot-headed idiots to choose February fill-dyke, the wettest month of the year. Dear Romany, I am sorry but you may have to swim.'

He leaned down and patted me on the neck. 'They said in the shop that the river was passable. Ah well, nothing venture nothing win!'

I had crossed rivers before but never one so deep and fierce, and now I was frightened of those dreadful rushing waters which bore sticks and branches along as though they were bits of straw. I blew through my nostrils and danced from side to side and Charlie said, 'Only cowards turn back.' Then he spurred me forward.

'God spare us,' he cried. 'Spare us, and I'll never gamble or drink heavily again. I'll mend my ways, dear Lord. But please first take us safely across this river!'

Behind us streams of water raced down the hill to join

the flood like children running to catch up with the crowd at a fair. The wind drove us from behind, sending my tail between my legs. Skip barked as lightning zig-zagged in the crazy sky. I hesitated, blew again through my nostrils and then plunged into the swirling waters. Charlie, knowing that a swimming horse must use his neck, threw down the reins. Skip barked more wildly standing up on my back to admonish the river for its fury. On the other side the trees swayed away from us, creaking and groaning like old men. The water pressed

hard against me as it rushed downstream. It rose up to the stirrups. It climbed Charlie's legs. It reached my mouth as the floor of the river seemed to give way under my feet. A moment later there was nothing but the water and myself battling against one another. The force of the river toppled me over on to my side. My mouth and throat filled with water and I thought that I should drown. I heard a stifled cry from Charlie and, with a choking snort, righted myself, then found that I was swimming for the first time in my life. My tail fanned out in the water to act as a rudder, my legs moved in the right motions without directions from myself. I forgot Charlie, Skip and the ride to Cornwall and thought only of reaching the other side where the lane led upwards between trees to meet the wild tempestuous sky.

A moment later my feet felt firm ground. I scrambled and plunged forward and came into shallower water covering the bank which had once marked the edge of the river, and then I was out and standing on the lane. I shook myself like a dog, I snorted to clear my nostrils and throat while my wet sides heaved up and down. My saddle was empty. Where was Charlie? And what should I do? My first impulse was to gallop until my legs were so tired that I could go no further. But where to? I stared at the raging river. I looked downstream where young trees were being dragged up from their roots by the current, where weeds and undergrowth were flattened and fencing posts split. I looked up the lane along which we had come, in case Charlie had somehow turned back, and into the darkness of the trembling wood. There was not a cottage or building in sight, not a human voice to guide me. I neighed and my neigh rose above the storm and hung for a moment in the air. I neighed again. And then I saw the little dog lying panting on a brown patch of sodden earth a few yards downstream, and Charlie still in the water hanging on to a tree, his black cloak swirling madly round his body.

I turned as another flash of lightning lit the sky and trotted up the hill, and at the top was a tiny thatched cottage. I neighed again and a little door opened and a wrinkled old man came out. He looked at me, at my soaking body and shaking sides, and then turned to find a sack to put over his head and shoulders. Then he took my reins and led me back down the hill with all the vigour of the storm beating in his face.

'Someone drowned,' he muttered. 'Some poor soul.' He turned his head, looked up and down the swollen river and spotted Charlie white and hatless with his wet hair plastered to his head. He left me then and climbed a fence and went to pull him out. But he wasn't strong enough.

'I'll die of cold, if I don't drown first. Make haste, get a rope. Help me, man, help me!' gasped Charlie between chattering teeth.

The old man leapt the fence with the agility of a mountain goat, jumped on my back and galloped me back to the cottage. He found a rope, broke down a bit of fence and led me to Charlie. He tied the rope round Charlie's chest, hitched the ends around the flaps of my saddle and urged me forward. The saddle moved. I pulled again. The old man pulled. The saddle slipped back but my well sprung ribs held it from passing over my flanks. I pulled again and with a cry of gratitude Charlie came to rest on a lump of undergrowth.

'Brandy in my cloak,' he whispered hoarsely.

And the old man found the flask and held it to my master's lips, and watched the colour come back into his face. Then the old man went to Skip and opening the little dog's jaws, persuaded him to drink also. And after a few moments the terrier got to his feet and shook himself as though he had just been for a pleasant dip on a summer's day.

Charlie sat up. 'I think I owe you my life,' he said simply.

'This 'oss fetched me,' the old man said. 'He neighed outside the cottage.'

150

'God be praised,' exclaimed Charlie with a fervour which was not natural to him. And then he laughed. 'I wager I look like a drowned rat!'

The old man said we had taken the wrong lane. The other ford was usually passable whereas this one was only useful in midsummer or at times when there was little rain. It was particularly treacherous because of a shelf which made the floor of the river fall suddenly away. He helped Charlie to climb on my back and we returned to the cottage with Skip trotting cheerfully and a little drunkenly at my side. Then the old man explained that he had a rabbit stew with dumplings hanging in a pot over the fire, but nothing that would adequately feed a horse. He could only give me chicken feed and a bit of straw. He took me to a hovel leaning against the cottage and, after removing various garden tools, he led me inside and fetched me a little water, maize and straw. He rubbed me down and made a rough rug for me out of sacks, using a jack-knife to slice them open and sewing them where necessary with a large needle and string. As he worked a plump black cat sat on his knees purring softly and looking with adoring emerald green eyes at his master's wrinkled face. And the old man talked to the cat and to me as though we were people.

Meanwhile Skip and my master were inside the cottage drying themselves before the wood fire, waiting to be joined by their host when he was sure I was comfortable.

'I'll have another think and if I can conjure up any more food for you, I'll be back,' said the old man before leaving.

The roof of that little hovel rocked terribly in the wildness of the storm, but it was well-made and nothing split or came apart, and I remained dry and snug all night. At dawn the old man came back, moving as softly as his cat and carrying a bucket which steamed and smelt delicious.

'I remembered that I had a little linseed put aside in case I needed a poultice, so I've made you a mash which will set you up for the day and make your coat shine like a jewel,' he said, speaking in the way of an educated man and moving like an animal of the woods accustomed to stalking its prey or escaping silently from enemies.

I whinnied politely for I loved that man, and he stroked me kindly as though he liked the feel of my coat.

We bade him goodbye as the sun streaked the eastern sky with ribbons of gold and red, and the country lay quiet at last after the tumult of the storm.

'I owe you my life,' Charlie said again, squeezing his hand.

'Don't say such things, that's blasphemy,' the old man said. 'We do not decide these things.'

'Please let me give you a sovereign. It would afford me such pleasure. You have looked after us capitally,' begged Charlie.

But the old man refused to accept anything, saying that he hoped to reap his reward in heaven and that money was of no importance to him. He lived all alone, Charlie said later, snaring rabbits and growing his own vegetables and earning a big hedging and ditching when that work was available. Perhaps in his heart he knew that Charlie was actually in debt with no money of his own to spare. Perhaps he knew many things without being told. There was something unforgettably wise about that brown wrinkled face which haunts me to this day.

## CHAPTER FIVE

# *Trouble at an inn*

After that frightening episode Charlie vowed that he would take no more risks and the next two days passed uneventfully. We stayed at inns with Skip sleeping in my manger as soon as I had finished my evening feed. Then every morning at daybreak the little dog would lick my muzzle and dance round me barking as though he was celebrating the dawn.

On the third afternoon we caught up with Archie on his weedy bay mare with two white socks.

'I thought you were lost. I heard bad news of you,' he told us. 'What a life!' he grinned, showing long white teeth. 'Is the dog your mascot, Charlie?' His voice mocked; his hazel eyes were heavily lidded and his nose curved like an eagle's beak.

'Just a little friend who has chosen to adopt us.'

'Oh, now you are being sentimental. I should part company with that cur, otherwise you are only adding to your weight and responsibility.'

'Romany is a substantial fellow. I only weigh eleven stone,' retorted Charlie. 'He's a nice little dog with engaging ways, and the word cur is objectionable to my ears.'

'Running out of money?' asked Archie with an impudent grin.

'Not at all, not at all, Archibald,' replied Charlie with his disarming laugh. 'You must not worry so much about me. We have been living very carefully.'

'No liquor?'

'Just enough to keep the wicked cold at bay.'

As the two men continued to exchange remarks of this kind half in mirth and half in earnest, I looked at my rival. She possessed, I noted, a finely cut head, rather nervous protruding eyes and a long slender neck. Her skin was so thin that here and there you could see the veins standing out like string, and her cannon bones were too narrow to suggest stamina. She walked nervously, looking more like a three year racehorse than a seven year-old hunter, her small hoofs picking their way daintily over stony ground. In contrast my own feet looked large as sunflowers and my cannon bones like fencing posts.

'I'm going to gallop to freshen up my mare. Coming?' asked Archie.

But Charlie declined saying we were taking the journey steadily. And we called goodbye to our rival, as Archie spurred the mare into a gallop, and presently we heard her hoofs on the stones growing fainter as she disappeared into the distance.

That night we took lodgings at an inn noisy with merrymaking. Someone played an accordion and there was much fine singing and many ribald jokes. Then around ten o'clock there was an uproar outside and I heard voices raised in anger, threats and curses and the sound of clashing sticks and thrown stones. Our ostler came running down from his loft and joined in the fray and occasional cheers contrasted with the groans and angry shouts of injured men. Little Skip barked wildly in the stable, jumping at the door as though he hoped to break it open and get out to join in the fray. Tied as I was with a rope and ball, I could see nothing although the noises seemed to tell their own story and I guessed that a fight between two different factions was going on.

Presently the latch of our door was lifted and Charlie came in, saying, 'Down, Skip, down, sir,' as the little dog tried to welcome his new master. 'There's been an affray,' he went on, as though we were humans who would understand. 'A lad is badly hurt. For heaven's sake, Romany, where is your bridle?'

A rough-looking man with blood on his arm, who had followed Charlie, said, ''Ere it is. Stand still, my beauty,' and as he spoke he gently took off my headstall and slipped the bit between my teeth. 'Now, sir, go right up this 'ere road till you get to the turnpike, then turn left and it's a white 'ouse 'alf a mile down close to an old oak tree. There's a brass plate on the door. If Jack kicks the bucket 'is Missus will be in sorry straits with a new baby and all.'

He led me out into the murky night, where bricks and stones and wooden sticks, upturned benches and a couple of knives glinting on the ground showed evidence of the fight.

'Say no more, I'll gallop as though my own life depends on it,' said Charlie dramatically, as the man gave him a leg-up on to my back.

He slapped me on the flank and aware of the urgency I sprang into a gallop, and people cheered or mocked as I raced up the road along which men were limping homewards, some supporting one another, others singing wild songs. Little Skip ran in our wake causing some amusement among some of those we overtook.

Charlie made a fine noise banging the doctor's knocker on his fine oak door and presently a white haired woman with a candle drew back bolts, unhitched a chain and lifted a bar to open up.

'Gone to bed,' she said, peering at us. 'Had an early morning delivering Rosie Greg's baby, he's that tired.'

'There's been a fight,' Charlie said. 'A lad's dying by all accounts. Two different factions trying to settle an old score . . . down at The Three Bells.'

'And who might you be?'

'A wayfarer, belonging to neither side. I'm only interested in saving a life. The lad needs a surgeon, he's little more than twenty years old.'

'I'll go and see. Wait a moment,' the old lady said.

She came back some moments later with a stout bleary-eyed doctor, who held a black case in his hand.

'No peace for the wicked, they say,' he remarked. 'The Three Bells, did you say? Well if it's that urgent I had best have your horse. Martha, look after the gentleman until I get back. I daresay he would not say no to a dram of whisky. A leg-up, sir, if you please. It's not the first time I've ridden bareback.'

The doctor's hand was light on the rein and he spoke to me softly as we jogged the mile or so back to the inn, where he sewed up the boy and dosed him with medicine. 'He'll live,' he said, simply. 'He won't lose the scar but a few cold compresses on the head would assist his recovery. Tell him to keep out of fights in the future, for he might not be so fortunate next time.'

The ostler had saddled me for the return journey, so the doctor trotted me briskly back and in no time his place was taken by Charlie, who was in high spirits after the glass of whisky. I was back in the stable just before the church clock struck twelve with faithful little Skip panting beside me, and was glad to find that the ostler had left a little feed for me in the manger and had filled my rack with fresh hay.

156

But I missed a proper night's rest and the next morning when we started I was tired. Indeed I yawned right in front of Charlie's face. And where was Archie and his bay mare? My master asked everyone he met. Eventually a farmer driving his cob to market told us that he was five miles ahead on the higher road. 'Saw 'im myself on a thoroughbred mare riding like the very devil.'

'He'll wear his horse out,' said Charlie. 'It's the story of the tortoise and the hare all over again. We'll win in the end.'

''E's no horseman or he wouldn't be galloping over them stones, enough to bruise the mare's soles,' the farmer said.

The sun came out and put my rider in good humour and he started to sing again with his arm round the little dog who was sitting on the pommel of the saddle.

'You animals are both such good friends to me,' he said, between one song and another. 'You are better than people, you don't scrap and fight.'

We stopped at an inn at midday where the stables were full and, tied outside, I watched Charlie eating at a table by the bar. Three ragged orphan girls came to the door with outstretched hands begging for bread. The inn-keeper's wife turned them away, but Charlie came out and gave them a few pence and they curtsied to him. 'Thank you, sir, thank you.' Then they ran off on their bare brown feet to buy bread at the baker's shop.

'Who looks after them?' asked Charlie.

'They look after themselves and sometimes the Rector spares them a bite of this or that and they begs the rest,' the woman said. 'But if I was to give them bread I should have every penniless man, woman and child at my door.'

All afternoon riding through Somerset Charlie was

trying to write a poem in his head about those orphans. He said he could not forget their little white pinched faces and dark troubled eyes. 'We look after our horses better than our children,' he told Skip.

So the day passed and another and we heard no more of Archie while we came through Devon and on to Cornwall, a wild place, where the men spoke with a dialect we could not understand. There was no railway here and much of the land was bare and uncultivated, and there were tin mines, in which children and adults worked from first light until dark.

Riding across a moor we came upon a man walking unsteadily, tripping over clumps of heather and boulders. He was wearing tweeds, a deerstalker hat and laced brown boots, and there was a drip at the end of his purple-veined nose.

'He must be drunk,' Charlie said, while Skip barked and leapt in the air with excitement. 'The poor old gentleman has lost his bearings altogether.'

As we drew nearer Charlie called out: 'Permit me to help you, sir. Can I be of any use?'

'That you can, for I canna see a thing,' answered the man in a loud clear voice.

'Scottish,' muttered Charlie. 'Come on.'

I cantered up to the lurching figure, who turned and showed us his scarred and rugged face, dominated by a large bushy moustache.

'I'm blind, ye perceive,' he said. 'I lost my sight at Waterloo.'

'But a moor is no place for a sightless man!' cried Charlie in great consternation. 'Can you ride?'

'Aye, I can ride, but let me have hold of your stirrup, that will serve me well enough.'

'No, I'm the younger man,' said Charlie, dismounting.
'I'll do the running if you please, sir.'

'I canna see you, but I ken you're a fine lad right
enough,' replied the blind man, putting out his hand for
guidance. 'Could you be the young lad I've heard tell of,
the man who's riding from Leicestershire to Tintagel for
the sake of a bet to, to, well, I'll not be going into
that.'

'That's me,' replied Charlie eagerly, taking the man's
hand. 'Have you heard news of my rival, Archibald
Hickstead?'

'I've heard say that his horse is lame, lad, and he's
raving like a frustrated bull.'

As we continued across the moor with the blind man on my back and Charlie at my head, we heard of our new friend's plight. A few miles back three men had ambushed his coach, knocked out his driver, and driven the horses to the moor where they had stripped the blind man of all his valuables and his bag of gold before dumping him in a clump of heather.

'It's a terrible place Cornwall to be sure and I wouldna have ventured so far had I not had a sister who's been waiting these ten years to see me, poor soul; she wed a sailor from Penzance and has been repenting of it ever since. But ye have a great journey in front of ye and will not be interested in the chatter of an old blind man. If ye could take me to the nearest inn I shall thank ye from the bottom of my heart. I have guid letters of credit with me right enough so will not be wanting my gold. I would not want to be slowing ye down.'

'With Archie's horse lame we can relax a little,' Charlie answered. 'And we're not the kind to leave a blind man on a moor, whatever the odds.'

'No, I ken that, I ken that, you're a great lad,' the blind man said.

So we walked on across the bleak sweep of moor that men call Bodmin and came at last to an inn where we left the Scotsman with a kindly innkeeper in a small town before continuing our journey at greater speed through unsheltered countryside, which lacked the pretty cottages, the little dells and dingles which had made much of Devon so pleasant for us. It grew very cold as the dusk fell on the rough fields and meadows and snow came with an easterly wind, so that we were glad to find lodgings in a posting house for the night. A kind groom rubbed me down and rugged me up and finding myself loose in a stable, I lay down and Skip cuddled up against me for warmth.

It was a rowdy place with much drinking and coming and going far into the night. Sometimes I could hear Charlie's voice as he joked or laughed with a crowd of other young men, and there were many toasts drunk.

## CHAPTER SIX

# I become a wild horse

In the morning several of Charlie's new friends came with much merriment to see him off and promised to meet him for a midday meal fifteen miles further on. They were going to catch a regular coach within the next hour.

I was glad to be on the road again and, trotting briskly, soon warmed up. My clipped coat had started to sprout little wiry hairs in an effort to protect me against the cold. The air was keen and invigorating, the landscape stark and bleak with the winding gear of the tin mines etched against a pale steely sky. Brave little Skip ran at my side, his bandy legs serving him well. Every now and then he looked up at Charlie and wagged his tail. He seemed so pleased to have found himself an owner.

By and by we overtook a little girl riding to school on a donkey. She was sitting sideways on his back and every now and then she shook a bunch of keys in his ears to urge him on.

'What a capital idea!' cried Charlie. 'My dear Romany, shall I try keys with you?'

We came to a grey slate-roofed inn just after midday and here I was tied in a shed next to a large white sow who lay wallowing in filth. The smell of her sty and the drains from the cow byre were very strong. There was no ostler but the innkeeper gave me a bit of chaff to eat and an armful of hay, while little Skip found chicken bones in the back yard and made a great show of eating them, growling most ferociously as though crowds of dogs were waiting to snatch them from him. The place was alive with rats and later he caught and killed three large males, leaving them in a heap by the back door as though wishing to draw attention to his skill. Meanwhile Charlie was drinking heavily and presently we heard him singing:

*Archie's horse is lame,*
*Isn't that a shame?*
*And who must we blame?*
*Hickstead is the name.*
*He galloped over stones,*
*Ignored his horse's groans,*
*And now he's full of moans,*
*For he will need some loans*
*Unless his granny dies.*

Several other young men took up the refrain. The inn-keeper's girl was busy refilling glasses, and every now and then a cheer went up.

It was three o'clock before we took to the pitted road again; the sun had drifted downwards in the west, and a few dark clouds were gathering behind us. We trotted between rows of hovels where whole families of ragged children and parents seemed to live, and we met a team of red oxen with a man sitting sideways on the leader. Then we came into a wood where Charlie started to sing his ridiculous song again. It was a strange rough place full of stunted trees, boulders, and, here and there, a collapsing wall or remains of a cottage. I hesitated, wanting to turn back, then suddenly Skip started to bark and at the same moment two men emerged from behind bushes. They had dark hair and small rat-like faces and looked as stunted as the trees. They spoke to Charlie in a dialect he could not understand.

'What's that? I'm sorry I can't catch what you are saying?' He leaned forward good naturedly the better to hear and in that instant, quick as a monkey, one of the pair leapt on my back behind the saddle and held a long bladed knife at Charlie's throat.

'Hand over the money. Come on before I slice you open and leave you to die like a suckling pig.'

'Money?' replied Charlie keeping his nerve. 'My dear fellow, I am a gentleman with many debts.'

I wanted to gallop off, to throw the evil smelling man from my back but his accomplice held me firmly by the bridle. And the next moment my poor silly master was on the ground, too drunk to fight. They dug in his cloak and found his little bag of coins, his brandy flask and his compass. Then they hit him in the jaw and, after seizing his cloak for themselves, they jumped on my back one behind the other and galloped me back the way I had come. Making a detour round the inn they came to the moor on which we had found the blind man, where eventually they reached their hideout, an old pit which they had covered over with branches and slates and stones, so that it merged with the landscape. Here they dismounted and, giving me a resounding wallop on the haunches with a stick, told me to be on my way.

I should have returned to Charlie, of course, but instead I galloped wildly and senselessly with the cold wind lifting my mane and stinging my eyes, across those wide acres. The moon rose. Winding tracks led in all directions, myrtle and broom bent under my frantic feet, stones jarred my pasterns and tendons. My heart pounded and my breath came at last in gasps. And then I could go no further. My sides were heaving as my throat tightened. My legs slowed down, grew weak as cotton-wool. And yet nobody was following me. My panic was unnecessary and ill-founded. I stopped and from my body there came a loud and desperate neigh which seemed to belong to that desolate moor rather than to myself; and caught by some outcrop of rock it came back as an echo, mocking me. I hung my head, ashamed that I had panicked and left my master and little Skip. Then, miraculously, I was answered by a little whinny of friendship. Excitedly, I strained my eyes but at first could see nothing except emptiness meeting the troubled grey sky. Yet I felt a presence and could smell ponies. I knew that I wasn't alone. Calming down, I now perceived that I had been looking too far ahead, scanning the horizon while in front of me there was a dell lower and cosier than the plateau on which I stood. A curly path led down into this haven, a small sheltered place with boulders and leafless trees bent and twisted by storms and tempests; and, picking my way down, I saw a group of ponies nibbling at a few jaded blades of grass that grew sparsely between rocks and boulders. They were thin little animals with hips jutting out like cliffs and sweet dish faces from which shone large eyes soft as velvet; and they reminded me of a Dartmoor pony I had met in my youth. As I drew nearer, a dark bay mare with a little white star whinnied gently and a young colt approached me mouthing in play as youngsters often do. He sniffed me from head to foot, paying special attention to my tack.

'You are tamed,' he said. 'You carry man. I shall never let them catch *me*!'

'Hush, he is a horse, not a little wild pony. He was bred by man, his father and mother chosen for mating no doubt,' said the mare.

Now the leader of the herd, a dark brown stallion with neat hoofs, high crest and wide-cheeked head stepped forward.

'Where are you from and why have you no hair?' he asked. And then I told them my story while night lay over the land and the moon turned the moor silver. And, as I talked, they all looked at me with wonderment through their long forelocks and pricked their delicate ears which were full of fluffy hair.

At last a yearling stamped a foot. 'What a terrible life, no freedom, no chance to be leader of a herd!'

'But plenty of food,' the dark bay mare commented, swishing her tail which swept the ground. 'He never goes hungry; see how fat he is compared with us. He is beautiful.' She came across to sniff muzzles with me and to run her whiskered face across my shoulder and down my sides.

'You smell of man, not of the moor,' she said, 'and this saddle? How can you bear it? It is strapped on so tight! I think I should burst under such constriction.'

'Roll on it,' advised the youngster. 'Break it into pieces. And bite through that iron in your mouth. Kill it!'

'I love my home,' I said simply, 'and I am thin-skinned. I could not survive a winter on this windswept moor. I need a warm stable and Paddy's kindness. How I would love at this moment to plunge my muzzle into one of his warm bran mashes, and to be covered in rugs, to have him fussing round me to make sure I was comfortable. We horses at Belvoir live better than many a human child, and I work willingly in exchange for such care and cherishment.'

'Your mane is stupidly short and as for your tail – what help is that pathetic thing against the storms of winter and the flies of summer?' asked the youngster.

'That is enough,' said the little mare, 'Romany is tired. Let him be.'

'You can stay with us, but I warn you to leave the mares alone. This is *my* herd,' said the stallion, 'every female and every foal is *mine*, and I give the orders.' He tossed his lovely dark mane which fell inches below his proud neck and wheeled around in a pirouette as if he wanted to demonstrate his beauty and strength.

I told him he should have no fear. I would not wish to stay long, for I couldn't live on lichen and old grass nor stand the bleakness of the moor. My master needed me and I was bred for work not breeding, so I would not touch his wives.

We remained in the dell all night, talking and dozing and at dawn the stallion led us up on to the moor where grass could be found among the stones.

Here, exposed to all the vigour of a biting wind, my poor clipped hair stood on end in an effort to protect me from the cold, and I must have looked a sad sight with broken reins, coat covered in dirt where I had rolled, and saddle askew. Several of the herd came to sniff at me as the dark bay mare had done, feeling my body and sampling my smell, as though I was something new in their experience. They asked me where my fetlocks had gone and how I came to have no whiskers and beard and, when I explained about clipping, they snorted and declared that *they* would not allow themselves to be treated in such a way. They needed their beards they said to protect their faces from the snow when they searched in winter for grass, and their whiskers helped them in the dark. I loved them, in spite of their derision and criticism, admiring their looks and the way they climbed over rocks and boulders with the agility of goats while I followed slowly, my big hoofs slipping on hard surfaces, my fetlocks twisting as I stumbled over crooks and crannies.

Towards evening I followed the herd to a farm where, the youngster said, a man put out food for them each day during winter.

'He thinks he owns us, but we belong to the moor and each other, and when I'm older I shall go off with some of the fillies and make a herd of my own,' the youngster told me. Not far from the farm gate we found a long curving line of hay, poor stuff compared with the fine mixture grown at Belvoir, but palatable enough to a horse as hungry as myself.

'Sometimes he only gives us straw, which is bitter and hard but better than nothing,' the dark bay mare said. 'Young Mountaineer sees himself as king of the ponies, but if he's chosen for breaking-in instead of breeding, he will be as much a slave as you are whether he likes it or not. It is the farmer who decides now whether or not we shall be free. He comes with other men on tall, fast horses like you and rounds us up and takes away most of our foals leaving just a few for breeding. We can't gallop fast enough to escape, however hard we try.'

I spent a second night with the herd in the same dell which had protected us from the wind and rain the first time, and tried to satisfy my empty stomach with twigs and lichen and what old grass I could find. It wasn't enough and I was glad when the next afternoon came and we started to make our way down to the farm again. This time the farmer saw me and came out of his yard calling softly.

'Whoa there, my beauty, whoa. Come along sweetheart.' He rattled a sieve of oats and walked lightly over the sodden earth while the herd of ponies began to move off.

'Don't go to him,' a dark bay two-year-old advised. 'If he catches you, he'll put ropes on you and throw you down and burn you with a red hot iron. See how I am branded with this terrible letter on my flank! I shall carry his mark for life and that means that he thinks I belong to him. And I don't want to belong to anyone. I want to be free.'

But I was tired of the moor. I was cold and hungry and the sound of the shaken oats made me long for a decent meal, and I knew that animals like me were never branded; we were too valuable to be mutilated.

The farmer was tall and well built. He walked with the step of a man accustomed to striding across rough ground and surmounting every kind of difficulty, and he spoke with an accent which belonged to the Shires of England rather than Cornwall. I was tempted to approach him, but the little mare who had been kind to me from the first neighed enticingly.

169

'Don't go, stay with us, be wild!' she called. I turned and saw the herd watching me, so many pairs of dark eyes peering out from under bushy forelocks, their nostrils wide, their little furry ears pricked and sharp.

'Come on, my beauty,' called the man. 'Come up. Let's take that saddle off.'

'We're going,' neighed the little mare. 'Follow us. Soon it will be spring with bright tender grass everywhere and sunshine to warm your back.'

A vision of Skip with his endearing brown patch over one ear and another on his flank, flashed before my eyes, and of Charlie with his fresh complexion and pleasant amused expression, and his foolishness.

'We're going,' called the mare. 'That man is dangerous.'

And then I pushed back the vision and turned to follow the herd, even though my stomach felt empty as a used bran sack.

Yesterday had been fine, but now it started to rain again, and the cruel wind howled relentlessly. The stallion took us to another dingle where we nibbled at dry stalks trying to keep our backs to the wind and rain. I started to shiver and then I started to cough, and the stallion said I was too delicate for their way of life. This moor was worse he said than Exmoor or Dartmoor. You had to be exceptionally strong to live on it.

'Look at our coats,' he said. 'It takes hours of rain to reach our skins, but you have nothing. And your legs are too long and slender and you still have that dreadful saddle, and those slippy shoes.' And now, standing there with the rain beating my quarters and the wind whistling round my short pulled tail, I was very homesick. I wanted Belvoir and Paddy and all my friends, my warm rugs and deep bed of straw.

'You are going,' the little mare said. 'You can't stand this. You're too large.' She looked at me sadly, her head on one side.

I stared at my little friends as they stood so stoically in the storm, their thick coats flattened by the rain, the water trickling from their manes and their untrimmed fetlocks, and I knew that they were right, so I went to the mare and sniffed her neck, which was my way of saying goodbye, and the youngster came again with his baby-mouthing and said, 'You were not born to be free,' and the little mare ran her muzzle over my flank and her breath was warm. And then I turned and trotted from the dingle up on to the main part of the moor. And here I galloped until I found the farm house. I came to the open gate and went into the yard and my shod hoofs made a clatter on a brick path that led to the house. The farmer saw me through a window and hurried to shut the gate so that I was trapped.

'You changed your mind, then,' he said. 'Whoa there!' I stood while he took my broken reins and stroked my wet neck. 'You're a fine horse,' he said. 'And your young master is fair demented with the worry of having lost you.'

He took me to a stall, removed my saddle and bridle, rubbed me down, rugged me up and then went to make me a bran mash. And I was very happy to be free of a saddle and to have a fine surcingle holding a jute rug instead of a tight girth and lopsided tack.

Much later in darkness Charlie arrived, driven by a man in a dog cart.

'He gave himself up, walked into the yard of his own

accord,' the farmer said. 'You're fortunate he's not caught the pneumonia.'

Meanwhile Skip looked up at me with shining eyes and barked his greetings.

## CHAPTER SEVEN

## Charlie says farewell

Charlie and Skip spent the night at the farm. My master was still feeling confident of winning the two hundred sovereigns because he had further confirmation that Archie's mare was lame, and one of the conditions of the race was that the winning horse must be sound in wind and limb.

The farmer made a sweet-tasting paste for my cough and showed Charlie how to put it on my tongue with a wooden spoon. He also oiled my tack so that it would be supple and comfortable for me to wear, and gave Charlie a pair of reins to replace the broken ones. He told us that he had been born in Northamptonshire and knew Belvoir, but had moved to Cornwall when he inherited the farm through his mother's side of the family.

'The Cornish are a peculiar people,' he told us, 'very deep and devious. I find it hard to get along with them, for they are like foreigners to me. Some are hardly better than outlaws. When I heard of your race to Tintagel I was naturally interested. Quite a number of people have been laying bets on who will win.'

'I do believe it will be me,' replied Charlie most earnestly. 'If it isn't I shall be ruined, I tell you truthfully, for I'm up to my ears in debt and had to go to the considerable expense of buying a new cloak and hat after I was robbed.'

'Well by all accounts the mare is lame and you are only a day's ride or less to Tintagel, and by God's grace your horse has not suffered from being out on the moor two nights. Did you see the herd as you came across? Lovely little fellows they are, the colts as courageous as bantam cocks and the fillies when broken gentle as kittens. They make capital ponies for children and are grand in a governess cart. Why, one I bred pulls the invalid carriage for Lord Carter's daughter and looks after her crippled mistress with the care of a nursery maid for a child.'

We had just over twenty miles to go and started before dawn, the farmer walking with us carrying a hurricane lantern to set us on the right road. Like the little old man by the river he would accept no payment for his hospitality.

'It's been a pleasure,' he said. 'And it was grand to converse again with a man who knows the Shires.'

The smell of the sea was in my nostrils and I could see the coastline meeting the pale sky as dawn broke over flat countryside. The roofs of the houses were blue in this early light and the grass and first flowers sparkled as the night frost melted and the sun rose flooding the eastern sky with pink and gold. Charlie started to sing again, and people came to garden gates and doorways to see us go by. We saw a group of children going to work in the fields and a man sitting sideways on a donkey who was laden with straw, and oxen ploughing. I trotted and cantered for the sea air made me lively and the farmer had fed me well with plenty of oats. When the Cornish sun comes out it is very warm and where we were sheltered from the wind it was hot on our backs and for the first time on the whole journey I was glad that I was clipped.

Charlie wanted to find out more about Archie, but the people we met were all taciturn and reserved. Their eyes and their straight faces did not seem to invite questions as they watched us in silence, deep, it seemed, in their own thoughts. This was the last day, these the final miles of the journey, yet my master did not hurry me. He seemed wrapped in optimism and hope. He had convinced himself that Archie was out of the race on the strength of information gathered from people he did not really know. And nothing would change his mind. He was already deciding how he would use the two hundred sovereigns, or rather the few which would be left after he had paid his debts. It must have been the same insane optimism which had made him lose so much at the gaming tables, a sort of fatal flaw in his character. But, of course, I did not understand all this at the time, only later after I had heard many people discuss the race and its outcome.

He stopped briefly for a glass of ale and a pie at midday, watering me at a common village trough which would have annoyed Paddy, who always claimed that horses caught dangerous diseases from drinking from such places. And then we continued on the road to Tintagel striped now with sunlight, and deep in woodland and forest. I could not resist contrasting this untended landscape with the green beauty of Belvoir with its great trees and its gardens so bright with flowers and shrubs of all kinds. I longed to see a copse again lying warm and brown on some winter hillside or a spinney winding its way like a dark muffler across the landscape. Now as we drew nearer to the sea the wind seemed to rise and rush towards us, but the low stone houses stood steady as rocks and the women we met on the road looked solid too with shawls over their heads and their faces rugged and brown with no spare flesh to soften the lines of age.

'We shall spend the night at the inn, a capital place by

all accounts,' said Charlie, 'if my information is correct. And I'll buy you a steak, little Skip, for you have been a faithful friend and companion and I confess I've grown to love you.'

Now we could see the castle standing out to sea on cliffs, grey and mighty, and a nearby ruined church and other buildings. We could hear the roar of the waves and the thunderous crash as they broke on rocks, and the cry of the seabirds. And, although the sun still shone, the strength of the wind defeated its warmth and whipped our faces and whistled over the fields and the blue roofs of the cottages. We overtook a farmer in a gig with a fine high-stepping horse and three donkeys pulling carts which seemed too big for their thin little bodies, and a waggon loaded with dung.

Now and then Skip went into backyards to bark at chained dogs and taunt them with his own freedom, until Charlie took him up in front of the saddle again.

'To keep you from making mischief, you little tyke,' he said. 'Anyway, should you not arrive riding like a knight? Romany, my dear fellow, do you not see the ghosts of King Arthur?'

As we came nearer to the village we noticed a group of people standing outside the inn including the three young men who had witnessed our departure from Leicestershire. I could not see Charlie's face as he waved, but I suspect it wore a smile of happiness and triumph. But there was no cheer in response, only a mocking cry from all but the young man with the fair moustache, who looked disconsolate. And then my master swore.

'Surely,' he cried, 'I have not been pipped at the post?'

'Archie arrived yesterday, he's drinking now in celebration,' the fair young man said. 'What kept you?'

'Robbers, and a lost horse, but Archie's mare is lame. I had reliable information,' said my poor master in a voice heavy with despair. 'I'm lost, Cedric.'

'I know, and I can't lend you even a sovereign for I betted on your winning and now have lost it all. You had the best horse Charlie but the least sense.'

'I lost him on a moor, but twenty-two miles from here.'

Archie came out of the inn then, his saturnine face split in a smile.

'Sorry, my dear Daintree, but I am the winner. But I do congratulate you on the condition of your horse. He looks remarkably fit.'

My master dismounted, lifting down Skip.

'I've hardly a sovereign left,' he said weakly.

'You can give me a letter of credit,' replied Archie Hickstead.

'I've no credit.'

'What a miserable fool you are, Charlie Daintree. Your

debts are renowned, your stupidity notorious. Perhaps it's time you saw inside a debtor's prison, for I'll not leave till I have the money or see you in jail. It's a matter of honour between gentlemen, my dear fellow. Have you no sense of decency, sir?'

'Let me see your horse, bring her out,' cried Charlie in desperation.

'Ostler!' yelled Archie.

Presently a mare with two white socks came blinking into the sunlight. She stepped daintily, her eyes bulging a little with apprehension, her nostrils distended. Her tail was high, and the veins stood out on her forearms like string.

'Her sole mended then?' said Charlie.

'It was nothing, just a prick, a farrier soon dealt with that,' answered Archie. 'It was no more than a trifling annoyance.'

'She looks full of life,' added Charlie miserably.

'A good night's rest does wonders with a tired horse,' replied Archie. 'Now I've waited sixteen or more hours for you, and I want satisfaction on one way or another.'

By this time a little crowd had gathered, farmers and local people who had heard of the race, and a short swarthy faced man shouted: 'Come on sir, pay up!'

I looked at the mare and she looked at me and I knew she wasn't the same horse as the one I had seen earlier in the race. The shape of her head was different and the way she carried her tail and, most plainly of all, her smell. But everyone else except Archie seemed to be deceived.

My master's friend went inside the inn and came out with a tankard of frothy ale. 'Drink that while you decide what to do,' he advised. 'A man with an empty stomach is likely to make unwise decisions.'

'I wish I was dead,' said Charlie. 'Truly I do. Has anyone a pistol? – for I would happily blow out my own brains.'

At this moment a small dark eyed farmer approached him.

'It may be that I 'ave the answer, sir,' he said. 'I'd gladly 'elp you out of this little difficulty by giving you two hundred sovereigns for your horse.'

'But, but. Oh heavens, pray sir let me think a little,' poor Charlie said. 'I am somewhat confused, for I am not at all anxious to part with such a loyal friend as this horse has been to me.' He took another gulp from his tankard. 'Ostler, take this horse and look after him while I talk more seriously inside. This wind is no pleasure to man nor beast.'

I knew then that he was going to lie and allow the farmer to think that I belonged to himself rather than to the Duke of Rutland; and as they walked towards the inn, I heard my master say, 'I could not part with such a fine beast for less than three hundred and you would have to take the dog as well, for the little fellow is devoted to that horse.'

Tied up in a stall, I was able to look at the mare properly although I could not speak with her, and knew for certain then that Archie had swopped mounts. Indeed I could see that her white socks had been made by man not nature and I could only suppose that he had bribed a number of people to remain silent. And now I despaired at the thought that I might never again see my beloved Belvoir. Miserably I played with a feed of oats, bran and chaff and nibbled at the musty hay in a rack. The stables here were dirty with the urine running straight out into an open drain where it remained until rain washed it away, or it overflowed into the yard.

Presently a chastened Charlie darkened the doorway carrying Skip in his arms.

'It's farewell,' he said simply and sadly. Then he patted me on the neck, fed me two lumps of sugar and chained the dog at the end of my stall. 'I wish you both good fortune,' he said, 'and I'll never forget you nor fail to rue this day.'

Standing there he looked very small and suddenly rather weak, as though a gust of wind would topple him over like a tree without proper roots.

Skip whined and barked as Charlie left us, furious to find himself chained like the dogs he had mocked as we had walked so merrily down that last stretch of road to the sound of the breaking waves.

CHAPTER EIGHT

## *Life on a Cornish farm*

My new owner, William Pardoe, was small, dark and as
silent as Paddy and Charlie had been talkative. He fetched
me out of the stall in late afternoon, hitched me to the
back of his gig, invited Skip to share his seat and set off
for home the way we had come, for he lived not far from
the moor where he had a flock of sheep and a score of
bullocks which he was fattening. He also grew potatoes
and daffodils and kept a hundred or more hens. His grey
house was long, low and shabby, and, looking at the
place, you would not expect the owner to have been able
to hand over a credit note for two hundred or more gold
sovereigns without so much as blinking an eyelid.

As I arrived, after a brisk trot for the best part of
twenty-one miles, I heard several cocks crow and out of
the house came three rather dirty, dark haired children,
and a mongrel collie dog who growled ominously at Skip
who was standing up in the gig with his ears raised.

Seagulls swooped and called above the house and not
far away in the twilight we could see a river hurrying on
its way to the sea. A westerly wind blew across the moor
and the pale impatient clouds were high in the sky sailing across the wide grey expanse like ships on calm
water.

The three little girls stroked my legs and rubbed their
faces against my chest. They had peat-brown eyes, bright
cheeks, short noses and pointed chins and in their ears
they wore gold rings like gipsies. They were called

Winifred, Rosalie and Mirabelle and seemed almost as wild and carefree as the young ponies I had met on the moor, for their dark hair fell over their eyes in almost exactly the same way and they were generally unkempt in appearance.

They greeted Skip with cries of delight, but he was overwhelmed by their welcome and hid under the gig, causing our new master to give a sardonic smile.

Soon I was installed in part of a cow byre standing in a pen fenced by hurdles with a sweet smelling brown cow as my neighbour, while the dun mare who had pulled the gig so briskly was put in a stall in a building that adjoined the house, which she shared with five brilliantly coloured bantam cocks who crowed almost incessantly and threatened each other through the bars of their cages.

Later in the evening Will (as he was known) came with his wife to see me, carrying a fisherman's lantern in his hand.

'And why would you be wanting a great horse like that and you such a mite of a man?' she asked him.

'I've always longed to own such a beast,' the Cornishman said. 'It's just because I'm small that I admire the big strong animals. Look at those legs, Rosabel!'

He stared at me, his little dark eyes bright with pride of ownership. Then he told his wife that he had promised not to sell me for a month while Charlie looked around to see whether he could raise the money to buy me back. 'And the little dog will keep down the rats,' he added, 'for old Floss has grown lazy of late.'

Spring comes early in Cornwall and next day I saw that there were already primroses and violets out in sheltered spots and Will's daffodils were nodding bud-laden stems in the warm breeze blowing across the moor. In just twenty-four hours the weather had changed dramatically.

After a few days I saw that my new master was nearly always busy. When I arrived his sheep were lambing and he was up at all hours of the night looking after his ewes, and in the daytime he mended fencing, dug his garden and trained his fighting cocks. His wife, a sluttish looking woman with dark hair hanging half way down her back, cared for the hens, and the three girls were sent into the fields most days to hoe around the potatoes. Each morning if it was fine I was turned out in a long meadow to rough-off, as Will put it, sometimes accompanied by the dun mare, Daisybell, and the cow, Buttercup.

Occasionally Daisybell would go out at night pulling a wagonette, and come back in the early hours her hoofs muffled with felt and rubber boots, and then kegs, barrels and boxes would be carried from the cart down into a small cellar at the back of the house. When I asked Daisybell about these journeys she said, 'I go to the sea and a rowing boat comes in, down in a little cove between rocks, and they unload the liquor and the tobacco and I bring them here for Will. And there are ponies taking loads away on their backs. That is all there is to it.'

But a man came one evening enquiring about the kegs and barrels, only it so happened that Daisybell had taken them all away to another farm the previous day, and when he searched the cellar he found it empty. Nevertheless, Will was obviously much distressed by the man's visit and an hour later he saddled me up and galloped me across the moor, down by the River Fowey and on towards the sea. In darkness I picked my way nervously along the edge of a cliff with the great ocean lashing the rocks below. Presently we saw lanterns down on a beach and we heard the splash of oars, muffled rowlocks and men's voices raised above the sound of the water. Will jumped from my back, tied me to a bush and made his way down to the shore along a dangerous twisting path. Staring down I could make out a boat and several figures in dark clothes and tall boots, and then I heard Will cry out like a sea bird and the men stopped and looked up towards the cliffs, and waved their arms and then signalled with a light. So steep was the path that I feared Will would fall, but he reached the bottom, and, immediately he arrived, the men started to carry kegs, boxes and barrels back to the rowing boat. They moved silently as though their lives depended on the job being done as quickly and quietly as possible. And the moon came out from behind a blanket of cloud and gave us a silver sea.

Presently Will started back up the path and, as he neared the top, the boat pushed off and disappeared round the corner of a great rock that jutted out to sea, and

then by the light of the moon I could see a small masted sailing ship anchored a mile or so from the shore.

Will lay down in the sparse cliff grass beside me, watching the cove. I could feel the tenseness in his body and knew that he was afraid. I nuzzled him gently but he bade me be quiet. After about half an hour he got up and led me down into a dell from which we could watch the path, and presently we heard men's voices and feet. And then Will held my nostrils so that I could not neigh. Four soldiers went by with guns slung over their shoulders, and two darkly clad men whom I was told later were customs officers. They took the path that Will had taken and when they were half way down and could not see us, Will jumped on my back and trotted me back the way I had come. I reached home in the early hours of the morning and great was Skip's welcome, for it was the first time we had been parted since my time with the herd of wild ponies, and he was afraid that I had gone for ever.

In the morning out in the meadow with the sun dappling the young spring grass, Daisybell said, 'So you went out smuggling last night. I heard you come in.'

'I don't know what a smuggler is, but you make it sound special,' I replied. 'I do know that Master was very frightened!'

'It's to save the tax. There's something called a duty on drink and other things that come over the sea. If you smuggle, you fetch it in secret and don't pay the tax. That's all I know. Don't ask me what tax is for; I can't answer. But I think you saved him from getting caught. That man who came was looking for trouble. He was a customs officer.'

We were half way into March now and there was no

news of Charlie and Will talked of selling me to a Sir George Wrightson-Smith who lived in Devon. Apparently Will knew the man's stud groom who was from Cornwall. The gentleman was rich he said and well accustomed to paying from three to four hundred guineas for a good horse and the stud groom would take Skip as his own and so Will would not break his promise to Charlie.

A strange contentment had crept over me down at this Cornish farm between the moor and the sea, where the days seemed to fold into one another and all around me was the fragrance of spring. Apart from the bantam cocks all Will's animals seemed calm and comfortable. There were few excitements and as a result few worries. There was no bustle, no aim at perfection as there had been at Belvoir, and Will himself was always the same: quiet, expert and kind. He never spoke to us except to give orders, but his hands were gentle and he never made mistakes. After the strain of living with Charlie and his foolishness, the Cornishman gave me peace of mind. And, although I longed to see Belvoir again, I grew fond of Daisybell, with whom I could have easily and happily spent the rest of my life. She wasn't beautiful, being plain in colour with a long face and rather ugly black stripe down her back, but she possessed such an air of calm friendliness that she was pleasant company, and I loved to stand with her under the trees.

However, it was not to be, for although Will admired me for my looks he had no real use for me and was never adverse to making a bit of money if the opportunity arose. He had bought me on the spur of the moment and was willing to sell me on a similar impulse.

In March the stud groom came in a coach to see

me, along with his master, the plump Sir George Wrightson-Smith.

The stud groom, a man of middle height with a lean boney face and hazel eyes, ran his hands down my legs, opened my mouth to check my age and inspected the lower lids of my eyes to see that my blood was red and strong.

'A beautiful hoss, sir,' he announced. 'Shall we see him out?'

Will had put up my mane and groomed me until I shone like a polished walking stick. My hoofs had been tarred and my mouth washed. I felt worth hundreds of guineas, yet I didn't want to leave my new home, and I didn't like the red faced Sir George, with his bristling grey moustache, his bloodshot rheumy eyes and his fat soft body. I left my pen reluctantly.

'Not nappy, is he?' asked the groom.

'No, willing as a sheep dog,' said my owner, giving his friend a meaningful glance.

The stud groom mounted me, swung me round as though I was a cow pony and sent me straight into a trot, so that I knew he wasn't a horseman, for a truly know-ledgeable rider always lets a horse that has been standing in a stable warm up slowly. I swished my tail with annoyance and offered to canter. Presently the groom sent me into a gallop to test my wind and then he brought me back to his employer, pulling me up sharply to halt beside Will who looked none too happy about the way I had been handled.

'Rides all right, sir, and he's well up to your weight. See what bone he has! Going to have a try, sir?' The man dismounted. 'Got a mounting block?'

'No, never had need of one,' Will said.

So the stud groom legged the fat Sir George into the saddle and adjusted the stirrups for him and checked the girth. And after Charlie and Will he felt like a sack of turf. He dug me with his spurs and I moved off, shying a little at a twig that was blown in my direction by a little gust of wind from the moor. Sir George stuck his legs forward and his hands moved up and down as I trotted, jerking my mouth. He made himself seem even heavier than he was by sitting too far back in the saddle, but he was firm and I didn't misbehave, because I had been well broken and trained to obey instructions automatically. He cantered me in circles, first one way and then the other, neck-reining me as though I was a polo pony. Then he asked for a jump and Will and the stud groom fetched three hurdles and drove them into the ground with a wooden mallet.

'You've taught him to go leap then?' he asked Will.

'He's been a hunter down in Leicestershire, jumping bullfinches and the like,' Will said.

Sir George galloped me at the hurdles and at the very moment when I wanted to stretch out my neck he raised his hands as though to lift me up, but hurdles are nothing to me, so I sailed over just the same and he seemed well pleased.

'A great leaper, no doubt about that,' he said, very proud of himself. 'Well, Ted, I leave you to check him over again. Look inside his hoofs, and take him out once more after he has stood in the stable for a while. Now Mr Pardoe let us talk business. I want to know more about his home in Leicestershire. I always like to know about a horse's background and pedigree. Indeed I never buy an animal without checking his credentials and antecedents.'

Will said he had a little bilberry wine inside and a

noggin was a good pick-up on a blustery day like this one. And then the two men went into the house, and Winifred, Rosalie and Mirabelle came out and put their arms round my neck.

'You are never going to buy him, and what about the little dog, Skip?'

The groom said that curiosity killed the cat and that it would be best if they held their tongues, but they continued to pet me, and to gaze up at the man with their appealing dark eyes. Unmoved, he looked inside my hoofs and pushed me with a stick to see whether I would grunt and peeped under my tail, and then he left me in the byre and went outside to smoke a cigarette.

The door of the house opened and Sir George came out followed by Will, who looked very grave.

'I shall write to the Duke,' Sir George said. 'I've met him on more than one occasion and an enquiry from me will be in good order. I recollect a piece about the race that appeared in *The Times* and, if my memory is not at fault, it was stated that this horse ridden by young Daintree was the Duke's property. If there's been any funny stuff it's best sorted out. But don't worry, my man, it goes without saying that you bought in good faith and shall be repaid, whatever the facts of the matter are.'

'The young man was a fool,' Will said. 'Why, a horse like this could cover fifty miles a day without coming to harm and he just played around doing twenty or thirty. And it's said the other fellow changed horses and the white socks on the mare he rode at the end were bleached, but I don't know the truth of it.'

'Trust me to get to the bottom of the business,' said Sir George puffing through his moustache like an overweight walrus. 'I'm not a man who stands any nonsense.'

Meanwhile the driver who had brought Sir George reappeared as if by magic with the coach and horses, and a moment later with a clatter of hoofs and the rattle of iron wheels on the stony lane, they were off with Skip barking in their wake. And somehow I knew then that their visit was going to mark the beginning of the end, and another change in my life would soon take place.

## CHAPTER NINE

# A happy ending

Of course it was all very disturbing. It is horrible for a horse to feel that his future is uncertain and frequent changes of home often make us nervous and unreliable. Charlie or Paddy would have chatted to me so that I should have known how things stood, but Will was as usual as silent as a bat in the rafters.

Two weeks passed like months and, with Daisybell busy taking eggs and flowers to market, Skip either ratting or trying to make friends with the unresponsive Floss and the three little girls busy in fields or garden, I was much alone.

By April my summer coat had grown, sleek and glossy as a raven's wing, and Will rode me over to the smithy to have a new set of shoes put on my feet. I thought I might learn something of the future from his talk with the farrier, but he only spoke in a general way about the potato crop, the price of daffodils and so on.

Then, two days later, everything changed again. I was in the long meadow with Daisybell talking sleepily about the plight of animals at the hands of men.

'Think of Master's sheep,' she said. 'Man takes every-thing from them. First their coats for wool, then their dear lambs for meat, and, last of all, their very skins for coats or rugs.'

'Yet all but the last comes again,' I objected. 'The ram gives them more lambs and nature provides them with new fleece. My mother for example loses her foals, one by one, but each time she is expecting another to arrive, so that although she may neigh and gallop up and down the fence she is soon happy again.'

'I don't agree,' began Daisybell. 'But what is that? Listen – a man is coming.'

Raising my head and pricking my ears I heard a merry whistling and footsteps brushing through wet grass, and the tune was wonderfully familiar. Indeed at the sound of it my heart seemed to jump and miss a beat. It was the *Londonderry Air*.

'Paddy! It's Paddy!' I said. 'I would know that whistle anywhere.' I galloped to the gate of the long meadow and almost hurt my eyes gazing through the mist in search of my friend.

'He's come for me,' I said to Daisybell, who was soon at my side. 'Isn't it a fine whistle?'

'It sounds to me very like any other whistle,' the dun mare replied. 'I can't see or hear anything special about it as a matter of fact, although I confess it's not a tune I've heard in these parts.'

'It's Paddy,' I said again. 'I know it's Paddy.'

Then I saw him walking with a light step, a knapsack on his back, and strong boots and gaiters on his feet and legs. I whinnied, pressing my chest against the gate, and the soft Irish voice said, 'It's me, Romany, for sure. Top of the morning to you!' And there he was standing before me like a person out of a dream, with his shock of red hair, freckled face, blue eyes and snub nose.

'Hello stranger,' he said with a merry laugh. 'It's been a long time, and the Duke has been making enquiries, and you're the winner, Romany, as I knew you must be.'

He patted my neck, as he spoke, and gently pulled my ears, and I nuzzled his pockets for tit-bits.

192

Then Will came across to us, a cap on his head and a rabbit snare in his hand.

'So you've arrived and came to the horse before the house,' he said with his sardonic smile, looking small, dark and wiry beside my Irish friend. 'He's been well cared for. You can see that with your own eyes.'

'He's grown a fine coat for sure,' said Paddy, looking me over with a critical eye. 'It's a fine thing that he's been in such good hands. Is this your mare, too? She's a handy sort.'

'Yes, that's old Daisybell, fifteen years old this May and always as good as gold.'

Paddy told the Cornishman then that three hundred guineas was waiting for him in a bank some twenty miles distant.

'I'll give you the note; just take it. They know what you look like, so don't send anyone in your place or he might be clapped in jail.'

'And Mr Charles Daintree?' asked Will.

'He fled to France, with the change without paying his debts, a wastrel for sure, good-natured enough, but weak as water. He's cleared, of course, and the other young rascal has paid up, but it's a bad man who sells another man's horse right enough.'

As he talked Paddy ran his hands down my legs.

'He's in fine fettle and he'll take me to the railhead all right. It'll be a welcome change from walking, for my feet are awful sore.'

'And the dog?' asked the Cornishman, looking up at Paddy from under the peak of his cap.

'What dog? Dammit man, no one spoke of a dog to me.'

'Didn't Sir Arthur tell the Duke that it was part of the

bargain? This horse can't go without that little terrier – I gave my word.'

'To a scoundrel.'

'It was my word, never mind to whom I gave it. My word is my word,' said the Cornishman, looking at Paddy with the full force of those dark slanting eyes. 'He's a grand terrier, and will not hold you back.'

'I'd be a grateful man for sure if you would have the charity to explain,' said Paddy.

So Will told him more about Skip and described the bay mare who had replaced Charlie's lame mount and the cruel way in which her fetlocks had been bleached.

'There's a lot round these parts who now know the truth about that, but we are not a people to talk unless we are asked. It was for the young man who rode this horse to spot the difference, but a drunk man is a poor judge and a poor master to a horse, too, and there it is. I expect you would like a nosebag, and a meal just now for yourself, so come along and we'll see what the wife will find you. I can give you the name of a farmer who'll put you up thirty miles from here, and when you've eaten I'll saddle old Daisybell and put you on your way.'

The two men went off to the house then, both talking in their own dialects, which I have not tried to reproduce here, for they are hard to understand until you have lived with them for a while.

An hour later we set out with our heads turned towards the moor, with the mist lifting as the midday sun broke through and lit the way with hazy gold. We came to parts which I had not crossed before, strong with the acrid scent of gorse, the distance dominated by tors which stood like mountains, their peaks shrouded in the last remnants of mist.

194

Later we reached a deep valley where we drank in a stream that fell from rocks in a cascade of white, pretty as blossom, but foaming like the froth on the crest of a glass of beer. We saw great crags standing like guardians either side of a ravine and in the distance a forest where men were cutting down trees to use as pit props in the tin mines.

We must have covered almost ten miles when we came upon a herd of wild ponies, their manes ruffled by the wind which never seemed to leave the moor, their winter fur falling to reveal the splendour of smooth summer coats, their bodies plumper now as they flourished on the spring grass. Startled, they looked at us with raised heads and pricked ears. And I realised that this was *my* herd and over to the west was the farm where I had spent a night. I stopped then, and the little mare recognised me and whinnied gazing at me again with those wonderful soft velvety eyes under a wild and tangled forelock. But the stallion wheeled around and started to urge the herd away and, after I had whinnied my greeting in return, the little mare turned too and followed the rest as they galloped across the moor, their tails streaming out behind them.

Soon afterwards we came to a turnpike where Will and Daisybell left us to make our own way, and then a long lane stretched before us leading through deep woods with not another soul in sight. I thought of the robbers and shied at shadows and jumped every time a twig cracked or a leaf rustled. But grooms are not robbed like gentlemen and we came to our first night's lodging without mishap.

Each day then passed more or less the same, without incident, for although Paddy could barely read he had an uncanny gift of knowing which way to go. Like a collie dog he knew his way home, and once he was given directions he never forgot them. Three days later fresh and relaxed we reached the railhead and I was persuaded to step inside a van, where I was tied. The movement of the train and the hiss of steam frightened me, but Paddy, close by in the groom's compartment, calmed me down and fed me oats, and by the time we reached Leicester many hours later, I was quite accustomed to bracing my legs to take the sway of the van on the lines.

The great moment came when I stepped out into the light of day and smelt again the air I knew so well, and then it was only a few hours' ride to Belvoir down the roads where a few months earlier the carriage horses had taken the Queen so quickly from Brooksby Gate to her train for London. The day was now overcast, with a thin, kind drizzle blowing in our faces, and the wild flowers smelling sweet on the banks. We stopped at a farm, where Paddy was known, for food and drink and then at last we saw the castellated walls of Belvoir Castle. And, as though to welcome me home, the sun came out, and the clouds cleared to show a sea-blue sky. Just before we reached the stable yard we rode under an arch made of laurel, like those constructed for the Queen and the Prince Consort, and on this arch a board cried out in white paint: 'Welcome Home Romany – The Winner.'

Paddy must have been told of it beforehand because he read it to me, although, as I have said, he was no reader. And in the yard lots of grooms and servants came out to see me as though I was a hero. Then Paddy said, 'And now, my friend, I have a happy surprise for you.' And he led me to a field and there, standing under a tree, was Pioneer. 'The Duke bought him back to replace you,' said Paddy with a laugh. 'And we have the pair of you again.'

I neighed and Paddy said I could go out there presently when I had been fed and given a drink and rubbed down, and so on. And he fussed around me as though I was worth a million pounds, while the stud groom's wife took Skip off for a meal of rabbit.

Much later when I was grazing with Pioneer the old Duke came across and looked me over, and said that I had come to no harm, and that I'd be all right for a full season's hunting next winter. And then he ordered beer to be brought out to the yard so that all the stable staff could drink my health, and there was a sing-song.

Skip soon attached himself to the stud groom's wife and lived in her cottage instead of my manger, which was just as well because I slept out for the rest of the summer. But in the winter when I was stabled he spent a good deal of each day with me and always danced around me first thing in the morning when work started.

One day about two years later I heard a familiar voice in the yard, and there was Charlie with the girl whom he had met at his cousin's house.

'May I introduce my wife,' he said.

197

Paddy was cold and unfriendly at first, but once again the young man's humour was infectious, and soon the grooms had more or less forgiven him his dishonesty. He had, it turned out, made himself useful to a rich nobleman whom he had met in France and somehow come into some money, so that he was talking of buying a place and settling down to farm. He made a great fuss of me and asked whether I would overlook his careless behaviour. Soon he told everyone of our adventures on the journey and with so many jokes against himself that presently Paddy was laughing against his will, and other grooms were asking, 'What next, sir?'

Now as I write I am near retirement. Times have changed and steam engines thresh the corn and roll the roads and more crops are being grown in the fields, but Paddy, who has married, is still my groom and, though old and lame, Skip still visits me most mornings, licking my legs as though to express his undying friendship. The old Duke has died, and his eldest son has taken his place and chosen me to be his special hunter. And now and then in the evenings, after a glass of beer, the servants still talk of the Queen's visit and the way Prince Albert rode to hounds and proved to them his worth as a horseman and Queen's Consort.

# BLOSSOM

✻

*by Christine Pullein-Thompson*

# Contents

ONE    I am born    203

TWO    Nutmeg    209

THREE    I start work    217

FOUR    A foal    221

FIVE    Jimmy Reed    226

SIX    A carrier's horse    229

SEVEN    Disaster!    234

EIGHT    A bad time    238

NINE    A rough journey    243

TEN    I become a coal horse    248

ELEVEN    Midnight    253

TWELVE    At the forge    258

THIRTEEN    I break my knees    262

FOURTEEN    Back to the country    268

FIFTEEN    Frances and May    275

SIXTEEN    Grandma!    280

# Black Beauty's Family

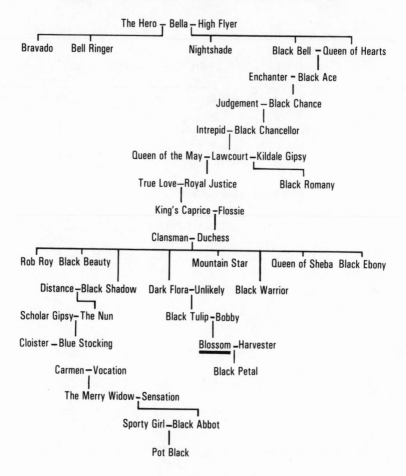

# *I am born*

My first memories are of my mother, tender, warm, black as night, with a star which gleamed white as snow on her dark face. Her name was Black Tulip and she had been well-known in the hunting field before becoming a brood mare. I was her sixth foal and her first filly. I came into the world on an April day, but it was not until June that I learned of something which was to affect my whole life. My mother and my master knew straight away, and my master never forgave me for being what I was. I remember him looking at me in disgust, his waxed moustache twitching. Once he said, 'She's fit for nothing but the tinkers and I thought we were going to have a good 'un this time.'

I was born on a small stud farm where there were twenty mares all with foals. They stood together under the trees when the weather was hot, talking about their offspring. On these occasions my mother always remained silent, though she would turn and nuzzle me from time to time trying to tell me how much she loved me. It was an old mare with grey hairs on her shoulders and a small, mean eye who finally revealed why I was so disliked by my master.

'Love matches are all right,' she said, looking at my mother, 'until your foal arrives. Now look at yours, Black Tulip. She will never be a beauty. You may be related to the great Black Beauty, but because you fell for a common young colt, she's piebald, and her fetlocks are growing already. She'll never be fit for gentlefolk. She'll be a common work horse all her life, and worn out by the time she's ten years old, and all because you wanted a change; because you were tired of Firecrest, one of the best stallions there's ever been; you had to run away with a useless young colt.'

My mother looked at me with sad eyes, but I was too young to care or understand. I butted her ribs with my black and white muzzle and stamped my tiny hoofs, two of which were pale coloured instead of the usual black.

'It is true of course,' said my mother at last. 'And my poor filly will grow to hate me. But it was love at first sight and there's no controlling that!'

My master refused to give me a name, so Luke, the old man who looked after us, called me Blossom. 'You and I are alike,' he said, stroking my forehead. 'I was an ugly little boy by all accounts, and my father used to beat me something terrible. But you do your best, Blossom, and you'll be all right.'

The other youngsters were always teasing me about my long fetlocks and soon my neck grew thicker than theirs, and my muzzle broader. I could see despair in my mother's eyes when she looked at me, but, though I could not gallop as fast as the other youngsters, I was stronger than them if it came to a fight, and in a kicking match I was always the winner. None of this pleased my master. 'She's going to injure the others,' he said one day, leaning against the field gate in frock coat and gaiters. 'She won't be hurt herself, that sort never is. I want her put on her own, Luke. And I want her tail off, and no fuss. Just fetch the chopper and take it off.'

'I'll put her in the paddock then,' said Luke uncertainly, 'I will have to get someone to hold her while I take her tail off.'

'Yes, of course,' snapped my master. 'Get young Tom. He's as strong as an ox and he's no good in the garden.'

'Yes, sir.'

So that afternoon I was separated from my mother and put in a small paddock beyond the walled garden which was by the house. I was quite alone now and I called to my mother for hours. I missed the other young horses too, and every sound frightened me. Luke came to see me often. One day he said, 'My family never cared for me neither. I was the odd one out.'

It was August and the little paddock was full of flies. 'We can't take your tail off now,' he said, 'not when it's so 'ot. It might get infected.' So for a time my tail was spared and I lived a lonely life, not knowing of the ordeal to come.

There was plenty of grass in the paddock and a pond from which to drink, but the only shade was that given by the wall, and I missed my friends more every day.

Sometimes I could see them playing in the distance, and I would trot up and down the fence neighing until I was exhausted.

Then, early in September, my master came to the paddock and stood staring at me, his face growing red with anger. After a minute, he started to shout, 'Luke. Come here will you. Come here at once.' And after a time the old man came stumbling and wheezing, crying, 'Yes, sir.'

'I thought I told you to take her tail off,' yelled my master. 'And it's still there. I've a good mind to sack you, Luke. Turn you out, and then where would you go?'

'I was waiting until the weather changed, master,' replied Luke. 'The flies won't do the stump any good.'

'Use something to seal the ends then – put some tar on, but take it off,' shouted my master, hitting nettles with the cane he always carried. 'If it isn't off by tomorrow, you'll have the sack, Luke. You're getting old for the job. I could do with a younger man.'

So, later that day, Luke came to the paddock with Tom, a rough lad of about sixteen. I trusted Luke and I let him slip on a halter and lead me to a gate. 'What you want to do, Tom? The chopping or the 'olding?' asked Luke.

'I might not chop it straight,' replied Tom. I don't want trouble with the master.'

'It seems a shame, doesn't it?' asked Luke.

'Let's get it over with,' replied Tom.

Luke stroked my head. Then he moved to my quarters while Tom twisted a cord round my lip and held my head steady. I was not ready for the pain which followed, but Luke's arm was strong and the hatchet was sharp, and in a moment it was over. He put something on the stump,

talking to me all the time, and I could see a tear running down his wrinkled, weather-beaten cheek. 'It's over now,' he said. 'It's done, Blossom. You won't feel no more pain,' and he threw my tail into the nettles.

But the pain was still there and I had nothing but a stump left now, nothing to swish against the flies, nor to protect my quarters from the wind, nor to hold high above my back when I played with other horses. It was gone for ever, and with it I lost my trust in human beings. In the distance I could see my former playmates chasing each other, their fluffy tails held high, and life seemed very hard indeed.

Luke visited me every day with oats in a sieve, but I was wary of him now. If he approached my quarters I kicked; if he tried to put the halter on I reared up. My master came once more to see that the job was done. He looked at me and gave a sigh of satisfaction. 'You will make a cart mare now,' he said. 'And your dam is in foal again, and this time she'll have a beauty, I can see it in her eye.' He turned away leaving me alone again with no tail to defend myself against the flies, and with all my trust in human beings gone.

## CHAPTER TWO

# Nutmeg

In the autumn Luke found a donkey to keep me company. He was a rough, tired animal, who had spent his life pulling a cart. Now he wanted nothing but rest. He taught me to eat the nettles when they were dry and the sting had gone from them. When he was not eating, he dozed, with his back to the wall. He was no company for a young filly, but at least I was no longer alone.

In December we were moved to another field, where there was an old thatched building where we could shelter in rough weather. I was much larger now and my mane had grown long and tangled. I had three white legs and one black, and my head was black except for a white streak down it. My mane was both black and white, as were my sides and quarters. I could still see my old friends in the distance, bigger than I was, but with slender legs and fine necks. They lived in a yard at night, and there were other horses near the house which were used to pull my master's carriage. Often I heard them stamping and neighing to each other, and sometimes I saw the carriage pass along the road below the fields, but we never spoke to one another. So, a whole year passed and now my mother had another foal, a colt as black as herself, but not the filly my master had desired. Luke had grown older during the winter, and now he coughed incessantly. Like me he was lonely, his wife having died, and he would stand in the paddock talking to me as though I were human.

'Your master's selling you,' he told me one day. 'You're going on Tuesday. He can't bear the sight of you. If your mother had had another filly it would have been different, but he's a hard man and he wanted a filly to carry on the line. Colts are no good he says, he can't be bothered with them, it's a filly he's wanting.'

Two days later he caught me and, putting the halter on with difficulty, led me away from the only home I had ever known. I saw my mother in the distance and neighed. The fields were dappled in sunlight, the trees were breaking into leaf. The brick buildings looked mellow. I was losing my coat which was blown hither and thither by the wind. Luke wore his trousers tied below the knees and a tattered shirt. An old cap covered what was left of his hair. 'It's a long way. The Master is a hard man,' he grumbled. 'I'm turned fifty and it's twelve miles to walk.'

At first we travelled along a road past cottages bursting with small children, past commons where geese plucked at the grass and goats were tethered. I stopped to look at everything. Luke was very patient. I was nervous and unsure of myself; the slightest rustle and I jumped. Carts passed us and once a carriage with the horses' heads strapped high and froth rising from their lips. I stood and stared, quivering in every limb.

Then we turned off the road and walked down a long straight track where nothing seemed to move but the wind. It was here we stopped while Luke ate his lunch – a piece of bread and half an onion. It was a strange silent world now. In the distance a pair of oxen were ploughing. The fields were flat, separated only by dykes. Far away something turned in the wind. I stopped and stared again. 'It be nothing but a windmill,' said Luke. 'Come on, my old darling. The Master's sending the gig for me at three and I can't keep it waiting.'

Women were hoeing in the fields, their long skirts billowing in the wind. The sky was full of dancing clouds. 'That be your new home, Blossom,' said Luke, pointing at a range of low buildings in the distance. 'You won't be lonely there; they keep a fair number of horses, I'm told. Not the fine sort we've been used to, but work horses.'

The ground was wet underfoot. I felt very nervous for it seemed to be drawing me down, but at last we reached a hard driveway. 'Not much further now,' said Luke, stopping to cough and then to spit. 'This be your new home, whether you like it or not.'

A carter met us, dressed in a smock. 'She's a bit small, ain't she?' he said.

'She's only a young 'un, and she's got good blood in her veins,' replied Luke.

'It's not blood we want, but strength,' answered the carter.

'She's got that too,' replied Luke. 'Give her time.'

A wagon filled with sacks was leaving the yard, drawn by four enormous bay horses with white fetlocks. Brasses hung on their chests. A carter led them, with a boy walking behind.

'That be wheat going to the mill. We've been waiting for a wind,' said the carter who had met us, whom I later learned was called Giles. 'We used to mill it here in the old mill house yonder, but it's easier to send it to the mill, and the master says it does a better job.' And he pointed to the windmill in the distance. 'It be the last of the wheat,' he said.

The farmer appeared now, a large man with a red face.

'This be the filly then,' he said. 'I don't like the colour, but since she only cost me ten pounds, I can't complain. Put her in the bottom meadow with old Nutmeg, Giles. What's her name? Or hasn't she got one yet?'

'We call her Blossom,' said Luke, handing the halter rope to Giles. 'I had best be getting along then. The Master's sending the gig for me and they don't like to be kept waiting.' He patted my neck and then was gone, walking along the drive into the distance. I never saw him again.

Nutmeg was a strange dark colour. 'So you've come to take my place,' she said, looking me up and down. 'I should be in foal, and I'm not, so it will be the knackers for me. I'm twelve, that's a good age, isn't it, for a work horse?'

'I wouldn't know,' I answered, walking round the field.

'That's the river down there,' she said. 'Lots of things happen on the river, you'd be surprised. Yesterday two boys drowned a dog down there. They tied a stone round its neck. How it struggled and how they laughed! It whined and pleaded for its life, but they had no mercy. When it was drowning, they threw stones at it. I see your tail is docked too. Do you suffer much with the flies?'

'Yes. Why do men do it?' I asked.

'It keeps our tails out of the way of the harness, and they don't have to be brushed any more. I wish we could cut their hands off,' said Nutmeg.

I felt very depressed by Nutmeg's talk. She had been alone for a long time with a swollen fetlock and was glad of company.

'You should be with gipsies,' she said. 'They like a piebald.'

'My mother came from a great family,' I answered, 'but my father was a common cart horse, so I am nothing, neither strong nor fine.'

'I am the same,' replied Nutmeg. 'And like me you will be a jack-of-all-trades. You will pull the muck cart and the hay rake and the pigs to market. You'll wear the worst set of harness which is stuffed with straw, with blinkers so big they hide everything, and breeching so low that you can't hold a load on a hill without almost breaking your legs in two. It will be the worst brush for you, without any bristles, and the youngest carter will learn his trade on you. Your manger will be dirty, and you will have the worst of the straw, and the oats which the rats have chewed. There are prize horses here, great Shires, and they have stables finer than the carters' cottages; but we are the misfits, born to slave day in, day out, to breed foals while we work to pay for our keep.'

'Foals?' I asked. 'Have you had many children?'

'Nine,' she replied. 'One a year and no rest in between.'

'Where are they now?'

'All gone – sold for meat or work. Oh, the master has made good money out of me, but I'll never be in foal again, the work has seen to that, and you are here to take my place.'

I refused to be further depressed by Nutmeg's talk. I was young and everything was new to me. I rolled over and over on the wet ground. I smelt the air and, cantering to the river, I drank and drank.

Nutmeg stood under a tree resting a leg. 'Rest when you can,' she said. 'Don't wear yourself out. You'll work soon enough.'

'I'm too young for work,' I answered. 'I'm not yet two.'

'They work children here,' she replied. 'Last year they were picking up potatoes all day in the pouring rain. How they cried. Then a policeman came and asked their ages. Their mothers told them to say ten, though you could see they were younger. It was a terrible day. I was glad of my stable in the evening, but they left in the dark to walk five miles home. Oh, it's a cruel world,' finished Nutmeg. 'The masters may be comfortable but their servants aren't.'

'Where do we live in the winter?' I asked.

'In stalls, tied day and night, except when you're working. You're let loose when it's time to foal, but after that it's work again. Often I've wanted to die. Working all day long when your foal is waiting for you, not knowing when he may be taken away for ever, that is the cruellest thing of all. Then one day he's gone and you know you'll never see him again. Oh, it's hard.'

'But soon you have another one,' I answered.

'But the worrying's always there until the next time comes and then it starts all over again. Why can't our masters leave us in peace? Why can't we keep our foals for a little time? Why must we always be separated?'

214

I trotted down to the river again, wearied by her talk. There were horses on the other side. I galloped up and down calling to them, but they soon grew bored with me, and dropped their heads to graze again. I looked back at the farm house, red-bricked, with a slate roof, newly built. I galloped round the field twice more bucking to try and impress the horses on the other side, my poor stump of a tail standing straight up.

I jumped a branch and kicked at a butterfly.

The next day was the same, only a boat passed along the river drawn by a horse and I saw the Shire horses working in the fields. And my master brought the mistress to look at me, and later his children, who were well dressed and clean. They laughed when they saw me.

'What a funny colour she is,' they cried. 'Like a patchwork. And her tail is so short. They cut it too short, didn't they, papa?'

'They never work in the fields,' sniffed Nutmeg, after they had gone.

So the days passed. Small incidents remain in my mind. I was very young and still full of youthful joys; even so some things affected me strongly. There was the day I saw the beautiful stallion who served all the mares on the farm, and the day a young woman threw her baby into the river and ran back across the meadow weeping, 'Better dead. Much better dead.'

There was the day when boys threw stones at us, and the day Nutmeg started work again and I waited for her all day by the fence. They were all days I would never forget. So, slowly, the days turned into weeks and the weeks into months. Another summer came and I suffered horribly without a tail. Nothing would rid me of the flies on my flanks and I spent much time galloping up and down the field to shake them off; only to be tormented by them again the minute I stopped. Nutmeg, who had more tail than I, suffered them in silence when she was not working in the fields from dawn to dusk. When winter came we were taken in each night to stand tied up in stalls in the large airy stable where the Shire horses lived. They were tall and proud and I think they looked down on us, though one of them, a tall horse called Admiral, would sometimes tell of the days when he worked in the woods clearing whole forests with his strength. He would describe the people who lived there. Kind, decent people, he said, who made their living by making barrels, chair legs, even clothes pegs. 'It is a different world,' he said, staring at the flat fields outside.

I found being tied up all night caused my legs to swell and I grew bad tempered as the weeks went by, but at last spring came again and Giles, the head carter, announced that it was time for my education to begin.

## CHAPTER THREE

# *I start work*

Giles was a patient man. He started my training by making me wear a bridle. It was a stiff dirty thing with a thin bit and blinkers across my eyes which stopped me seeing anything but that which lay straight ahead. It was very unpleasant. Next he put on my harness, talking to me all the time, for I was very nervous. One of the younger carters held my head while another held up a front hoof while he slipped the crupper under my tail. The collar was very heavy, even though the hames and traces had been taken off, and the pad across my back was broad and smelt of sweat. It was not the fine harness carriage horses wear, but a work harness, heavy for the most part with broad straps and dull unpolished buckles. When it was on, I felt frightened and uncomfortable, but Giles talked to me all the time, calling me all sorts of pretty names, like 'his little cherry', and after a time I felt less nervous and followed him round the yard only trembling occasionally. The next day I wore the hames on my collar – heavy metal bars which were attached to the traces – and Giles made me walk while one of the young carters, who was called Ted, hung on to the traces, making me pull him along. I had seen Nutmeg in harness and I did my best, but I was still very nervous and disliked the blinkers intensely, for they made me feel half blind and shut out the sunlight. The crupper was not much better, and the breeching felt uncomfortable against my haunches.

Giles was very patient, but Ted, who was to be my carter, was always in a hurry. It was his job to brush me now, and instead of being gentle he would scratch me all over with a metal tool called a curry comb. I look coarsely bred but I have my mother's fine skin and I found the curry comb difficult to bear.

After three days I was harnessed to a plough alongside Admiral. I was nervous of him and nervous of the plough and the work was very heavy. Giles drove us himself, walking behind the plough and Admiral snapped at me when I went too fast and kicked at me when I went too slow. He liked to plough with his partner, Consort, who matched him perfectly in size and strength.

'You'll never make a plough horse,' he said. 'You haven't the stamina. I am pulling you as well as the plough. Throw your weight into your collar.'

Giles shouted at me from time to time and used a whip on my quarters. I found the work unbearably hard, and soon my shoulders and quarters were aching. Then I started to stumble. By midday I could hardly walk and I was soaked in sweat. I was taken out of harness then and allowed to rest; but three hours later Ted put me in the tip cart and I spent two hours trotting round a field with Ted and his friends jumping up and down inside. I had no spirit left by this time and was now considered broken to harness. The next day Giles took me to the farrier himself to see that I was treated kindly but I was too tired to resist and in an hour I was shod.

Days began early at the farm. The carters arrived first at five a.m. and by six we were on our way to the fields. Ted usually overslept, so my breakfast of oats and chaff, tipped into the manger, had to be eaten in a hurry. Often he forgot to water me and I would go all day without a

drink. This was almost worse than the work, which was hard enough. We would all break off at midday and either we were allowed to graze or were given nosebags. If there was a pond nearby we would be watered, if not we had to wait until dusk when our work ended, and how we drank then! Sunday was our day of rest when we were turned out to pasture. Many the talks we had then, standing under the trees resting. Nutmeg was a great one for stories. She had a way of tossing her head and saying, 'Men! If there were no men in the world what a happy place it would be!'

But my most interesting friend was Dewdrop, a grey mare, whom the Master rode. Sometimes she was turned out in a field next to ours and we would talk over the fence. She was grey with small ears and a sweet face. One day she told me not to grumble too much about our home. 'There are worse places,' she said. 'Here we have enough to eat and, though you may work all day from dawn to dusk, it is slow work. I have seen horses galloped to death in the hunting field. I have seen them whipped and spurred to death over fences they knew they could never jump. I have met ponies which have worked under the ground, never seeing grass or light of day for years on end, some only coming up to die. Nutmeg grumbles, but their lives are worse than hers.'

'But carrying the Master cannot be as hard as pulling a plough all day. Why, sometimes you leave at midday and are back before dark,' I answered.

'But I go much faster. Often we gallop and I am expected to show my paces, to hold my head high and step out. You can go as you like,' replied Dewdrop. 'I wear an uncomfortable bridle, because that is the fashion. I have two bits in my mouth and a chain round my chin. And I used to carry a side-saddle when all the weight was on one side, or so it seemed at times.'

'So I shouldn't be sorry to be a work horse?' I asked.

'No, it is a more peaceful life. You will never wear a bearing rein; and on farms there is always plenty of everything. You need never go short of food or bedding.'

I felt better after this conversation. I started to look at life in a different way. I was determined to do my best and, as winter came and the work grew less, I remembered what Dewdrop had said and knew it was true, for we were never short of food nor bedding, and when Giles caught Ted feeding me before I had had water, there was a great to-do and it never happened again.

## CHAPTER FOUR

# *A foal*

Several months passed in this way. Hard weather came and the roads were made impassable by snow. We stayed in our stables for several weeks, while the carters polished the harness and cleaned the windows and painted the walls. Giles kept an eye on us seeing that our hoofs were picked out regularly and that we were given bran mashes to compensate for lack of exercise. It was warm and friendly in the stable, and the yard was cleared of snow so that we could be led up and down it twice a day to stretch our legs. Of course it was irksome to be tied up for hours on end, especially for us younger horses. But when the snow was gone, spring came and Giles insisted that we start work gently as our muscles had grown slack with lack of work.

I shall never forget spring coming. The grass was suddenly miraculously green, birds sang from dawn to dusk, hens cackled, calves frolicked. Even the Master seemed more cheerful than usual. Then one day the stallion walker came with his stallion. He was a little man with bandy legs who came every year and slept in the loft above our stable. The stallion was called Harvester and was well known. He was a chestnut colour with three white socks. And I think I fell in love with him at sight, which was just as well, for he had been chosen to be the father of my first foal.

With spring and summer came more work. Once again, we were in the fields from dawn to dusk, pulling the hay rake and the plough. It was about this time that a sad thing happened. Nutmeg was taken away. She had been expecting this to happen ever since I had been announced in foal. 'I won't be wanted any more now,' she had said, shaking her worn dun head. 'You can do my work and produce the foal a year our master wants. I shall go to the horse slaughterer. I have known it ever since you came.'

Giles was fond of all of us and sad to see her go. 'It's a pity she couldn't have a last summer here in peace,' he said. 'She's worked well all these years; but there it is, that's money for you. The more men have the more they want and the beasts and the poor must suffer for it.'

And young Ted, who was growing into a fine young man, said, 'One day things will change. It won't go on, because many of the poor won't stand for it any more.'

I missed Nutmeg. The Shire horses were kind enough. There were eight of them. They had been together for several years and were related to one another, so were very close, most of them having been born and bred on the farm. They found me young and ignorant. With Nutmeg gone, I had all the casual work to do. I took animals to market, and carted muck to the fields. There was hardly a day when I was not busy from dawn to dusk, and by the winter I was heavy in foal and the work seemed harder. I would lie down in my stall now whenever the opportunity arose. We were carting potatoes at this time and the fields were full of small children who earned sixpence a day for their labour. They picked up the potatoes and put them in sacks, which I carted to the barn. Often they were crying with cold, for a cold wind blew all the time bringing with it sleet and hail. They wore no gloves and their boots let in the rain. I felt very sorry for them. The Master would come to see how the work was going and sometimes he would cuff one over the ear if he wasn't working hard enough, and their mothers were always shouting at them to work harder or there would be no supper. The girls suffered more than the boys, being even smaller. There was ale for the mothers when we broke off at midday, but nothing for the children, although many of them managed to get at the ale.

Nobody needed to lead me now. I would walk on and halt to order while Ted walked behind picking up the sacks. After the potatoes were lifted, there were cabbages to be cut and carried; and threshing to be done in the big barn. One of the carters left to better himself and Ted left me to work with the Shire horses and a new boy came called Jack. He was a silly young man and given to teasing, which made me very bad tempered. He would hold out a bucket of feed and when I put out my nose for it, he would snatch it away. Or he would tickle my nose with a piece of straw when I was tied up and unable to move away. Ted caught him at it one day and boxed his ears. After that he only teased me when no-one was about.

Jack was a very rough driver. When he wanted me to move off, he would jerk the reins and shout at me, which hurt my mouth. When he wanted to stop he would lean back and haul on the reins nearly pulling my lips in two. When we went to market, he would forget to put the drag on when we came to the hill above the town, which meant I had to hold all the weight on my haunches, which was very tiring. He would forget to water me and hang about the town instead of returning immediately, and then he would drive very fast home to make up for the lost time. My harness was very heavy and the cart had iron wheels and was not made for fast travelling and, being in foal, I grew very tired. I would arrive back sweating and exhausted. After a time there wasn't much spirit left in me.

My foal arrived in April, after a long and painful labour. Giles sat up with me all night sponging me with cold water where I sweated, feeding me a bran mash with his own hand, talking kindly to me. He helped my foal to suckle and for several days we lived in peace in a shed where I was free to turn round and get up and lie down as I pleased, and how pleasant that was! My foal was black like my mother with all her slender grace. 'A real throwback,' said the Master happily. 'We can sell him for a hunter.' And he gave me something sweet to eat, which he called sugar.

They called my foal Black Petal and our master came often to look at him. He had grown much stouter and his side-whiskers had turned grey and his face was very red. I think he drank too much, for often his speech was slurred and he smelt very strongly of drink. After a week, I started work again. At first only for a few hours, but how long they seemed, for all the time I was yearning for my foal. Sometimes I could hear his little voice calling to me. Then, when work was finished, how I rushed back to him, hardly stopping to drink though I was very thirsty. I would rush into the shed with my harness still on, whinnying to him, fearing he might be gone. Gradually, as I worked longer hours, my fears grew worse. I could hardly concentrate on my work and whenever I could, I would call to him across the fields hoping he would hear me. So what Nutmeg had foretold came true. I think Giles knew how I felt, but he had no choice in the matter. The Master set the rules and he needed money to keep up his fine house and servants and drink.

So weeks passed and one day in the evening my foal had gone. How I neighed then! If only men could know how sad it is to lose a foal. When they are older we can bear it, but to be separated from your own child when he is still small and needs you is unbearable.

I couldn't eat. Next day I went to work again, but all the time I was calling for my foal. My eyes searched for him, my heart ached for him. I remembered what Nutmeg had said to me. I knew it could go on year after year, and I wished myself dead.

CHAPTER FIVE

# *Jimmy Reed*

Shortly after my foal was taken away from me, the Master died. People said it was drink that killed him. At any rate, the farm was put up for sale, and we were all to be sold too. I wasn't sorry, because I was still pining for my foal. But the carters were very upset.

'We'll all be looking for jobs then,' said Giles, 'and with these new steam engines coming in, there will be less jobs about.'

He had lived on the farm for a long time in a small cottage by the gate. Now he was to lose his home and his job. It was very hard. The Shire horses were to be bought by a neighbouring farmer, but I, like the carters, was to go to the next fair in search of a home.

I shall never forget the fair. The pleasant town was completely transformed. The market place was full of tents; gipsies were everywhere; the inns were bursting with people. Men stood in lines looking for work, the carters and the thatchers with twisted cord and straw round their hats, the shepherds with crooks in their hands. It was a sad day for Giles after fifteen years as a head carter. There were cows mooing, and small ponies straight from the moors, wild-eyed and untamed. There were mares searching for their foals, and foals searching for their mothers. There were proud thoroughbreds who had come down in the world through no fault of their own, and odd coloured gipsy horses, and old cart horses, their lower lips hanging, their fetlocks swollen by years of work. There were gipsies telling fortunes in booths, and performing fleas, and the fattest woman in the world on show. There was cock fighting out of sight in the courtyard of an inn. Nearly everyone seemed to have a beer tankard in their hand. I was tied up and left. I was very nervous. I neighed for friends. I searched with my eyes for my foal.

Horses were run up and down. Men cracked whips to drive them faster. There were horses with swollen withers and horses that coughed. There was a horse that lay down and would never get up again. Dogs ran between our legs. A lady in a fine dress walked up and down among us begging everyone to be kind to dumb animals. 'Think of the Lord,' she said. 'Do as you would be judged. Be kind to these poor animals. They are God's animals.' She stopped to stroke my nose. Her hand was very soft and white. Her eyes were full of tears.

Men came and pulled open our mouths. We were trotted up and down. Our legs were picked up and put down again.

Soon the air smelt of sweat and drink. Men's faces grew redder. There was one man who liked me particularly. He kept returning to feel my legs and pick up my hoofs. Finally he said, 'I'll give you eighteen guineas for her,' and after some haggling I was sold.

'Blossom; it's a pretty name,' said my new master. 'I hope you and I get on well together. You're a little on the small side, but you look strong enough.'

My new master was a carrier by the name of Jimmy Reed. He lived in a cottage with an orchard and the neatest stable you've ever seen, with a level floor and a door I could look over. He had a dimple-faced wife and five children. His horse had just died and he had bought me to replace him.

When we arrived after walking six miles through the dusk, his wife and children came running out to meet us, crying, 'What have you bought? Have you bought a good one?'

They fetched a piece of bread for me to eat, which was something I had never tasted before, and the two little girls were put on my back.

'Now, keep quiet,' said Jimmy. 'Remember horses have feelings too. She'll need a bit of time to settle down. Don't rush her.'

'Can I feed her?' asked one little boy.

'Can I brush her?' asked another, while their mother stood smiling, saying, 'I think you've made a good choice Jimmy, for she has a sweet, kind eye.'

I looked at the orchard. The boughs on the trees were heavy with apples. There were bee hives under the trees, and a cat sitting on a window ledge. The children were bedding down the stable now and filling the rack with hay. There was a carrier's cart in the shed next to the stable. Jimmy took me to a pond to drink before turning me loose in the stable. Everything smelt fresh and clean. The hay was sweet and when I had eaten my fill I lay down, thinking that I would be very happy.

## CHAPTER SIX

# A carrier's horse

My new master was a kind man. 'Treat others as you would be treated yourself,' was a favourite saying of his and he would add, 'Man or beast'. My stable was always clean, the hay sweet and the oats in my nose bag were never musty. His cottage was small but always neat and tidy.

The day after my arrival was Sunday and I was turned out in the orchard to rest. The elder children sang in the church choir and I could hear the church bells ringing on and off all day.

The next day I was fed and groomed early and soon after that the children came to bid me and my master goodbye. The little girls were called Meg and Rosie and they kissed my nose while the boys, trying to appear more manly, patted my neck. Henry was the eldest, closely followed by Mark and John.

The covered carrier's cart was heavy, but my master always walked when we came to a hill, and never forgot to put the drag on when needed. He was very well known in the district and on this first morning, all his regular customers came out to look at his new horse. They were a merry crowd; there were plump women with baskets who wished to be transported to town, and others who wanted us to call and take parcels to the station. After three miles we were nearly full, with four women in the back, a baby, two young geese and half a dozen parcels. Whenever we saw a sign put out on a gate, we stopped to pick up something. At eleven we reached the town, a distance of some nine miles, and I was taken to a small inn, unharnessed and tied in a clean stall and given food and water. 'This is where you stay, Blossom,' said Jimmy, 'until we start for home again.'

I wondered what he did all day in the town. There was one other horse in the stable, a tired bay, who had once been an army horse, but was now used for delivering and fetching drink.

'So you are the new carrier's horse,' he said. 'The last one never had anything to say, but you look a bit more sprightly.'

'Except for losing my foal, I am a very happy mare,' I answered. 'I could have borne it if he had been a little older, but he had only just begun to nibble grass when they took him away for good, and I cannot forget him.' And I fell to wondering where he was now and whether I would ever see him again.

'They took off a lot of your tail,' said the old horse, next. 'I was a gunner's horse before I came here, but I never saw battle, which is just as well for it's terrible I am told.'

At three o'clock my master harnessed me again and drove me to the newly built station. I was very frightened of the great steam engines, for I had never seen one before, but he talked quietly to me, and after a time I grew calm. Once again, we were soon loaded with parcels and people, and two tiny kittens in a basket, and now we completed the journey the other way round, stopping to leave parcels at homes and for people to get out. Several of our passengers remarked on my good looks and I think Jimmy was pleased. 'At least we can see this one coming,' cried one little old lady. 'And she has such a kind face.'

'Yes, the other was a sour old horse,' said a child.

'He had a hard life,' replied Jimmy, 'with never a kind word till he came to me. He wore a muzzle I know, but he never bit me, because he trusted me.'

Jimmy stopped to light the lamps on my van and when we reached home the children were waiting for us. Jimmy took me to the window of the cottage and they fed me titbits from inside, and what a pretty sight it was, with a clean cloth on the table and lots to eat and everyone merry and smiling and full of fun. My spirits rose immediately, for we horses don't mind work if we are well treated; it's doing our best and being punished just the same that breaks our spirits.

Soon I was well known in the area. People would look for 'the black and white horse'. Some ignorant people even thought I brought them luck. At first I was lonely, but after a time I grew used to being alone. I became part of the family. The work was hard but Jimmy was a kind, patient man. If the passengers were in a hurry, he would say, 'This is only a one horse van, if you're in a hurry catch the stage coach, or one of those new fangled steam engines in the station. Only it will cost you more than sixpence.' The town was always full of horses, gentlemen's horse that pranced, high stepping butchers' ponies, sad cab horses, greengrocers' ponies. I never had time to talk to them. I still looked for my foal, but I never saw him.

As I've said before, I never knew what my master did when I stood comfortably fed and rested at the inn. But I am certain he did not rest, for sometimes he came back quite morose, while other times he was laughing and joking with the passengers all the way home. On these occasions he usually had presents for all the family and extra oats for me. He did not smell of smoke or tobacco, but when he was merry, his pockets were full of money.

The village where we lived was quite small with a thatched church, a row of cottages, a baker and some outlying farms, all of which belonged to The Hall, the property of a Lord Chadwick. Sometimes we called at The Hall. We went round the back and my master would be given a cup of tea before collecting whatever we were required to take to town. The stables were very grand and there was always a great bustle going on with stable boys running here and there and fine horses being led backwards and forwards, and everything clean and tidy. There was a great array of harness in the harness room, polished to perfection, and many magnificent carts and carriages. The coachmen wore liveries and there were footmen in the house and butlers, housemaids, laundry maids, parlour maids, cooks, kitchen maids, pantry maids, scullery maids. Everyone seemed to know their place, but it must have been a happy place because they were always laughing. Once I saw Lord Chadwick himself. He asked Jimmy Reed how my mistress was and was very friendly and quite ordinary to look at. Of course the horses there didn't talk to me, considering themselves very superior and not stooping to talk to a mere carrier's horse. I didn't mind this, for I was perfectly happy to look at them from a distance, and, since I was content with my humble stable and pretty orchard, I did not envy them their fine stalls.

Gradually I learned where to stop for parcels and my way round the town, so my master hardly needed to guide me. I knew my stall at the inn and the way to the water trough. So two years passed; happy years. I was accustomed to my way of life now and wanted nothing better. As Christmas drew near I was very busy. Everyone wanted to shop and often my van was so full, that passengers had to dismount and walk up the hills. It was my second Christmas as a carrier's horse and it was about this time that my master started taking me out at night and disaster befell us.

## CHAPTER SEVEN

# *Disaster!*

It happened like this: I had finished my day's work and was resting in my stable, when my master came in with a lantern and saying, 'Come on, Blossom, we've still got work to do.' I raised my head and saw that there was a moon shining down on us, and everything had turned white with frost. It was not the first time my master had taken me out like this at night and I knew what to expect. Before we left, my mistress came out and pleaded with Jimmy not to go. 'Blossom has done enough,' she said, 'and you know what you are doing is wrong. None of us mind about a Christmas dinner, so please stay with us and forget the job you are doing tonight.'

'I've given my word, and I won't break it,' my master said, pushing her away so roughly that tears started to well up in her eyes.

'If you didn't gamble, it wouldn't be necessary,' she said in a voice so low it was hardly audible. 'You are trading with the devil, Jimmy.' And with that, she went inside and shut the door.

I was much perturbed by this conversation. But my master went about his work briskly, and I was soon harnessed and trotting along the road without time for thought. He was always in a hurry when we went out like this at night. It was as though he couldn't wait for the job to be finished.

Soon we turned down a rough lane full of stones and there was no sound now but the creaking of the wheels on the van. The lane turned into a track, which led through a wood and then to a cottage which stood quite alone at the edge of a field. Here we stopped and Jimmy gave a long low whistle. A man came out carrying a tea chest. 'Dead on time,' he said. 'Now, don't let anyone see them. And you know where to go tomorrow. Don't waste time. If anyone asks what's inside, say you don't know. I've sealed it up, and here's a brace for you,' he said, handing my master a pair of plump pheasants. 'The money will be waiting for you at The Four Bells tomorrow night,' he added. 'And then we'll lie low until after Christmas, for I think his lordship is growing suspicious.'

'Aye, he'll want a good shoot for Boxing Day,' agreed Jimmy.

The man was a rough, unshaven fellow who smelt strongly of drink and tobacco. The tea chest was hastily loaded into my van and Jimmy jumped up in front. 'The Four Bells tomorrow, then,' he cried, using the whip across my quarters. 'I won't be late, you can be sure of that. And thanks for the Christmas dinner.'

There were stones on the track and the moon had moved behind a cloud and everything was dark. We had gone barely a hundred yards, before we heard the barking of dogs and loud voices. 'We're done for, Blossom. Gallop, for God's sake,' shouted my master.

I threw my weight into my collar, but we had no chance, for in a moment the lane was full of men, some with lanterns, some without, but all of them bearing sticks or guns.

One grabbed my bridle. Another seized my master, crying, 'So, we've caught you, Jimmy Reed. You'll be in trouble for this. You'll get six months for certain.'

Two men climbed into my van and levered the tea chest open. 'I didn't know what was inside, I swear I didn't,' pleaded Jimmy.

'What? With a brace beside you on the seat? Come off it, Jimmy,' cried the man at my head.

'Think of my missus and children. I'll never do it again. I swear I won't. It was only because of Christmas,' pleaded Jimmy.

But no one listened. Two men came along the lane now, dragging my master's accomplice. 'That's it,' they said. 'We'll take them to the station.'

A man drove me home. He was quiet and gentle with me and obviously used to horses. We soon reached the cottage, and he called, 'Missus, are you there? I've brought your mare back.' And my poor mistress came to the window, her hair in plaits, a candle in her hand.

'Has there been an accident?' she called, though I think she knew the truth already.

'If you want to know about your husband, you had best go to the police station. I'll put the mare away for you,' said the man.

'I'll do that then,' she called back in a faint voice, trying to pretend that she knew nothing.

Next day the children came to the stable early and wept into my mane. The van stayed in its shed and there was no one to take passengers and parcels to the town.

Later, Henry, the eldest boy, turned me out into the orchard for exercise and cleaned my stable. My mistress was beside herself with grief. After a time she put on her best bonnet and went to see his lordship, but it can't have done much good, for she came back crying, 'We're all disgraced. There's nothing but the workhouse for us now.'

Later some men came with a fine looking horse in a dog cart and took away the tea chest. 'His lordship wants his property back,' they said.

'What will become of us?' wept my mistress.

'They say he'll get three years,' said one of the men. 'But it will soon pass, missus. He's lucky not to be transported.'

'It was the gambling which did it,' she said. 'Why must men gamble? We were quite comfortable. We wanted for nothing. Why did he do it?'

## CHAPTER EIGHT

## *A bad time*

After a few days, bailiffs appeared at the cottage and took away the furniture. Apparently my master owed many people money, which he had lost gambling. My mistress was often in tears, and when a dark haired gipsy-like man took away my oats, I had little to eat.

One day my mistress put my halter on and led me to the river. At first I thought she intended throwing herself in, for she stood looking at it and muttering, 'It would be the best way out.' I remembered the girl who had thrown her baby in the river, and was very nervous. But presently my mistress led me on along the towpath and soon

we came to a row of barges moored by a little inn called The Sparrow's Nest. Horses were tethered near the barges and they raised their heads and whinnied to me. A man climbed out of a barge and looked at us; brown-eyed, brown-skinned children followed him.

'What is it, missus? What be you wanting?' asked the man.

'A home for my mare,' replied my mistress. 'She's

good and kind and I don't want a lot for her. We've fallen on hard times, otherwise she would not be for sale. I think she would be happy with you.'

The man started to laugh. 'Buy your mare?' he cried. 'Just take a look at our barges, missus. They are half empty. There's not enough work for our own horses, missus. Our children are nearly starving. The railways have taken the work away from us; they've killed our trade. I'm sorry, missus, for she looks a good mare.'

'So am I,' replied my mistress, turning away, 'for there's no home for her now, but the coal merchant, and he's a hard man if ever there was one. And she will have to work in the town, and the streets are cruel to a horse's legs I'm told, and she's been a good mare.' She was sobbing now. She put an arm over my neck. 'It's the end of us all, Blossom. Just a little dishonesty and we're all finished,' she said.

The children were crying outside the cottage when we returned. 'Our beds have gone. They even locked the door,' cried Mark.

'I tried to stop them,' said Henry. 'But they were too big and strong.' He had a black eye and he looked crest-fallen. 'If I had been a man, they might have listened,' he added.

My mistress started to weep and wail, then crying, 'What will become of us? Blessed Lord, how did it happen? Is there no kindness in this world?' while Henry put me in my stable.

The next day the coal merchant came to look me over. He pulled my mouth open and knocked my knees with a hammer. Henry trotted me up and down the road.

'She's too small,' the man said. 'And I don't like a

piebald, you can't keep them clean. Her neck looks weak too. And isn't this a spavin on her hindleg?'

My legs were as clean as a whistle, but my poor mistress knew nothing about horses and became very downcast. 'I can't give you much for her because I don't think she'll last more than a year on the coal carts. Her hocks look narrow and you need good hocks for the hills,' he said.

'She's never been sick or sorry with us,' said Henry stoutly. 'She's a good mare and willing. Ask anyone around here.'

'Why don't they buy her then?' asked the coal merchant, turning away.

'Because they're too poor,' replied Henry.

'I thought you wanted to sell her, but I see you don't,' said the coal merchant, looking angry.

'But we must,' cried my mistress. 'We are in terrible straits. Have pity on us.'

'That sounds a bit better,' said the coal merchant, 'and a lot more like the truth. Now, you said you wanted twenty pounds, but I haven't that sort of money for a mare like her, for she's small for our carts and will have to be given the easy runs, unless there's a cock horse available on the hills. So I can't give you much. She needs shoeing too. One way and another, it's ten pounds or nothing,' he finished, stroking his chin as though giving the matter great thought.

My mistress turned a little pale. 'It's very little for a mare just turned six,' she replied. 'Couldn't you make it twelve, for you can see we're in a bad way.'

'No,' replied the coal merchant, starting to walk away, 'for I'm not keen on the mare at all. I was looking for a different animal altogether. I like a bay myself, and failing that a chestnut. You know the saying about white legs? "One buy him, two try him, three suspect him, four reject him".'

'What does that mean?' asked Henry.

'That three white legs mean trouble,' cried the coal merchant. 'On second thoughts, I don't want the mare at all. I see nothing but trouble with her. My men won't like her white legs – too much work keeping them clean.'

'Oh, please buy her,' cried my mistress. 'Please. We have to leave here tonight. I will accept anything, only be kind to her.'

'Ten pounds then,' said the coal merchant. 'Here's the money, my dear and I will send a man for her in the morning.' And he pinched my mistress's cheek. All the children were weeping now. They clung to my neck and cried, 'Don't go, Blossom, please don't go. Run away. Hide. You will hate pulling a coal cart.' Then the girls clung to their poor mother's skirts, saying, 'Must she pull a coal cart? Isn't there anyone else who wants her? Can't we try at the big house?'

'After your father stole his lordship's pheasants?' asked my mistress. 'Come, help me. We have to be gone tonight.'

'What about Blossom?' asked Henry.

'She must stay in the stable until the morning. And then take her chance. Hurry now. We must get our things together and leave.'

Henry gave me the last of the hay. His whole bearing had changed. He slapped my neck and said, 'Goodbye Blossom,' and turned away with tears running down his face. There was much crying coming from the cottage, but at last they all came out of it with small bundles over their shoulders. They turned once to look at the cottage, and then they were gone, walking away in the dark, and I was alone with nothing left to eat, waiting for the morning.

## CHAPTER NINE

# A rough journey

Morning came, wet and dismal. There was no one to feed me and no merry voices coming from the cottage. Horses have small stomachs. We need to be fed often. I neighed for help but no help came. Soon I was both hungry and thirsty. I walked round and round my stable and banged the door with my knees. Henry had shut the door completely, top and bottom, and I could hear nothing but the falling rain. I had grown used to a regular routine and we horses like a routine; it suits our stomachs and gives us confidence. After a few hours I feared I would be forgotten for ever. Then at last, towards evening, I heard hoof-beats coming up the road, and presently a small man wearing breeches and gaiters and a tweed coat looked inside my stable. I was mad to get out now, but I had to wait while he forced my head into a bridle with blinkers and a Liverpool bit and led me out. A horse and cart were waiting by the cottage. He tied my reins to the cart and, with a click of the tongue to the horse, we set off. I felt very nervous for he had not spoken one word to me. I had no choice but to follow the cart, which was pulled by a black horse with a fast trot. Soon I was cantering to keep up and, because I was accustomed to nothing more than a steady trot, I was soon drenched in sweat. After a time we stopped outside an inn and the man went inside. I was very tired by this time what with no food inside me, no water and a lot of worry. To make things worse, it started to rain again and the sky grew dark.

'He's Jacob,' said the horse pulling the cart. 'I am called Nobby. What is your name?'

'Blossom.' Nobby was a black horse of barely 14.2 hands, not highly bred but well put together, with a long mane and tail.

'I am a Dale pony,' he said. 'For a long time I was a pack pony bringing slates down from the hills. There were twenty of us working together and it was pleasant, peaceful work; but there are trains now, so we are not wanted; and I was sent to a fair, and here I am driven to death by Jacob or the Master, badly fed, badly shod and always dirty.'

'You don't pull the coal carts then?' I asked.

'No. I am not big enough, though sometimes if there's a rush on I deliver small loads. Mostly the Master drives me. I miss the hills. Sometimes I think that I shall never see them again.'

Jacob came out then and we set off again, hammer, hammer on the hard road for three more miles, until we reached another public house and stopped again. It was dark now and Jacob smelt of drink. I felt very miserable, hot one minute, cold the next.

'Are our stables comfortable?' I asked Nobby.

'If you don't mind being tied up all the time, staring at nothing but a blank wall,' he answered, shaking his mane. 'If we could go out to pasture sometimes, I could bear it . . .'

I felt very disheartened by this time. Jacob returned again and drove us very fast and so, at last, we came to the town which was lit by lamps. It was a very big town and a great pall of smoke hung over it. In spite of the hour the centre was full of horses and carriages. Cab horses waited in a long line by the station for the last train to come in. I was too tired to be nervous and soon we left the centre and trotted over cobbles, down mean streets with houses so close that there was barely room for a horse and cart to pass between. The windows had no curtains and everything looked dejected and poor. The air was very unpleasant after the country air I was accustomed to. My shoes were nearly worn out and I found it difficult to stand up on the cobbles. We passed a public house where children sat on the pavement waiting for their parents to come out. Finally we turned into a yard and stopped. My new master, who was called Hudson, came out with a light.

'You're late, Jacob,' he said. 'Have you been drinking again?'

'No, sir, it was the mare; she wouldn't come along. She kept jibbing, sir. She needs a lot of whip. I was afraid she might break the reins, the way she hung back.'

'Well, dry them off properly, Jacob,' said my new master. 'And see they are given grub and water, and here's two shillings for your trouble.'

I felt very disheartened by what Jacob had said for I have always done my best, and he had given me a bad name to cover up that he had stopped to drink. He led us into a long stable which consisted of nothing but stalls. Everything smelt of coal, the horses, the bedding, the very wood on the partitions which separated us. Nineteen tired heads turned to look at me. Most of them had no forelocks or manes, having had them cut off to save trouble. Some were resting forelegs, others hind legs. They were all tied short and the stalls sloped down to a centre drain. Jacob tied me up and fetched me water and hay. I was wet and cold but he made no attempt to dry me. A chestnut horse spoke to me over the partition

which separated us. 'You smell nice,' he said. 'You smell of the country. Are the trees in blossom there? Is there much grass? I have almost forgotten what it is like to graze, or roll, or simply stand under a tree. We only leave here for the knacker's. Have you ever pulled a coal cart?'

'No,' I answered, much perturbed. 'I am a carrier's horse.'

Jacob shut the double stable doors and went away. I could hear the rumbling of a train. Most of the horses were asleep now standing up. But even in their sleep, they moved from one hoof to another trying to relieve the strain on their tired legs. I ate for a long time. The hay rack was built for a tall horse and as I ate the hay seeds fell into my eyes. I found the slope of my stall very trying. I wanted to lie down, but I was tied too short. A little thought and we could have been saved much misery and discomfort at no cost at all. But Mr Hudson was not a clever man and it never crossed his mind that horses come in different shapes and sizes, so hay racks should be hung lower for ponies and small horses. He never looked to see how tightly we were tied and the drivers tied us tight so that, in the morning, we were clean, not having lain down all night. We would have lasted much longer, with a little thought, but though Hudson was careful to sell underweight sacks of coal, it never occurred to him that there were also honest ways of saving money. We were shod with calkins on our shoes to help us pull our laden carts over the cobbles, but these caused terrible strain to our legs. And because of the coal dust, most of us soon developed a cough which, in time, would break our wind.

The morning after my arrival I was given to a man named Ralph to drive; a thin, haggard man, with a perpetual stoop from carrying coal. 'She's called Blossom, and she's got a lot of wear in her yet. Her legs are clean all the way down, not a splint or a spavin anywhere. She needs shoeing and the farrier will be here this evening. I want calkins behind. I'm told by Jacob she's stubborn, so remember to take a whip. I think that's all,' said Hudson.

'Yes, sir,' said Ralph.

And so my life as a coal cart-horse began.

## CHAPTER TEN

# I become a coal horse

I won't dwell too long on the hardships of my life as a coal cart-horse. Some horses have good, considerate drivers who make work possible to endure; others have cruel, thoughtless drivers who make work a torment and a misery. Ralph fell somewhere in between. He was an underfed exhausted man with nine children to feed. He worked seven days a week, doing the other men's work on Sundays when they wanted the day off. He suffered from rheumatism, and was worried about his wife, Bessie, who was always ailing. Often he would drive to his house when we should have been having a rest and something to eat. She would come to the door, still in her night clothes, clutching a baby, with three or more children behind her, barefoot and badly clothed. Washing hung across the street. It was a completely different life to that which I had known in the country; there, the children had had rosy cheeks, here they were mostly thin and pale and undersize.

Most of our time was spent carting coal from the station to the great steel works on the outside of the town. At first, I was terrified of the steam engines and even more of the great steel furnaces, where men worked naked to the waist, sweat glistening like drops of rain on their bodies. We would stand by the trains while the coal was loaded and then we would trot through the cobbled streets to the steel works, where it was unloaded again. Sometimes we would do as many as ten trips a day and, as the distance was some three miles, we would be quite exhausted by the end. Hudson also supplied coal to private houses and this was usually delivered on Saturdays. Sundays we stayed in our stalls resting our exhausted bodies.

Soon I was as dirty as the other horses. I smelt all over of coal. I longed to roll. Rolling is as good as a bath to a horse and if I could have rolled in a green field, or in wet earth and then shaken myself, I would have been much happier, but this was impossible being kept as we were. We all suffered a good deal from never having enough to drink. Often we were watered when we came in from work and had nothing to drink again until next morning.

On Sundays, when the stables had been cleaned and we were fed and watered and shut up until the afternoon, we would talk. None of us had been in the stables for more than a few years. Dauntless, a sixteen-hand dark brown horse was the exception. He had worked at some brick works before in a village called Nettlebed. 'There were twenty of us,' he said. 'And the work was hard, but we didn't mind because we were well treated. There were fields all around, and whenever possible we were turned out to rest. The Master was fair to the men who worked for him, so they were fair to us, and we were well fed and well shod. Once a year the brick works shut down completely and we had a holiday, and how well that suited us!'

'I worked as a brewery horse,' chipped in a big bay with three white socks. 'We had a holiday every year. We were walked six miles to a farm and turned out for a month; our master said it was worth it, for it added ten years on to our lives.'

'I worked on the buses,' said a bay mare, with a small

neat star on her forehead. 'But I was too highly strung. I could not bear the stopping and the starting and I always wanted to go before all the passengers were on board. It was terrible work. No horse lasts longer than three years on the buses. But I never learned to endure it, so I am here.'

'The trams are little better,' spoke up a mealy coloured horse, 'though I've never worked on them, for I worked for a baker before I came here. It wasn't a bad life, except my master drank and when he had had too much he became a different man.'

'We've all gone down in the world then,' said Dauntless. 'I've been here seven years and I think I have navicular; my off pastern aches very much at times. If we had level floors and more bedding, and were turned out sometimes to rest, it might be less painful, but there is little hope of that. Last week a lady spoke to my driver about it, for I was resting my hoof. She said that I should be turned out for a rest and that in three months I would be a changed horse. But my driver just said, "Yes, m'lady, and no m'lady" and that is as far as it's likely to go. He doesn't care; and the Master doesn't care, because he knows he can buy another horse for twenty pounds when I'm no use any more.'

'There was an accident yesterday in the centre of the town,' said the mealy coloured horse. 'My driver had taken me there because he wanted to meet a friend, when I should have been resting with a nose bag. A fine young horse came galloping down the High Street driven very fast by a young man, just as a carriage and pair came out of New Street, and a shaft went right through the young horse's shoulder. They were all down in the road with gentlemen crying, "Sit on their heads", and "cut the

traces", and women screaming. It was a terrible sight.
They shot the fine young horse. The carriage horses had
their heads strapped high with bearing reins, and hadn't a
chance of getting up. Both their knees were broken, so
they'll never work for gentry again. And all because of a
young man showing off!'

'What about the passengers?' I asked.

'Oh, they were all right of course, though the ladies
were escorted to a posting inn so that they would not see
the horse shot. Very grand they were, clutching smelling
salts and the like. I wish they would try pulling a cart for a
day or two, it might teach them a lesson. My driver was
helping everyone, and was given a handsome tip, but I
had no nosebag and no drink all day. And he lost a lot

more time looking for his friend, a kitchen maid in one of the big houses, so I had to go at full speed for the rest of the day to get back here on time for him to meet the young woman somewhere else.'

'If money was shared out a bit fairer we would all be better off,' said Dauntless. 'If our drivers were worked less hard they might look after us a bit better, and if they had a holiday, we would have one too.'

Three days later Dauntless was led away. We all missed him for he always seemed to lead us into conversation. There was no time for saying goodbye. He came in from work tired and dusty, his head low, limping badly, and presently Hudson came in and said, 'Take him away, Jacob. He's no more use to me.' And we never saw him again.

In his place came a spirited black mare called Midnight. She was known for her flighty manners and for her bad temper and Hudson had bought her cheap because of this. 'We will soon break her spirit, Jacob,' he said. 'You take her out tomorrow with an extra full load. Don't spare the whip, and she'll be a different horse by the evening.'

And so she was, a poor exhausted animal, soaked in sweat, with heaving flanks and weals from a whip across her quarters. She came staggering home in the dusk with Jacob shouting at her, though he must have known she had no strength left.

## CHAPTER ELEVEN

# *Midnight*

One Sunday Midnight told us about her life. 'I was born across the sea in a place called Ireland,' she said. 'It is very wild there and I grew up roaming the moors with my dear mother. In the winter we went to the farmstead for food and shelter, the rest of the time we went where we pleased. It was a rough, carefree life and I was happy. At two years old I was broken in and drew the plough and my master's cart. It was hard, for I was not fully grown, but I did my best. The harness was old and tied together in places with string, the stables were tumbledown and we shared them with pigs and hens, but I never saw any cruelty there and the grass was always green and the hay sweet. So I grew up believing that men were my friends. Then one spring day, I was led to some crossroads by my master. Other farmers had gathered there and each of them had hold of a black horse. I discovered why, when a man appeared and started to look us over. "She's got to match his lordship's mare, and nothing but a mare will do; a mare with a blaze right down her face and with a snip between her nostrils. This one should do," he said, slapping my neck, "she's the right size and the right age. Now what about the price?" My master and this man, who had come from England, haggled for a long time, but I think my master got a good price for me for he sang all the way home.

'It is terrible to leave the place where you were born and it was a long tiring journey to the coast. The last part I travelled on a train, which was terrifying, but mostly I was ridden, which was tiring enough for I was barely four and had never carried a saddle before. When at last we reached the sea, I was put in slings and raised high in the air and then dropped into the hold of a ship where I was tied so tight I could hardly move. It was very dark and the ship seemed to be shaking all the time, and you know how we like firm ground under our feet. There were several other horses and we were all sweating and trembling. I was the youngest there, most of the others being hunters.

'After a time the ship started to move and then we could hardly stand on our legs at all. I won't dwell too long on that journey. I felt very ill and I couldn't eat or drink. Several times I neighed for my dear mother, but I knew now that I should never see Ireland again. Then at last we were lifted out of the hold on to firm ground again, shaking and trembling, our heads sore and aching from swaying against the ropes that held us in the hold. I was led away and left at an inn for the night. I was too ill to eat much but the ostler there persuaded me to drink some gruel. He was a very kind man; if all men were like him, I think we would all be happy. I couldn't bear him to touch my head, but he sat talking to me, rubbing my aching muscles, calling me "a poor wee mare".

'The next day his lordship arrived by carriage to look at his new horse. I was still very tired and frightened. "She's had a bad journey," the ostler said. "They're all like that when they come off the ships; it takes weeks for them to settle down."

'My new master was middle-aged, with narrow lips, a strong chin, and side-whiskers. He looked at me with dislike. "She's too heavy, and I never said anything about white socks; she's got two behind and that won't match my mare. Jeffreys, where are you? Come here at once."

'The man who had chosen me in Ireland appeared, suddenly humble. He had been a sprightly man in Ireland, but now he seemed much cast down.

'"You won't get anything a better match," he said. "She'll slim down with work, and we can black out her socks, your lordship. But you never said anything about legs, sir. I swear to God you didn't. She's the right size, your lordship, and the right age, and her blaze is right too, right down to the snip here, sir. You won't do better, sir. I swear to God, sir, I searched all Ireland for her, your lordship."

'"I won't pay three hundred guineas for that mare and that's my last word," shouted his lordship. "She's more suited to a hearse than my carriage. I want quality. I repeat it, Jeffreys – quality."

'And with that he climbed into his fine carriage and was driven away.'

'What happened to you then?' I asked.

'The ostler said he knew of a home and two days later I was led to a fine house set in a park, and then to stables which were like a palace after my home in Ireland. But I was still very nervous. I was frightened to step off one piece of ground on to another for fear it might move like the hold of a ship. I wouldn't let the grooms touch my ears, so they put a twitch on my lip which was very painful and made me more nervous. I hadn't worn blinkers in Ireland and they frightened me, for I couldn't see what was happening on each side of me, and I was afraid to go under a railway bridge. The stud groom was called Johnson. He was a very handsome man more interested in impressing the ladies than in how we horses were cared for, and he had little patience. He would whip me without mercy when I was afraid, when a kind word was all that was needed, and the more he whipped me the more nervous I became. Finally, one day when I was in the dog cart, I bolted. Johnson was driving me with a message for the vicar, because he wanted a word with the parlourmaid there and was happy to make this his excuse. I galloped for two miles and, when I stopped at last, there was only one wheel on the dogcart, and no one holding the reins. I think Johnson was badly hurt for I never saw him again. Three days later I was sent to a sale with no reputation and our present master bought me for twenty pounds. So here I am for the rest of my life, through no fault of my own, for I always wanted to do my best. A little kindness and I would have been all right, but ever since I left my old home it has been nothing but whip, whip all the time. And how ever hard I try, I can't cure my fear; Jacob may whip me all he likes, but I can't change myself. I was very young when I went on the ship, straight off the farm with no experience of life. I can't forget that journey and no amount of whipping will erase it from my mind.

'In Ireland my master was my friend and the hard work didn't worry me, and if our stable was like a pig sty, that didn't worry me either. It was a lot better than a fine stable loaded with cruelty.'

Three days after this conversation, Midnight bolted again. We were waiting by the station with nosebags for a train to come in, when a factory hooter went off, and she must have thought it was a ship's hooter. She hadn't been eating her oats and chaff, but standing fretfully as she always did throwing her head up and down. She broke her reins and, although the drag was on the cart, it was empty and she still managed a gallop. We neighed to her to stop but, scared as she was, she didn't hear. Her cart turned over some crates and knocked over a child, and the child's screams frightened her even more. Her driver caught up with her and started to whip her and she seemed to fall to the ground with fear, and never got up again.

Her driver said she had broken her neck in the fall, but I think she died of fear. We all felt very sad for some time afterwards, for she was only five and, handled properly, she could have lasted a long time and been happy, but being tied up at night and worked all day was no life for her. If there was nothing else in store for her, she was better dead.

CHAPTER TWELVE

## *At the forge*

Hudson was angry at losing Midnight and we were now one horse short, which meant more work for all of us. My fetlocks were swollen with wind-galls, which were very painful at times. Summer had come and the town was always hot and stuffy and full of flies. I was finding the loads very heavy, being not as large as the other horses and part thoroughbred. Struggling up cobbled streets with a heavy load behind you is hard at the best of times, but after a night standing up on a sloping floor it becomes even harder. Ralph did his best to make my life easier. He always walked when I had a full load, and he put tassels on my bridle to try and protect my eyes from the flies. In his own way he was quite fond of me, but his wife was often ill, and sometimes he would be in such a hurry to get back to her he would neglect to pick out my hoofs or check my shoes. So, one day I found myself without a shoe and Ralph was forced to take me to the nearest farrier. We had to wait some time. Three farriers were working and I was tied to a ring while Ralph sat telling everyone of his troubles.

'There's rats in the house,' he said. 'And I can't get rid of them. And my wife's ill with a cough and I can't afford the medicine. What sort of life is that, I ask you? Times have got to change; there's no other way. I've got nine children to feed on twenty shillings a week, and three of that goes on the rent. If I had a bit of ground I could grow something.'

Nobody paid much attention to poor Ralph and presently a fine black horse came in and was tied next to me. He wore a rug with initials on it and was led by a young groom.

'The Master said he was to be done at once,' said the young groom. 'For the Mistress is to ride him in the park in half an hour. If you shoe him straight away there's a shilling extra for you,' he added. There was something familiar about the horse. He reminded me of my mother.

'And where do you come from then?' I asked.

'I have two homes,' he answered. 'One is in the country and one is in town. I like the country one best, but I am kindly treated in both. I am my mistress's favourite horse. I have come up in the world for my mother was a

259

simple cart mare, piebald like you, though my father was finely bred, and my grandmother was related to the sire of Black Beauty, I believe. I am in fact half good and half bad, but my mistress sees nothing but the good in me and I am very happy.'

'And where is your mother now?' I asked, my lip trembling a little.

'I don't know. I was taken away from her when I was very young and put with finely bred colts. I have no idea what has become of her. She was only a simple farm horse but kind and good I believe.'

My shoe was now replaced. Ralph untied me. I turned to look at the young black horse. He looked very fine and I was proud to think that he was my son and glad that he was happy. I wanted to say one last word to him, but we had been in the forge a long time already and Ralph was in a hurry. 'Get up,' he shouted. 'What's the matter with you, Blossom?' At the word Blossom, the young horse turned and looked at me, his eyes growing wide with recognition. But there was no more time for words. I was pushed between the shafts, the traces were attached, the breeching straps and the belly band fastened, and then it was back to the railway station full speed, hammer, hammer, on the road and that is how it went all day; Ralph trying to make up for the time he lost at the forge, driving me fast with a full load. As the days went by I could feel my strength failing. Ralph's wife's health was growing worse and he would rush through the day's work in his haste to get back to her. He grew absent-minded with worry; he would forget my nosebag, to put the drag on the cart until I was half way down a hill, and the time he spent grooming me grew less and less. All this helped to undermine my strength still further.

My hindquarters grew thin and I found the cobbled streets increasingly hard on my legs. I had a perpetual cough now, due to the coal dust, and was given cough powders by Jacob. Ralph was ordered to damp all my food and to make sure that my oats were free from dust. My legs were bandaged at night to try to reduce the swelling and Hudson, who was afraid of losing another horse, inspected me daily. But it wasn't just the work that was undermining my health; it was the lack of green grass and sunshine and the unhealthy state of my skin and coat. If I could have been turned out for a few weeks in lush pastures I would have come back a different horse, but the air we breathed was either thick with coal dust or with smoke, and it got into our coats and into our lungs. This affected our drivers too and their health was little better than ours. Sometimes they even fared worse; most of them were bent by middle age, with lined faces and shabby clothes. They shambled rather than walked and nearly all had money troubles of one kind or another.

I don't know how much longer I would have lasted as a coal horse. I was only seven but I looked and felt much older. I had not been bred for such heavy work and I had not the strength of the other horses. And in a way this saved me, for Hudson ordered that I was to be put to the easier work of carting coal to private houses. 'She'll have a cock horse to help her up the hill,' he said. 'And the air will be better for her a little way out of town.'

## CHAPTER THIRTEEN

## I break my knees

The next day Ralph loaded my cart from the stack near our stable and we set off for the pleasanter part of the town. Soon we had left the drab streets behind and crossed the railway by the fine new bridge. Next we crossed the river. Then we came to a steep hill. Here Ralph stopped and gave a long whistle and almost immediately a man came from under some trees leading a fine chestnut horse. This was the cock horse, a horse used to help pull a load up a hill. This one was called Jack, and his driver was known as Walter. You could see they were fond of one another and, though Jack was hitched in front of me in seconds, no cross word was spoken. And what a difference Jack made! He was seventeen hands high and I think he could have pulled two coal carts up the hill. When we reached the top he was unhitched and Ralph said, 'I wouldn't have made it without you.'

'Yes, many a horse has died trying to get to the top of this hill. But the ladies, God bless them, decided it had to stop and I'm here as a result and paid by charity – Jack too. It just shows what a little good will and charity can do. Now if you'll excuse me, I'll go back to our little house under the trees,' replied Walter with a smile.

After a few days I knew Jack well and the pleasant air above the town did much to raise my spirits, though I did not lose my cough. Pulling the cart up the hill was no effort with Jack in front, and returning, it was always empty. The outskirts of the town were full of pretty houses and there was a common with a windmill. I think the air did Ralph good too. But some weeks later he came to the stable very sad and disturbed, with a black band on his arm, saying that his missus had died, and one of the children was sickly too, and there wasn't a lot of hope for her. He wanted to stay away but Hudson insisted that he had to take a load of coal to the Manor on the common. 'Mr Heyworth is a good customer of ours and he asked particularly that the coal should be delivered today, for they have barely enough to cook on. If you had come early we could have made other arrangements, but seeing you are late and all the other carts are out already, there's no two ways about it. Old Mrs Wison at Sunny Side wants two bags too, so you can put them on the back and kill two birds with one stone,' he said. 'And make haste, my man, the sooner you are gone, the sooner you will be back.'

Ralph was in a dreadful state. His hands were trembling so much he could hardly buckle my harness. But eventually we were ready and he jerked my mouth and shouted at me to get going. And how we raced through the traffic, narrowly missing other carts! There was such a jam of vehicles on the railway bridge, we were forced to stop. I was dripping with sweat by this time, the load being unusually heavy owing to the extra two hundred-weight on the back.

'Steady on,' called a driver. 'What's the hurry, mate? You'll kill your horse driving like that. Have a little sense.'

But Ralph was in no mood to wait and as soon as there was a space in the traffic, he laid into me with the whip again. By the time we reached the hill, I was sweating all over with my breath coming in sobs. Ralph gave the

263

usual whistle and then started to shout, 'Cock horse' in a loud, demanding voice, which I had never heard before. But no cock horse came. 'Drat them,' he shouted, after barely a minute. 'We can't hang about.' And he whistled again, louder this time.

'Well, we can't go back,' he said after a moment. 'Where is he, the fool?' And then, when no one came, he said, 'Well, the Manor must have its coal or there will be the devil to pay; so we will have to get to the top of this hill, Blossom, cock horse or no cock horse.' And with that he seized my bridle and shouted at me to get moving. The first part of the hill was quite a gentle slope, but it grew steeper. I did my best, but now I was moving more and more slowly. Ralph was frantic by this time, pulling at one shaft and shouting, lashing me with the whip, even kicking my stomach with his feet. Half way up, the surface became very slippery; it was easy enough with Jack in front, but without his extra power the iron on my wheels wouldn't grip. I threw my weight into my collar.

I strained every sinew of my being. My heart pounded inside me like a hammer, but I could not move the cart another inch.

Ralph put the drag on and waited for me to get my breath. Sweat dripped off me like rain. I hung my head. My legs trembled. My sides moved in and out like bellows. 'Now then,' cried Ralph, after a moment, 'get up, Blossom,' and he leapt into the cart and laid into me with the whip like a madman. I strained and struggled, too distressed to feel the whip cutting weals across my quarters. There was a humming in my head, and then I felt my hoofs slipping from under me and I knew I was going down.

I heard Ralph shouting at me as though through a mist, his voice growing more desperate each passing second. I heard hoofs going along the footpath by the road and Walter calling that he was coming. Then I was down on the road with blood spurting from both my knees, my collar choking me, the traces broken.

I don't know how long I lay there. It felt like a minute but it could have been much longer. I think all the breath was knocked out of me. Then I heard Walter's voice. 'Steady there, steady. Not to worry. Steady.'

I heard a horse neighing and it sounded like my own son. I thought I was dreaming or dying as I lay there, the road wet with my blood. Then there was a crowd around me, all talking at once and above it all, a lady's voice crying, 'I'll have you summoned for this. If it hadn't been for my horse, I would never have stopped, for I couldn't see you through the trees. But Black Petal would not go on. He knew what had happened, and people call beasts stupid! He knew there was a horse down and in trouble and he was trying to tell me.'

Walter was sponging my head now with cold water. 'Couldn't you wait? I would have been there in five minutes. I had only gone for some water,' he said.

'Don't summons me, please, Madam,' said Ralph. 'My wife has just died and I hardly know what I am doing. I've got to make the funeral arrangements, and one of my little girls is desperately ill too. I should have the day off. I'm sick with grief, but the Master said I had to work. It's a cruel world, Madam.'

I was on my feet now. I felt very weak. 'I'll take her to Jack's stable and bathe her knees; she's losing joint oil and will be scarred for life,' Walter said, stroking me.

'The Manor wants the coal,' said Ralph, wiping sweat from his face. 'I don't know what to do.'

'They will have to want the coal. Now, where do you come from? I am going to see your master. This mare isn't big enough to pull a coal cart, and hers was overloaded, as you know yourself. Now, you go straight home, my man, and I will speak to your master and see that you are not out of pocket. It's a terrible thing when a man can't have a day off to arrange his wife's funeral,' said the lady.

Walter led me down the hill to Jack's stable under the trees. It was made of wood with a tarpaulin for the roof. He only used it in the day time, but it was cosy enough inside. He took off my harness and sponged my knees, talking to me all the time in a quiet, soothing voice, which made me feel better straight away. If men only knew what a difference a kind, friendly voice makes to a horse, they might not shout at us so much. While this was going on, Jack stood outside as good and patient as a horse can be. Then Walter made me a warm mash and bandaged my legs with wet bandages to stop the bleeding. After that he made himself a cup of tea and sang a song called 'Dolly Gray', before a whistle summoned him and Jack back to work.

He stopped to pat my neck before he went and, when he was gone, I lay down in the straw to rest my legs. It was very peaceful under the trees and I think I slept.

Later, Jacob came for me. I was very stiff by this time.

'I should turn her out as soon as the wounds have healed,' said Walter. 'Otherwise she'll never be the same again.'

'That's for the Governor to say,' replied Jacob. 'He might rather send her to the knackers than have the bother of getting her right. I always said she was too small for our job.'

'She's not an old mare either,' said Walter. 'She might breed a nice foal. She's a good natured sort, too, by the look of her. It would be a pity to have her destroyed.'

It was a long painful walk to Hudson's yard. Jacob let me go at my own pace. It was tea time and the streets were quiet.

Hudson was waiting for us in the yard. He was in a bad humour.

'She's caused us plenty of trouble,' he fumed, looking at me. 'The young lady who called is threatening to summons me for cruelty. Was it my fault the cock horse wasn't on the hill? And now there's another horse ruined. If Ralph had had a bit of patience it would never have happened.'

'If you had given Ralph the day off, Blossom would still be sound,' muttered Jacob, leading me to my stall.

## CHAPTER FOURTEEN

# Back to the country

The young lady called the next day and the day after. She brought a groom with her, who held Black Petal and his own horse, while she looked at my knees. Her hands were very gentle and she talked to me as though I was a child.

'I know who you are,' she said. 'You are Black Petal's mother. You've fallen on hard times, but I am going to have you taken from here quite soon.'

She looked strange in the yard in her riding habit and veil, and Black Petal would grow impatient to be gone after a few minutes. My knees were painful; if it hadn't been for the young lady, who was called Florence, I believe I would have been shot. While Florence was visiting the stable all our conditions improved. We were watered more often; our hoofs were picked out without fail and we were groomed more thoroughly. The men touched their caps to her and Hudson would inspect the stables before each visit, putting everything in order. She had a sharp eye. She complained about the sloping floors and had my hay rack lowered. The groom, who was tall and good looking, always stayed outside in the yard, a look of disapproval on his face.

After her third visit, she had a long talk with Hudson. 'If you turned your horses out for a holiday each year, they would work much better,' she said. 'They would return full of strength and vigour. As it is, they are all coughing and all poor. Now I am going to give you

fifteen pounds for Blossom, for I've found her a home. I
want her taken to the station tomorrow and put on a
train. It is quite a long journey, but she will have a happy
home when she gets there and a long rest. Will you bring
her out into the daylight so that I can look at her? She
needs to move about. She will never get well confined in
a stall.'

Slowly and painfully I hobbled out into the sunlight,
which hurt my eyes. Black Petal whinnied to me and
pricked his ears. 'Try to walk, try,' he said.

I was very stiff. 'Walk her up and down or she'll never
make the station tomorrow,' cried Florence in great distress.

'You can't replace joint oil,' said Jacob. 'She will never
be the same again.'

'She'll be as right as rain in a week or two,' replied
Hudson, afraid of losing fifteen pounds.

'Oh, I do hope so,' cried Florence. 'And I'm sure Black
Petal does too.'

Next day Ralph came back. 'Just to say goodbye,' he
said. 'Who said piebald horses weren't lucky? My little
girl is better and the young lady has found me a garden-
ing job in the country, so I shall be all right. I'll be making
a new start.'

He led me to the station himself. My friends were
waiting there in their coal carts, hanging tired heads.
Nobby looked rough and tired. He tossed his head and
called, 'Goodbye.'

Ralph talked to me kindly and the stall in the carriage
was comfortable and bedded thickly with straw. He
fetched me water and tied me up. 'Goodbye. Do your
best,' he said.

It was not a very long journey, but my knees were

painful and I found the shaking difficult to bear. When I came to the end of it, a groom was waiting for me. He looked at my knees and said, 'Well, you are in bad shape. And piebald as well; that won't please the Master. Come along now, gently does it.' The air felt fresh and clean. Birds were singing. Trees hung pink and white with blossom. I felt better already.

It wasn't a long walk to my new home. On my arrival, the head groom rubbed ointment into my knees and I was then turned out into a shady paddock with a mare in foal. I smelt the ground and rolled over and over trying to rid myself of the coal dust which had been in my coat for so many months. The head groom watched me over the gate. 'The Master won't like her colour and he won't like her scarred knees, but he'll do anything to please that particular young lady, so she'll stay,' he said.

'Fair enough,' replied the young groom who had fetched me from the station and was called Percy. 'She deserves a rest. She looks as though she's had a rough time, and when all is said and done, she's God's beast, just the same as the thoroughbreds.'

My new home was a stud farm for thoroughbreds. It had bred several winners. My master lived in a pleasant house with fine pillars and a beautiful garden. He was bearded and usually wore a top hat and carried a cane. When he saw me he said, 'Is this Miss Florence's good deed? Hide her away, will you George. I don't want her out with the brood mares. I shall be the laughing stock of the neighbourhood.'

'She's only resting, sir. Later on she can cart the hay and straw. I want her close by so that I can keep an eye on her knees,' replied George, the head groom.

'She's a disaster. There's nothing fine about her. Even her tail has been docked too short,' said my new master. 'As soon as her knees are better, see if Farmer Collings will have her with his cart colts.'

'They'll chase her, sir,' said George.

'The Mistress mustn't see her from the windows of the house. She'll think she's a gipsy horse. Move her as soon as possible. And if you must use her for carting later on, hide her round the back somewhere. I don't want her in the front. Whatever will my customers say if they see her in a fine loose-box? It's unthinkable,' said my master. 'Is that understood?'

George touched his cap. 'It doesn't seem fair,' he said later to Percy. 'She's just the same as the other horses, only a little less fine.'

Three days later I was turned out on Farmer Collings's farm. He was a large, bluff man with broad shoulders and side whiskers, but kind enough. My field had a pond in it and a little coppice where we could shelter. The cart colts were rough and given to biting and kicking and I kept away from them as much as possible. My knees were completely healed by now and my stiffness was going. Farmer Collings would visit us every day and I grew quite fond of him. There was plenty of grass in the field and my jaded spirits soon rose and my coat grew sleek and glossy again. I was hardly the same horse by the autumn. When George saw me he exclaimed, 'What a few months at grass do for a horse! You look a different mare altogether, Blossom, my dear. Surely, even the Master will not mind so much about your colour now.' He slipped a halter over my ears, talking to me kindly, and led me across the fields to the stud farm. The stables were very grand. The horses were all in loose-boxes and

271

there was not a piece of straw to be seen anywhere in the yard. I lifted my head and whinnied.

'Not there,' said George. 'You are to live round the back,' and he gave my halter rope to Percy. 'Put her in the shed, and don't tie her too tight,' he said.

There were chickens in the shed scratching in my manger. 'This is your home now,' said Percy. 'It's not any great shakes, I know, but a lot better than a coal merchant's no doubt.' And with that he tied me up and went away.

The roof was so low that if I raised my head I banged it on the ceiling. My manger smelt sour and of chickens, and a hen had nested in my hay rack. I missed the cart colts, for we horses hate being alone and any company, however rough, is better than none. The window was shrouded with cobwebs, but I could just make out horses in the distance roaming free. After being free myself, it was very irksome to be tied up hour after hour with little to see and only chickens for company. I pawed the ground and whinnied. I stamped my hoofs on the floor. I pulled with all my might on the halter rope. But nothing gave.

In the evening Percy came to feed me. He was tired and in a hurry. He gave me hay and a bucket of water and shut the door after him. The chickens started to perch on my hay rack. In the distance I could hear the clatter of buckets and men's voices. I neighed again and again, but only the hens cackled. If only men knew how we suffer, tied up hour after hour. How lonely it is! I was still quite young and no longer exhausted by work. I neighed and stamped all that night, but by dawn I had become resigned and, in spite of the work and the coal dust, I almost wished myself back in Hudson's yard. Later that day I was put to work. My driver was the odd job man, Albert. He wore a broad brimmed hat and was old, with bandy legs and a weather-beaten face. His job was to repair the fences, to cut the hedges and to cart the hay and straw to the yard when needed. He had made a great bonfire in one of the meadows and I carted the hedge trimmings to it. I did my best and I didn't mind the fire, which greatly impressed Albert. Later I heard him telling Percy that I must have worked for the fire brigade. ''Cos she don't mind fire at all,' he said. 'She'll come right up to a fire, so close it almost singes her coat. She's a funny one.'

'More like a gipsy horse; they have fires, don't they?' asked Percy.

'Either way, she don't mind, that's the wonder of it,' said Albert.

My harness did not fit well, but no one troubled. It was not that they did not know how to fit a set, it was simply that they were busy with more important things and could not be bothered. The breeching was too low and the crupper too tight, causing it to chafe what was left of my tail. The tugs were set wrong, so that too much of the weight fell on the shafts putting strain on my back. But otherwise the work was easy, and often I would stand a whole day in my shed with no work at all, which I found most irksome. When I had been a carrier's horse I had been alone, but I could turn round in my stable and was put out to grass on Sundays and on fine evenings, so I could endure the loneliness. Now it was almost unbearable. I became very headstrong. Once untied I could not wait to get out into the daylight. I grew snappish and would refuse to pick up my hoofs when required, because I wanted to delay Percy, to make him stay longer. My head grew tender straining against the halter and I became difficult to bridle. I wanted to do my best but I could no longer control my temper. There was plenty of good food, and water was always available. It was not that I was badly looked after; it was boredom which was ruining my temper. I knew I was becoming peevish and ill tempered, but I could do nothing about it. I don't know how vicious I would have become with time, had something not occurred which was to alter my life. I had a very bad name by this time and Percy and Albert disliked me for it. Albert would shout at me and twice Percy hit me with a whip to try and curb my temper. I knew I was going down hill fast. I think if Florence and Black Petal had seen me at this time they would scarcely have recognised me.

CHAPTER FIFTEEN

# Frances and May

One afternoon when I had no work to do and was standing tied in my stable, I heard children's voices in the
distance. I had heard them before but this time they
seemed to be coming nearer. Presently I heard a little
girl calling, 'Nana, what lives in that little shed over
there?'

'Nothing, May,' answered the nurse. 'It's a hen house.'

'Yesterday I heard a horse's whinny. Do let's look,'
cried another voice.

'Frances, May, come back. That is no place for girls in
pretty frocks. Come back at once. I will tell your Papa,'
called the nurse.

'It moves. It's a rocking horse,' cried May.

'It's real, it moves. Oh, Nana, it's a lovely black and
white horse – all alone, poor thing.'

In a moment the two little girls were in my stable
fondling my nose with soft hands, running out to pick
me grass. 'Why is it here all alone?' cried May, who was
the smallest with ringlets and a pretty pink frock.

I remembered Jimmy Reed's children; all my bad
temper faded away. I nuzzled their hair while they cried
with delight. 'It must be a girl. She's so soft and sweet,'
cried Frances. 'She's not like the other horses.'

'She's cuddly like a teddy bear,' said May. 'I shall ask
Papa why she's here all alone. I shall ask him tonight.
Why should she be here – it's a hen house.'

'She is only a common cart horse May,' said Nana.

275

'She isn't fit to stand in a fine stable, any more than a common man is fit to live in a palace.'

'It is not the same, and she should not be tied up,' said May. 'Not one of the other horses is, not even the carriage horses. Papa always gives orders for them to be loose at night and when they are not working. He says it is better for them. So why is she tied up? It is not fair. I shall speak to Papa tonight.'

'So shall I,' said Frances.

'Your hands and dresses are all dirty now,' said Nana. 'You look a proper sight. Come indoors at once.'

'I don't care. We love this horse. Don't we?' asked May.

Nana took their hands and pulled them away from me. She wore a starched apron and her hair was piled on her head in a neat bun. 'Your Papa is a busy man. He won't wish to be bothered over a cart horse,' she said.

The next day Albert fixed a bar across the doorway of my stable and let me loose. I stretched my neck and all my legs in turn. Now I could see the house in the distance, and the sky, and the trees, and everything which was happening around me. I shook myself and felt easier all over. Later that day the children came again with carrots and lumps of sugar for me. They put their arms round my neck. 'Blossom, lovely Blossom,' murmured May.

'You are our horse now,' said Frances.

After that they came every evening with titbits for me, usually with Nana in hot pursuit. Once they fetched a bucket and climbed on to my back and sat untangling my mane with their fingers. I started to look out for them, to whinny when they came.

Albert told them that I was not safe. 'She'll bite you,' he

said. 'She'll bite your fingers right off and then what will your Papa say?'

'She won't. She's not like that,' said May.

'You make her like that. You are a horrible, cruel man,' retorted Frances.

'She should be with the other horses. She is lonely here,' said May.

The children changed my life. They complained that I had a sore under my chin from straining against the halter, and it was treated. They complained when I was dirty. They tried to teach me tricks and were always in trouble for the state of their frocks.

One day I heard their mother calling, 'Children, where are you? Come away from that dirty old horse at once. She is nothing but a gipsy horse. Next year Papa will buy you a pony – your very own pony.'

It was Nana's day off and in a minute she stood looking at me, her eyes filled with disgust. 'She's just a common cart mare,' she said. 'Come indoors at once.'

'She is a circus horse. She is not afraid of anything. Look, I can even light a match in front of her nose and she does not mind,' retorted Frances.

'How dare you have matches? You will set the yard on fire,' said their mother, who was a very fine lady dressed in silk and wearing fine gloves. 'Give me those matches at once. I shall tell your Papa to forbid you to come here.'


Slowly, a whole winter passed. I carted hay and straw and sacks of oats. I fetched bran from the mill. Albert was a slow patient man. He never hurried me, for he liked a job to last as long as possible, because that way he had less to do. I was much more comfortable now, but I saw the little girls less in the winter, and I grew lonely again. When spring came my head was filled with daydreams. I neighed to imaginary horses in the distance, and imagined that every hedge held a strange animal inside it. I took to chewing my stable door to relieve my boredom. Often there was no work for me for days at a time, which would make me very restless. I was stabled behind all the other buildings and there was little to see, and now everyone was busy with mares foaling. I was often neglected and left unfed until dark.

May became ill and when she recovered both the little girls were taken to the seaside for a holiday. Percy suggested that I should be turned out, but the master said that I was not to be with the brood mares and that every paddock was taken. 'I am sorry. She is too ugly for one thing,' he finished. 'Everything is wrong with her; look at her tail. Whatever made anyone dock it so short? And her fetlocks need trimming. I know she comes from a good line, but it doesn't show, does it?'

I felt very miserable after this, for the fields were full of buttercups and I was bursting with health, but there was nothing to be done. I was not well bred enough to be seen among the thoroughbreds.

Then the little girls came back and their visits began all over again. I felt much better then. They had something new for me most days – sometimes a bit of cake smuggled from the tea table, or some morsel from the kitchen when cook's back was turned. They would throw their arms round my neck crying, 'We don't want a pony. We only want Blossom.' One day they dressed me up in a bonnet. They put ribbons in my mane and draped my quarters with a table cloth. Nana was very angry when

she found them. But in the end she could not help laughing for I looked so comic.

I did my best to be patient, but sometimes I felt sorely tried by the strange games they played. One day I was a highwayman's horse, the next a fine lady on her way to the races, another day they dressed me in their father's top hat. They tied my legs together with rope and I became a robber. I liked it best when they sang hymns to me and lullabies. I dreaded the thought of winter coming again, for then their visits would grow less frequent and I would watch for them in vain. But something happened before then which was to change my whole life.

CHAPTER SIXTEEN

# *Grandma!*

I shall never forget that day. I had been carting wood in the afternoon from the spinney to the house ready for the winter. Albert had been even slower than usual, grunting and grumbling over each log of wood which had to be lifted into my cart. There was a keen wind blowing and the trees were turning yellow and brown. I was feeling frisky and I found Albert's slowness very trying. When we had finished, I was put away as usual, but the children didn't come that evening so I was quite alone. The night came early without a moon. Percy was going to a dance at the village hall. I think it was to do with the harvest festival. He had little time for the horses, and neither did George. They kept discussing the girls who would be there. Later, I could hear music coming from the village and laughter and a great clapping of hands. I stood by my door dozing, while the night grew blacker. Sometime later I heard a crackling noise and smelt smoke. It seemed to be coming through the cracks in my stable and the hens started to flap their wings and cackle. I was very nervous now. Next, I heard a great shouting coming from the yard, my master's voice the loudest of them all. 'Where are the men?' he shouted. 'Get the horses out. Don't worry about anything else, just get them out.'

I heard later that he had gone into the stables himself, but none of the horses would move for him. The grooms were still at the dance and not to be seen. And Albert had no understanding of horses and none of them trusted him. Soon the smoke was seeping into my stable, filling the air. Then I was coughing and distressed. I threw myself against the door and neighed. I could hear a great clatter coming from the yard and more shouting. I knew I would be forgotten and I became frantic. I charged my door again and again and suddenly it gave.

The next minute I was in the main yard, and what a sight it was there! Flames were leaping out of the lofts and the horses below were whinnying with terror, but they were too frightened to move in any direction. The Master was frantic and the Mistress was sobbing as if her heart would break and crying, 'We're ruined. There's no hope.'

Frances and May were standing with Nana and when they saw me, they let out a great cry. 'Blossom will save them. She is all right in fire. Look she's come to help. They will follow Blossom. Try, do try.'

The grooms were coming from the dance now having seen the smoke and the flames bright in the night sky. Someone put a halter over my ears and led me into the stables. The doors were all open, but the horses wouldn't move. Some had been blindfolded but it made no difference. I was not afraid because I had seen so much smoke and fire in my life and it was no worse than that of the steel furnaces; so I neighed to them, 'Come out. Follow me. Come out before you are burnt to death.' And one by one they followed me. I think I went back three times and by then the timbers were cracking. Another minute and the whole stable collapsed, but the horses were safe. I stood in the yard and coughed. My throat and my eyes were sore with smoke. The grooms' faces were black. The Master came across to me. 'You have done a good night's work, Blossom,' he said. 'And it won't be forgotten.' He patted my neck and pulled my ears. As he had never touched me before, I was very surprised.

The horses had to be taken to fresh stables on Mr Collings' farm. They were not nearly as grand, but somehow they were all found somewhere to sleep. Everyone wanted to know how the fire had started. Several of the grooms smoked when the master was not around, but none of them confessed to it. Albert said there had been a tramp about and George said that it had been done on purpose by someone who was jealous of so fine a stud.

In the middle of it all the fire engine arrived pulled by two fine black horses who pulled the hearse at other times. The firemen put out the last of the fire while I was taken back to my stable and given a feed of oats. Everyone kept patting me. I had never been patted so much before. Frances and May were beside themselves with delight. 'She is a heroine now,' May cried. 'You must love her now, Mamma and Papa. You must love her for ever and ever.'

After the fire my whole life changed. The stables were rebuilt and in the middle a special stall was built for me with a door I can look over and a hay rack which is neither too high nor too low, and a level floor, and a manger which is always clean. On the door there is a plaque which reads BLOSSOM. THE BRAVEST OF THEM ALL. The smart visitors who call to see the thoroughbreds, stop at my stable and read it and then the master explains, 'She saved them all. There wouldn't be a horse left if she hadn't gone in among the flames to bring them out.'

The hard work when I was in foal has made it impossible for me to be in foal again, but I spend my time in the summer with the brood mares. I am a great favourite with their children who call me Grandma, for though I am only ten, I feel old having seen so much. They love to listen to my stories about the great city where I worked.

So I hope to end my life, not as a piebald misfit, but as a horse much loved. I don't pull a cart any more, and Frances and May still visit me daily. One day last summer we had special visitors – Florence and Black Petal. He was looking very well and before he left he told me, 'I am proud to call you "mother". For handsome is as handsome does and you have done so much.'

So all my troubles are over and I have nothing to look forward to but peace and happiness. I only wish that all the horses in this hard world could say the same.

## About the Authors

The Pullein-Thompson sisters have been involved with horses all their lives. They shared their first pony, an elderly polo pony that was too tall for them, and which they mounted by a stepladder. They opened their first riding school when Josephine was fifteen and her twin sisters Diana and Christine were fourteen. They have all kept up their interest in horses and riding. Josephine is District Commissioner of the Woodland Pony Club. Diana and Christine are married, and have four and two children respectively, who also like horses. Among them the sisters have written nearly one hundred books. They live in England.